The Pawn
Against the Odds

Kate Sherwood

Published by Kate Sherwood

Cover Art by Aaron Anderson

Print ISBN #978-1-988752-23-5
ebook ISBN# 978-1-988752-24-2

Second Edition Issued 2019

CHAPTER ONE

THE hallway was familiar. Too familiar. Remy wondered how many times he'd stepped out of that mirrored elevator into the carefully perfumed air of this hall, or one just like it. Well, no, not *just* like it, and Remy would do well to remember that. This was the luxury floor, the level reserved for the wealthiest clients of the hotel. The walls were the same subtle shades of gold, the carpet the same rich red as the other floors, but the doors were spread further apart, spaced for entrances to luxury suites, not just rooms. The biggest difference in this hallway, though, was the absence of security cameras. They were still there, Remy was sure, but they were hidden better than they were everywhere else. The people behind these doors thought of themselves as the observers, not the observed.

Remy gave himself a quick once-over in a gilded hallway mirror, straightened his tie, and followed the white-uniformed room service waiters as they guided their cart on its silent wheels. They probably didn't know exactly why he was accompanying them, but they knew better than to ask.

A quick, deep breath when the procession reached the doorway, to steady his nerves. He'd already taken his pill, down in the kitchen, when the call came in. Ten minutes later, he could feel its effects. He'd be ready when the time came. The tip of his tongue played over the small ampule wedged behind his back molar; it was a routine check that had turned into a ritual. Another deep breath and he nodded to the head waiter. "Okay, let's go."

The waiter knocked on the door, an old-fashioned gesture that the hotel insisted on. Then he pressed the comm screen button and quietly said, "Room service, Mr. Challoner."

"Enter" came the reply, and the door slid open. Challoner wasn't in sight, but the door would have been calibrated to his voice when he'd checked in, and it responded to the command. "Set it up in there, please." The words came through the half-open bedroom door, not over the comm, but the waiters reacted with the same obedience as the outer door had displayed. Remy stood aside as they efficiently draped a white cloth on the polished wood dining table, lit candles, laid a single place setting, and artfully arranged several silver dishes within easy reach. The dishes were covered with ornate lids, but subtle aromas escaped to tantalize Remy's nose. He tried to ignore them, focusing on the suite instead.

There weren't many clues. The bottle of wine that the waiters opened and poured was a good sign; Challoner wasn't completely pure, not totally without appreciation for the finer things. There was a comm tablet on the coffee table, but that was standard at this level. The people who stayed in these rooms only needed to send their wishes into the world in order to see them come true, and the comms were the primary means of letting people know what was needed. They also carried information to their holders, of course, and information was power.

There was nothing else in the room that didn't belong there, nothing that Remy hadn't seen before. He'd hoped to find something that would give him an idea about what sort of man Challoner was, and what sort of strategy might be effective. Another deep breath as the waiters finished up and wheeled the cart toward the door. They ignored Remy. The head waiter made a quick inspection of their work, nodded in satisfaction, and followed the others out. The door shut behind them, and Remy heard a subtle, musical tone in the other room. The suite comm, letting Challoner know that the meal was ready and the servers were gone. Remy found a seat at the table, arranged himself in a flattering posture, and waited.

It was only a few moments before Challoner stepped into the room. Into the trap, hopefully. He was wearing dress pants and a tailored shirt, but it was open at the neck, exposing a triangle of pale skin and just a hint of dark chest hair. The man was a good size, about the same height as Remy but thicker, solid without looking fat. He was probably in his forties, but fit and obviously wealthy enough to take care of himself. He stopped short when he saw Remy, and looked almost alarmed, but his voice was level and calm as he said, "I thought you all left. Was there something more you needed?"

Showtime. Remy gave his best slow, seductive smile. "Nothing *I* need, no. But Mr. Baryman thought there might be something *you* need, or at least want. He thought maybe I could help you with that."

"Oh, for fuck's sake," Challoner said. It really wasn't the reaction Remy had been hoping for. "Does he honestly never give up? I think I've made my feelings pretty clear in the past. This isn't being friendly, and it isn't *customer service*, or whatever the fuck he's calling it. It's harassment, and I'm getting tired of it."

Remy let his eyes widen, and tried to remember what it felt like to be embarrassed. "I—I'm sorry," he stuttered. "Mr. Baryman... he seemed to think you'd be... you know." Remy looked down at the floor, waited a moment, then looked back up with a concerned, confused expression. "He seemed to think I'd be welcome."

"He seemed to think that? He's sent me whores every time I've come to town for the past eight months, and every time I've sent them away, and he seems to think that I *like* going through it all? Really?"

A moment to let the man realize he'd just called Remy a whore. Most of Remy's clients wouldn't worry about that; hell, most of them used the word like it was his name. But Remy had a feeling that Challoner might be a little different in that regard. "I don't know about any of that," he said, just a hint of wounded dignity coming through in his voice. "I just know that he said you were in town alone, and that I was your type. He... he acted as if this was a nice present." Another confused look, with a touch of hurt feelings, and then Remy stood up. He was wearing a suit that would have been conservative if it had been cut just a little looser, but as it was... well, as it was, it showed off his assets. He ran his hand down over his fly, cupped his fingers around his drug-hardened cock, and pouted. "Don't you like me?"

Challoner looked stumped. "It's not that I don't like you. It's that I don't *know* you."

"I'm here all night. You can *get* to know me."

"You're not here all night. You're on your way out." Challoner headed for the door. "I have work to do, and even if I didn't, I'm sorry, but I don't do this."

"You don't have sex?" Remy was clearly expected to follow Challoner, but he couldn't give up so easily. Mr. Baryman had made it clear that Remy was expected to make this happen, and it was not good to disappoint Mr. Baryman. So it was back to playing confused. "You don't have sex *at all*? Or do you mean... no, Mr. Baryman does his research. He wouldn't have sent me if he didn't think I was the right type. The right sex."

"I don't have sex with... with prostitutes." Challoner stepped a little closer, away from the door, and Remy was considering it a small victory until Challoner earnestly said, "It's nothing personal. Well, it's completely personal, for me. But it's nothing against you. I'm sure you're—I don't know. Good at your job."

"Mr. Baryman is going to be so angry," Remy said quietly, as if to himself. "I've already—" But he stopped, and turned his wide eyes to Challoner. "Please, sir. I'll do whatever you want. *Be* whatever you want. I need this job, and Mr. Baryman thinks I don't try hard enough, and I need the money, sir. I have a family to support." He took a few steps forward before falling to his knees. It was a good position for looking supplicant, but it also brought his mouth to the perfect level. He looked up, his lips just a little bit open, innocent and ready and desperate, and he knew just what came next. But then he saw the expression on Challoner's face.

"You don't try hard enough?" Challoner smiled sardonically. "You try pretty damn hard, kid. And you almost had me. But why the hell would he send someone who doesn't make an effort? And you got further than anyone else ever has. The others, I turned away at the door, but you weaseled your way right inside. Okay, I didn't *let* you in, but you showed some initiative. You gave me the spiel, the innocent act... it was really good, kid. An excellent effort. I mean, there was still no way we were going to have sex, but I might have let you stick around for a while, long enough so you could tell your boss that we did." Challoner stepped back a little and let his gaze run down Remy's body. "And he *definitely* got the type right. Damn." His laugh was rough. "He's playing for keeps, isn't he?" He stepped back to the door and raised his eyebrows at Remy. "But now it's time for you to go. Before I call security."

Remy rose to his feet gracefully. Plan A hadn't worked, but that didn't mean he was giving up. Instead, he gave Challoner his own smirk, jaded enough to make Challoner look like the innocent one. "You have no idea what you're turning down here." He stretched his fingers out and ran his palm across his chest, his hard abs, and back down to his cock. "You've got a luxury suite, a luxury meal, and a luxury bottle of wine... why the hell wouldn't you top that off with a luxury fuck?" Challoner didn't answer, just stood at the door, waiting. Remy brought his hands to the front of his shirt. "You want to see the goods?" He gave just a little shimmy of his hips as he stepped forward and loosened his tie. Then he reached under the silk and undid one button of his shirt. "You're so strong, so pure. I'm sure you wouldn't be tempted by just a little skin, right?" He undid another button.

"It's not about being pure," Challoner said. His voice was strained, but he was keeping his gaze resolutely on Remy's face. "Not me. But prostitution is demeaning. It turns human beings into commodities, and I don't believe in that."

Remy snorted a laugh. "It's demeaning? Me doing what I want with a guy who wants the same thing—that's demeaning?"

Challoner looked startled. "But you *don't* want to do it. You're doing it for money."

"And you telling me what I do and don't want, and telling me why I'm doing things... that's respectful too. Of course." Remy grinned, and he undid another button.

"You're a *prostitute.* The whole point of that is that you have sex for money. That's... that's what it means."

Whether it was the argument or the increasing amount of skin Remy was exposing, *something* seemed to be flustering Challoner, and Remy pushed his advantage. "I like sex. I like money. How is it more demeaning for me to do something I *like* for money than it would be to...." Remy cast his attention around the room, and then brought it to bear on Challoner's chest. "... to work in the factory that made that shirt? That's a DeBraust, right? That's a nice shirt. I used to know a guy who worked in that factory. He told me that it would take him his wages for two *months* to actually buy one of the shirts that he spent his days making. And trust me, he didn't enjoy his job."

Remy went in for the kill. He undid the last button of his shirt and slipped it a little sideways so Challoner could see the label on the collar. "DeBraust," he said softly. "I do something I like, and I get paid enough to enjoy the finer things. And you're telling me that I'm being demeaned by that?" He ran his hand under the fabric of the shirt, then shifted it aside to let Challoner see his fingers as they played lightly over his pierced nipple. "I want you. I saw your picture in the file, and I asked for the job. Begged for it, practically." He let his hand drift down to his waistband and dipped his fingers beneath the fabric to find the hot skin beneath. Challoner's eyes followed the motion. "If you don't want me, I guess that's just something I have to accept. But don't insult me by treating me like I'm too stupid to make my own decisions."

Remy slid the button of his pants open and brazenly shoved his hand further inside. "So go ahead. Call security, if you think that getting me kicked out of here is the way to keep me from being *demeaned*."

He closed his eyes and let his head fall back. He felt vulnerable, exposed, and as much as he hated the sensation, he was pretty sure that it was just what a guy like Challoner wanted to see. This wasn't a tawdry, rough affair, here; Remy was trusting Challoner, allowing himself to be weak in the face of Challoner's strength. Remy was a spunky kid, cocky and bold, not being taken advantage of but naturally submitting to Challoner's superiority. Whatever. This was the job, and Remy would damn well do it.

He wrapped his fingers tight around his cock and moaned softly as he found a slow, sensual rhythm. It would be a hell of a lot more efficient to open his pants completely and get some more space for it all, but this wasn't about him getting off. It was about tantalizing Challoner, and that would go best with limited visuals.

It was a rare experience in Remy's career, but he really wasn't sure this was going to work. Wasn't sure that the client wanted him. It was unnerving, and he was tempted to open his eyes to look for a reaction, but he forced himself to resist. Challoner wasn't calling security, so that was something. And unless the guy moved *really* quietly, he hadn't left, either. So he was still standing there, still watching. Remy licked his lips, making it look unplanned, and ran his free hand over his chest, down to the faint line of hair below his navel, and then he felt the back of his fingers brush against the silk of the tie that was still hanging from his neck. Yeah. That was another angle.

He played absentmindedly with the fabric at first, as if his focus were elsewhere and the silk was just one more pleasant sensation for his body. Then he built it up, wrapping his fingers in the tie and pulling it forward against the strong muscles on the back of his neck, tension increasing, then relaxing. He tried to picture what Challoner was seeing. Lean muscles, dark hair and eyes, skin that was always too dark or too light to fit any of the current fashions, but smooth and unblemished and soft-looking. Challoner would be focused on one of Remy's hands, either the one in his pants or the one wrapped around the tie, and maybe that meant Remy could cheat a little. He needed to know where to take this.

He kept his head back as he opened his eyes just enough to catch a glimpse. Challoner was watching, that was for sure. But he didn't look as lust-besotted as Remy had hoped. Instead, he looked thoughtful. Remy tilted his head forward and opened his eyes enough to be noticed. Challoner said, "Why does he care so much? Baryman. I've got to assume he could be making a lot of money from having you doing something else tonight. So why is it so important to him that you be with me?"

It was a good question, and Remy wasn't sure which answer would best serve his purpose, so he replied honestly, "You make him nervous. He doesn't understand you, can't figure you out. If you don't like whores, then you're not one of them. And if you're not one of them, then what the hell *are* you?"

Challoner thought about that for a moment, then said, "I'd really prefer that I not make him nervous."

Remy grinned. "Well, then... I have a good way to make *everyone* feel a bit more relaxed...." He stepped forward, slow but steady, and when he got close enough, he stretched the end of his tie out, offered it to Challoner. And just as slowly, reluctantly, Challoner reached out and wrapped his fingers around the silk. For a moment, they both stood frozen, but then Challoner tugged experimentally on the tie, and Remy responded. He wasn't sure exactly what Challoner had meant, but he knew a good way to keep things moving in the proper direction. He sank gracefully to his knees and looked up. Challoner had loosened his grip on the tie to allow Remy's movement and was watching him with the same thoughtful, almost confused look he'd worn earlier. His face looked remote, as if he were thinking about a philosophical conundrum or something, but when Remy leaned in, he found a rock-hard cock to rest his cheek against. And then to rub along, like a cat claiming its favorite master.

Teasing was good, but Remy needed to make sure that Challoner didn't get distracted, didn't call himself back to his boring, prudish ways. At least not until Remy had earned his night's pay. So another quick smile as Remy efficiently dealt with Challoner's belt and fly, and then the trademark wide-eyes-of-amazement-and-lust at the first sight of Challoner's cock. It was actually a pretty good specimen, just like the rest of the man, but Remy really didn't care about any of that. This was his job, not his hobby. He eased Challoner's pants down with one hand while he steadied the man's cock with the other.

It was no time for subtlety, he decided, and he gave a few hard sucks to the head before sliding his lips right down the shaft. He'd done this thousands of times, and he knew all the tricks. Suction, pressure, tongue action, humming and moaning, using his hands on the client's balls, his ass, occasionally running one up over his chest or down over his thighs for variety. If the corporations ever actually got around to building the sexbots they were always promising, they could hire Remy to program the blowjob function. But just like mechanization in the factories, there was no real need for robots in the bedroom, not when there was so much labor out there willing to do the work for cheap. Remy wondered how important it would be for a sexbot to look human; he bet some guys would get a kick out of fucking something that looked like a machine, as long as it felt right. Maybe there was a market for that... and then Challoner was pulling on his hair, on the tie, and Remy made himself moan in reluctance. *Oh, no, sexy Mr. Challoner, please let me keep sucking your cock.* But he was an obedient whore, so he released his prize and looked up with wide eyes.

"You're here all night?" Challoner asked. His voice was different now, husky and strained instead of calm and controlled, and for once, Remy's smile was genuine.

"Absolutely," he purred. "So can I finish this?"

Challoner's fingers were gentle as they traced over Remy's cheekbones and down to his spit-slicked lips. He looked strange, maybe sad, but he said, "Yeah. Thanks."

"My pleasure." Another grin, and then back to work.

It didn't take much longer. Challoner's body tensed, his cock jerked in Remy's mouth, and Remy swallowed and moaned as if he were tasting the sweetest ambrosia. He kept working until Challoner pulled himself away, then looked up at the client with a self-satisfied grin. It was a big treat to suck this guy's cock, and Remy was sure lucky that he'd been given the privilege.

But Challoner's expression, as usual, was not what Remy had expected. Instead of his own version of satisfaction, he was frowning as if back to his original thoughts. "You report back?" he asked seriously.

"Of course not." Remy rose to his feet in a graceful motion. "This is just you and me."

Challoner shook his head. "You report back. Do you tell him details, or just the general ideas?"

"For tonight, Mr. Challoner, I work for you. I'll tell him whatever you want me to tell him." Remy lowered his chin enough so he could look at Challoner through his long, dark lashes. "I'll *do* whatever you want me to do."

"Yeah, okay. And suppose I say I want you to tell me the truth?" Challoner sounded like he couldn't decide whether to be amused or disgusted.

"Of course, Mr. Challoner. I can tell you the truth." And Remy knew he shouldn't, but he raised his chin and looked the client in the eye, showing the lie behind the words. "I can tell you everything you want to hear."

Challoner frowned, but nodded, then looked down at himself and tidied his clothes. "Go in the bedroom," he said. "Please. You can sleep, or watch the holos, but keep the volume down, please."

"And you'll join me later?" Remy made his voice hopeful, but not demanding.

Challoner looked sad again. "Yeah. I will."

"Can I do anything special for you? Get anything ready?" Remy raised an eyebrow and nodded to the comm panel on the wall. "I can have just about anything delivered in half an hour. Maybe an hour if you want something *really* fun."

"No. Nothing special. Thank you."

Remy was clearly dismissed, and this time he didn't resist. Things were going... well, they were a bit strange, but they were progressing. Challoner certainly wasn't one of Remy's more enthusiastic clients, but Mr. Baryman's instructions had been to "knock the fucker off his high horse and get him to stop being such a fucking prude." It wasn't Remy's job to actually make the sour bastard enjoy himself. A blowjob probably wouldn't be enough to satisfy Mr. Baryman's orders, but it was a start. Remy headed for the bedroom, shedding his shirt as he went. He was tempted to drop it on the floor, like a breadcrumb path to the bed, but resisted the urge. Mr. Baryman provided Remy's wardrobe, and he'd accept it if something was damaged by a client, but not if it was ruined by Remy's carelessness. Remy assumed the room was at least bugged, but there might also be cameras, and he couldn't take the chance. Not with Mr. Baryman. Just the thought made him wish he'd kept the shirt on to help smooth the goose bumps along his spine.

He carefully untied his shoes—genuine leather, and he did *not* want to think about how Baryman would respond if they were damaged—and draped his shirt and pants on one of the bedroom chairs. Socks off, and after a moment's thought, underwear too. Challoner might miss the fun of unwrapping the present, but Remy couldn't afford to have any extra obstacles, no matter how small, between his ass and Challoner's cock.

It was too early, but Remy fished another arousal pill out of the envelope in the pocket of his pants. Challoner hadn't shown any interest in getting Remy off, and that was nice, but he seemed like the sort who would at least want his whore hard. Remy dry-swallowed the orange pill and straightened his pants on the chair before pulling back the down comforter and arranging himself on the dark sheets. He leaned over to aim the light on the bedside table in a better direction, thinking about the way the shadows would play over his body. If he shifted like this, and raised his arm like that... yeah. That would look good. Hopefully Challoner would come in soon so Remy wouldn't need to stay posed for too long, but even if he didn't, Remy would stay strong. He would be the best whore he could be.

CHAPTER TWO

REMY's body was fit and well-disciplined, but he really hadn't anticipated holding his pose for very long. Challoner was starting to piss him off. The man had enjoyed the blowjob, Remy was sure of that. And his gaze had roamed over Remy's body with clear appreciation and approval; Remy had seen enough of that look to recognize it for what it was. So why the hell was Remy lying naked in Challoner's bed, completely alone? A challenge was one thing, but Challoner was taking it way too far. This was a matter of professional pride, but also of self-preservation. Mr. Baryman had given Remy a job, and Mr. Baryman would not want to hear excuses if the job wasn't done.

Remy was considering his next move when the bed shook, and he felt a deep rumble that seemed to be coming through the floor and walls. His first thought was earthquake, but then he heard the dull thud, all that could penetrate the soundproofing of the luxury floor, and he understood. Another fucking bomb.

He had no idea how close the attack was, or whether he was in any danger, but he rolled off the bed and began pulling his clothes on with calm efficiency. The luxury suites were always evacuated at the first sign of trouble. He was still only in his underwear when there was a knock at the open door and Challoner's face appeared. "We need to go," he said. "There was an explosion somewhere near street level, and the hotel's being evacuated."

Remy just nodded. He stepped into his pants, wishing he

hadn't taken the second arousal pill. He wasn't quite hard, but every bit of friction moved him uncomfortably in that direction. He tried to focus on other matters. "They'll have shuttles for you on the roof. You know the way?"

"You aren't coming with me?"

Remy bent over to find his socks and covered his surprised laugh under a cough. "I don't really think your friends would appreciate my company, Mr. Challoner. Some of them are here with their wives."

Challoner thought about that while Remy tied his shoes. "But you're going somewhere safe? You'll be taken care of?"

Remy was getting a little tired of soothing this guy's conscience, but he supposed it was all part of the job. "Of course. I'll be fine." And then, because Challoner didn't look convinced, Remy gave him a cocky grin. "I'm valuable merchandise, you know. They're not going to let me get scratched up." Remy took a step forward and lowered his voice to a purr as he added, "Unless you *like* scratches...."

It was Challoner's turn to laugh in surprise. "You never stop, huh?" He looked over his shoulder toward the outer door. "Look, I really need to go. If you're not sure you'll be safe on your own, you can come with me. You don't need to worry about what my 'friends' will think."

"I'll be fine," Remy said, and he finished the last button on his shirt and scooped his tie up from its spot on the chair. He didn't bother explaining that there was no way hotel security would allow him anywhere near the roof, and that if he did somehow make it up that far, they'd push him off the edge before they let him on a shuttle with the more respectable guests. Let the man retain his illusions. "It was really nice to meet you, Mr. Challoner. It'd be great to see you again, maybe when we have a little more time." This was probably a total lost cause, but it wasn't like Remy had any pride to worry about. He reached into the inner pocket of his suit jacket and pulled out a card. "You can reach me at this code. Probably not live, but I respond to my messages promptly."

Challoner reached out and took the card, but it felt more like he was being polite than like he was actually interested. "David," he read. "That's all? No last name?"

"It's a private comm code. You don't even need the first name, really." But some clients liked to think they knew their whores, so all the Baryman stable had names on their cards. Names given to them by their trainers, or by the marketing department. Remy really had no idea where "David" had come from. The rumor had been that he was taking over the identity of a whore who'd killed himself a couple of weeks before Remy arrived, but he'd never tried to confirm that; he didn't really want to know. "You ready?"

Challoner nodded, and led the way to the door. The hallway was crowded, a sharp contrast to its earlier serenity, full of well-dressed people looking either panicked or irritated. A uniformed guard stepped forward from his spot across the hall from the suite's door. "Mr. Challoner?" he said politely. "If you'll follow me, please. We apologize for the inconvenience, but feel that evacuation is the best approach at this time." He ignored Remy completely, but Challoner was apparently not easily distracted.

"And my guest?" he asked the guard. "He'll be evacuated as well?"

The guard smiled. "Of course," he said. "Everyone's being taken care of." And then, because Challoner still wasn't moving, the guard finally acknowledged Remy's existence. "Staircase four," he grunted, and he jerked his head in the appropriate direction.

Remy wasn't going to argue. "I hope to see you again," he said quietly to Challoner, then turned and worked his way toward the staircase. He was swimming upstream against the flow of hotel guests and security personnel, but he wasn't the only one moving in that direction. He saw Elina, her thin body wrapped in a conservative shawl, and Rheanne, her voluptuous curves barely contained by the sequined dress she was wearing. They were both dressed for the preferences of whichever clients they'd been with, and now were both heading toward the exit.

A security guard jostled Rheanne and she stumbled in her five-inch stilettos. Remy took a quick step and steadied her before she fell. Once he was that close, he saw that her eyes were clouded and unfocused. Great. "Elina," Remy hissed. "Give me a hand." The whores were supposed to be subtle and unobtrusive; Elina didn't look enthusiastic about being part of a spectacle. But the hall was emptying, and Elina reluctantly turned around.

"She was with the colonel," Elina said flatly, and that was all Remy needed to know. The man had no taste for males, thankfully, but he was well-known for pushing chemicals of various kinds on his female whores. "Keep her still a second." Remy obliged, and Elina crouched down and slipped Rheanne's feet out of her shoes. "Hope the fucker tried some of his own medicine," Elina growled quietly. "Hope he falls off the goddamn roof."

Remy didn't bother to respond; they both knew there was no chance of the colonel meeting with that sort of accident. There were probably ten security guards for each guest on the roof, and they'd be taking special care of someone who seemed less aware of his surroundings. Just like Elina and Remy would try to take care of Rheanne.

"Get the doors," Remy instructed, and he and Rheanne staggered down the hall together. It was too bad that the colonel liked his women large; Remy could have picked Elina up and tossed her over his shoulder. Rheanne, however... Rheanne was going to be a challenge. And there was really no reason to believe that they were going to be any safer on a lower floor.

"You need to get moving, Remy." The quiet voice, using his real name, came from right behind him, and Remy turned his head in surprise, then stared in shock.

"Dar? What the fuck are you doing here?" Remy took in the security guard uniform and felt a sick lurch in his stomach. "Jesus, Dar. What are you into?" There was no way his old friend would ever have gotten his record clean enough for a job with hotel security.

"Don't worry about that. But you've got about two minutes before things get a hell of a lot hotter up here, Remy. You need to get moving."

Remy looked ahead to where Elina was holding the stairway door open. Damn it. "Give me a hand, Dar. Grab her other arm."

"Remy, I'm a little busy."

"Then slow down whatever it is and give us a bit more time."

"Can't do it. Things are in motion." But Dar obligingly shifted Rheanne's arm up and over his shoulder, and between the two of them, they dragged her down the hall at a half jog. Elina gave Dar a strange look when they reached the door, but asked no questions. If a security guard had suddenly decided to give a damn about a drugged whore, who was she to wonder why?

The stairs were tricky, and Remy wasn't sure how he would have managed without Dar. One or two flights, sure, but the luxury suites were on the forty-second floor. They were about ten floors down when the whole building shuddered, a low rumbling that grew in volume and intensity as Dar and Remy exchanged a glance. "Twenty-third floor," Remy said. "There's a safe room. Is that going to be enough? What's happening?"

"The shuttles." Dar sounded triumphant. "The bomb downstairs was just a diversion. The real target was the VIP floor, and there was no way we could actually get inside past all that security. The shuttles, on the other hand...." His grin was full of bloody triumph. Remy thought about Challoner, not wanting to take advantage of a prostitute, and forced his mind away from the memory.

Dar saw his expression and said, "The worst is over." But he didn't slow down, and Remy matched his pace. "We should be clear of the explosions. We'll get you to the safe room so you're not caught up in whatever the security forces come up with, and you'll be fine."

"And what about you?" Remy wasn't sure he wanted to know, but Dar flashed him another cocky smile.

"I'm good. Got a plan." He lowered his voice a little. "They're going to see me helping you, on surveillance. They'll ask if you know me. Tell the truth. I'm deep underground, and they already know my name."

"Jesus, Dar. What are you mixed up with?" Remy wasn't sure that he wanted to know, but it was impossible to not ask.

"I'm mixed up with *freedom*, Remy." Dar's eyes were fierce and proud. "You should give it a try. I think you'd like it."

"You're killing people." Remy kept his voice flat, kept his eyes on the stairs he was struggling down. "And you're going to get yourself killed too. You're calling that freedom?"

"'Better to die on your feet than live on your knees.'" Dar nodded sagely.

"I make a pretty good living on my knees," Remy said. He jerked his head at the tasteful sign on the next landing's door. "Twenty-three. You should go—I've got her from here."

Dar shifted Rheanne's arm off his shoulders and Remy started walking her forward. He needed to get her, and himself, to the safe room before they were caught in the inevitable security sweep. And he needed to get the hell away from Dar. But he found himself turning to look back at his childhood friend. The cameras would pick up every look, every word, but they weren't very good at catching nuances. "The security forces will be here soon, and they'll make you pay for what you did," he said out loud, but he knew Dar would catch the warning, and the concern.

"Everyone pays for everything, sooner or later," Dar responded. "Your friends on the roof just paid a little earlier." But there was no anger in his tone, at least not directed toward Remy, and his smile was as open and genuine as it had ever been. "Take care of yourself."

And then he was gone, sprinting back up the staircase to

complete whatever his mission was, leaving Remy to maneuver Rheanne toward the open door. As they passed Elina, she hissed, "You know him? I have to report that, Remy!"

"Of course you do." It wasn't as if she would have anything to add to the security footage, but the government liked its citizens to prove their loyalty as frequently as possible. "I'll be reporting it as well. Now, can you run ahead and punch the codes in for us? I can't hold Rheanne up a whole lot longer."

Elina gave him an unreadable look, but she scurried ahead to the safe room door and started poking at the touch screen. It was an old-fashioned system, but it worked, and the door was open by the time Remy and Rheanne made their way down the hall. There were helping hands to guide Rheanne through the doorway, and a roomful of irritated, bored whores to greet the new arrivals. Remy was home. He looked at the familiar faces, and forced himself, again, to not think about the lives lost on the roof.

CHAPTER THREE

"He gave you *permission* to speak to us. How are we to know what you would have done if he *hadn't* given you permission?" The investigator had already asked the question about twenty times, and Remy wondered what answer the man was looking for. It had been countless hours, days probably, since the hotel explosions, and Remy still hadn't been allowed to sleep. At this point, he'd have been willing to give the investigator any answer he wanted, but luckily, Mr. Baryman looked after his merchandise.

"You can't hold Mr. Stone responsible for something that someone else said," Baryman's lawyer said calmly. He was the fourth one who'd cycled through the interrogation, or possibly he was the first one, back after having a nice meal and a sound sleep. Remy couldn't keep track, and didn't really care. "And Mr. Stone has been more than cooperative in every aspect not only of this investigation, but also in similar incidents in the past. He is a model citizen, and is completely loyal to the government."

"Similar incidents?" Remy realized that the investigator had been changed a few times as well, but they were all so deliberately similar-looking that it was hard for his addled brain to keep track. And they were all asking the same damned questions, and making the same statements. "This incident was unprecedented. Mr. Stone's so-called loyalty was clearly just a way to lull us into overlooking him and forgetting his terrorist past. He has finally shown his true colors, and we intend to make a clear example of him."

"His terrorist past? Mr. Stone was eight years old during the Colony Seventeen Rebellion. He can't be held responsible for the actions of his family members on a distant planet almost two decades ago! He's been a valuable member of the Baryman team since shortly after that time, and we have *never* had reason to question his actions or his intentions."

There was a scuff mark on the outside of the investigator's black shoe. It showed a pale, plastic gray beneath the leather-look surface, and Remy wondered where his own shoes were. And his DeBraust shirt, and the specially tailored suit, and his silk tie. He wondered how much the outfit had cost, and wondered how much Baryman was charging for his services, to make that cost worthwhile. Not to mention the cost of the lawyers. At what point would the expense exceed the income, and what would happen to Remy then?

"We're wasting time," a voice said, and Remy was alarmed to realize that it was his own. He seemed to have separated into two parts, one of which was unable to do anything but watch in horror as the other tried to antagonize a government investigator. He turned toward the Baryman lawyer. "I appreciate you being here, but we all know that you're just being a witness, right? There's nothing you can say that's going to change anyone's mind." And then he turned back to the investigator. "And you're not high up enough to actually do anything to me, either, or you would have done it already. One of you would have. So we're just killing time, waiting for Baryman to decide whether it's worth paying whatever bribe they're asking. I don't know. What's the going price to spring an almost-overage whore from a totally bogus terrorism charge?"

"Please stop talking, Mr. Stone." It was his lawyer, frowning at Remy with enough authority that the mouth Remy himself couldn't control fell silent and still.

They all sat quietly for a moment, and then the investigator said, "You going to Terrell's this weekend?"

Remy couldn't understand the question, and couldn't decide whether it was a good or bad thing that there was finally a new line of inquiry, even if it was one that he couldn't decipher. Then his lawyer responded with, "Yeah, probably, if Alison's cold clears up."

"She's still got that? She was sniffling two weeks ago."

"It's down in her chest now." The lawyer sounded almost amused. "She's up half the night, hacking away." His tone barely changed when he added, "Look, Mr. Baryman doesn't want him marked up, and doesn't want him too crazy to work. But if you want to shoot him up with truth serum or something, that's not a problem. If you want to use interrogation techniques that won't leave a scar, that's fine too. But Mr. Baryman wants him back at work as soon as possible, and he looks like shit right now. Could you at least lay off the sleep-deprivation bullshit?"

"It's cheap, is the thing. The rest of that stuff... we need special rooms for that, and they're pretty crowded right now."

"Yeah, crowded with people who might actually have had something to do with this." The lawyer glanced down at his wrist, apparently in response to a vibration of his comm watch, and then looked back up at the interrogator. "Bet you a beer he's out of here in ten minutes."

The interrogator hadn't even finished making his scoffing noise when his own comm called his attention, and he frowned at the lawyer, then looked down to read his own message. "Bullshit," he responded, and he frowned at the lawyer again. "I'm going to request a review of this order. Freeing him doesn't make sense, not when we've got an investigation this big going on."

But the lawyer was already standing up and gathering his belongings. He shook his head and looked at Remy with something that looked a lot like disgust. He turned back to the investigator. "He's a whore, Wilson. He sucks cock and takes it up the ass for a living. You want an example of someone who's rolled over and showed his damn belly to authority? Find one better than him." Another head shake. "He hasn't got the balls to be involved in something like this. We both know that."

But the investigator wasn't nodding in agreement, and his scowl, this time, wasn't directed at Remy. "You must be aware of what you just said, Anders. Did you honestly just suggest that these terrorists are somehow brave? That's...." His frown deepened. "I'm very troubled by that comment."

The lawyer's eyes were wide, and Remy wondered whether this new wrinkle was going to get in the way of his own imminent release. "I didn't...," the lawyer began. "I wasn't saying that at all!" Remy had seen people die, had seen the panicked confusion that spread across their faces right before the end, and he saw the same expression now on the face of the lawyer. "I didn't mean it like that. I misspoke, that's all. The terrorists are scum! Cowardly scum!"

"But braver than this man, whom, according to your earlier statement, is a paragon of loyalty and service to the government."

The door opened, then, and two security guards stood in the doorway. The investigator looked at them and said, "Fine. Take the whore, process him for release. But keep Mr. Anders in the room, please. I need to make a report."

"This is bullshit!" the lawyer screamed, but Remy was out of the room, letting himself be led down the hall, trying to keep from stumbling, or running, or anything else that might call attention.

He signed what he was told to sign without bothering to read any of it; the electronic documents were easily altered if the government decided that they needed to be, and it wasn't like anyone cared about getting Remy's consent for anything anyway. Then he was led into a smaller room and handed the clothes he'd been wearing when he was arrested. He looked down at the bright orange jumpsuit he had on and turned to the guard who was watching him. "Is there someone here to pick me up? Did they bring a change of clothes for me?"

"What's wrong with those clothes?" the guard asked, nodding

at the crumpled bundle in Remy's hands.

"They're...." How to put it? "They're my uniform. And I'm off duty." *They're expensive and I'm filthy and smelly.* But the guard seemed to find Remy's spoken version compelling enough to lift his wrist comm to his mouth and mutter something into it.

Remy couldn't hear the initial question and he didn't catch the eventual response, but he saw the guard grin as he asked, "Seriously?" and was apparently reassured. "Okay, then," he said, and he looked at Remy. "You're supposed to just wear the underwear. Give the rest to me so you don't get it dirty." He shook his head. "That's some uniform."

Remy obediently pulled the underwear from the pile of clothes and handed the rest to the guard. There wasn't much to the garment in his hands; it had the form of boxer-briefs but was made of practically transparent material. He slid out of the orange jumpsuit and stepped into the underwear, and hoped he wasn't about to get arrested again, this time for public indecency. The guard, carrying Remy's clothes in a loose pile, led him out of the room, past other security personnel who were apparently jaded enough to do little more than raise an eyebrow, and into the front waiting area.

The room was already cacophonous, crowded with people waiting for news of their loved ones, but Remy's arrival made the din lessen, and then explode. He tried not to look at anyone, and then Sasha was there, frowning in his lovingly disgusted manner as he took Remy's clothing from the guard and carefully straightened the folds. "David, David, David. You *are* a challenge to me." He looked down at his own overcoat as if considering making the sacrifice, then shook his head decisively. "The cold will do you good. Help wake you up." He led the way through the crowd, and Remy kept his eyes on the back of Sasha's carefully coiffed head. He couldn't really get a read from the crowd, couldn't decide whether they were curious or angry or afraid. Probably a little of each, and none of it was his problem or his business.

The outside air was immediately refreshing, but Remy was shivering by his second breath. Sasha was heading down the sidewalk at a mercifully brisk pace, and Remy scrambled to keep up while still being careful of his bare feet on the littered concrete. He knew where they were going; this trip to the security center had been longer than earlier visits, but the general pattern was the same.

In only a few minutes they were at the heavy metal door, and Sasha punched in the required codes before allowing Remy to precede him into the building and up a flight of stairs. The hallway was barely warmer than outside and Remy stood shivering as Sasha entered another code. "Get in the shower," Sasha ordered as he opened the door. "These clothes need more help than I can manage, but I'll find something for you in wardrobe."

"Wait. What? Can't I just sleep?" That had been the previous pattern. Here to get cleaned up enough to not alarm the other whores, then back to the residence for rest before the next job.

"Command performance, darling," Sasha said. "Only *you* will do. We'll clean you here, get you shaved and pretty, and then you can eat and sleep a bit in the shuttle—it's a fair distance. I'll give you a stim shot before you arrive and you can take some extra pills with you. You'll be fine. And we'll try to get you some time for real rest when you get back." He smiled happily. "Although you're booked for two days, so hopefully you'll be able to get a little sleep while you're there."

Remy thought about arguing but knew it was pointless. There was a reason for the suddenness of his release from custody, and this was it. Baryman had been fine with letting him be interrogated as long as he wasn't required elsewhere. But when a client wanted him, Remy needed to be available. "Where am I going?" he asked, stumbling toward the shower in the corner. "What kind of job?"

"No details," Sasha responded. He'd been a whore himself, when he was younger, and was fully aware of what Remy wanted to know. Not answering Remy's question—it might be because

Sasha genuinely didn't know, or it might be because he thought Remy would rest better if he didn't have the answer. "No special wardrobe requests, though, so that's nice."

Remy turned the water on and dropped his underwear, then stepped under the spray. His body was too cold for him to be sure of the water temperature; it felt burning, so it was probably lukewarm. That was good. As much as he'd like to boil himself, it was hard on his skin, especially in the dry winter air. And Mr. Baryman's whores had nice skin.

The whole section of the room was designed to be waterproof, so there was no need for a shower curtain. Remy knew Sasha would be keeping an eye on him, and tried to make his actions at least somewhat purposeful: lather, rinse, shave, thank electrolysis for the areas that needed no attention, then turn the water off and moisturize. The routine was soothing, but it was also lulling, as Remy realized when he felt a sharp sting on his cheek and opened his eyes to see Sasha standing before him.

"Not yet, darling," Sasha scolded gently, and when he saw Remy making an effort, he lowered his hand from its slapping position. Even the few moments of sleep had sharpened Remy enough to notice Sasha's critical gaze.

"I must look like crap," Remy said.

"You certainly do." Sasha nodded toward his satchel. "But I have my tools with me. I'll fix you up in the shuttle. For now, I think we're going with a retro, rent-boy look. Maybe if you seem a bit out of it, the client will just think you're getting into the role." He nodded to the clothes on a nearby table. "I can do your hair in the shuttle. Get dressed and let's go."

No underwear, Remy wasn't surprised to find, and a pair of denim jeans so ripped they were more hole than fabric. A snug black T-shirt, a pair of cheap black boots that were at least three sizes too large, and that was all. Remy was ready. He followed Sasha to the back stairs, then up flight after flight. Mr. Baryman had obviously chosen to put the safe room in that building because of the private shuttle pad on the roof, and had just as obviously not worried too much about his staff keeping themselves fit by making the climb.

The shuttle that was waiting for them was one of the better models in Baryman's fleet. Not as good as the ones used for clients, of course, but significantly better than the type whores were usually transported in. Sasha noticed, and raised his eyebrows. "Mr. Baryman's pleased with you, it would seem." He gently shoved Remy toward the shuttle. "Let's see what we can do to keep it that way."

They climbed into the sleek black vehicle and Remy let his exhausted body collapse onto the bench seat. He was dimly aware of Sasha bustling around, and came back to himself with a surprised gasp of pain when the anti-inflammatories were injected into the bags under his eyes, but otherwise he rested. It seemed like he'd barely shut his lids when there was another sharp pain, this time in his thigh, and he gasped awake as he felt the stim surging through his body. It was like an orgasm in reverse, taking him from relaxed and happy to tense and restless.

"Take this now," Sasha instructed, holding out a familiar orange arousal pill. "The others are in your back right pocket. Capsules are there too, but get a couple ready now." Remy obediently slid a capsule behind each of his back molars, and ran his tongue over them in his ritual check. When the time came, he'd use his strong tongue to fish out one of the capsules and crush it between his teeth. A quick inhalation of the fumes and his body would obediently climax. The chemicals didn't provide any of the buildup of a regular orgasm, but Remy was used to faking that. They didn't really give any pleasure, either, just a physiological response, but none of this was about Remy's pleasure.

Sasha nodded approvingly. "Stim tabs are in your back left pocket. You know the dosage. Now, look up...," he said, and he dabbed some tone-blending makeup on Remy's face, then skillfully added some eyeliner and smudged it with his thumb. "Gorgeous," he declared. "Damn. I'm an artist." He sprayed something into his palms and ran them through Remy's dark hair. It felt like Sasha was going more for "artistically mussed" than any real style, and that seemed just fine to Remy.

He stood up as he heard the tone of the shuttle engines change. They were shifting into landing mode, and he looked out the window to see a sprawling mansion below them. It didn't look familiar but that didn't mean too much; many of his clients had multiple homes.

He stretched his shoulders and wriggled his face muscles around, loosening them up to take on whatever expression might be required. He tried to think of the worst possible situation he might be getting into; that was his usual strategy for facing the unknown. Go in expecting the worst and maybe he'd have a pleasant surprise. A gang bang... that would suck. But at least there wouldn't likely be much required of him. Hold a pose, moan a little, and let his mind drift. No, a gang bang wouldn't be the worst. Nothing physical would be all that bad; he was so tired, it would probably be easier than usual to tolerate a little pain.

He thought of Mr. Hesterman and looked anxiously back out the window. Hesterman's homes all had an ostentatious stylized "H" on their roofs, and Remy didn't see one below. So unless the man was visiting one of his friends, this wasn't a Hesterman call. That was a relief, but Remy would keep it as his worst-case scenario. Having to put on a stupid outfit and walk around pretending to be Hesterman's fucking boyfriend, making small talk with strangers who all knew exactly what Remy was but were too afraid of Hesterman to say anything... yeah, that would be the worst thing right now. Remy was absolutely not up for that level of mental effort, but he couldn't afford to fail on any of his jobs. Mr. Baryman had spent good money to keep Remy out of the security detention system, and Remy needed to show that he was worth the expense.

There was a gentle thud as the shuttle landed, a shudder that reminded Remy too much of the way the hotel had shaken when the bombs went off. He remembered Challoner being concerned for Remy's safety, and thought about the shuttles exploding on the roof. He turned to look over his shoulder at Sasha as the shuttle doors opened before them. "Have you been watching the news? At the hotel, with the shuttles... how many people died? Did the shuttles kill everyone?"

"No, not everyone," came the answer, but Sasha's lips hadn't moved, and Remy realized that the voice was coming from outside the shuttle, and was strangely familiar. He turned back around to face the exit, and there, standing in the doorway, was Challoner. The man smiled gently. "I hope this isn't an unpleasant surprise," he said, as if it actually mattered what Remy thought. He looked past Remy to Sasha and nodded politely. "Thanks for delivering him." Then he lifted an arm toward Remy, who automatically placed his own hand in Challoner's larger and somehow rougher paw and allowed himself to be guided down the ramp and off the shuttle. "Welcome to my home," Challoner said. He smiled like he really meant it.

CHAPTER FOUR

REMY wasn't sure if it was the lack of sleep or the stim shot or something else entirely, but he was definitely off his game. He'd somehow allowed himself to be led inside the opulent home, made comfortable in an armchair by the fire, and then fed soup. Soup. The whole thing was bewildering, but somehow it was the soup that was confusing Remy the most.

He needed to remember what he was there for. Or, possibly, just *figure out* what he was there for, because this seemed to be a whole new kink he was dealing with. He'd had clients who wanted to torture him, clients who wanted to dress him up as various things, and clients who wanted to pretend he was someone he wasn't. This seemed like a variation on the latter, but what the hell was Remy supposed to be?

"How's the soup?" Challoner asked from the matching armchair on the other side of the fire. They both had little trays attached to the sides of their chairs, and in addition to soup, they were eating something that might be tea biscuits. Remy had never really been sure quite what those were.

"It's delicious, thank you," Remy said. He supposed it was true. And then, because Challoner was waiting for more, he said, "Very hearty." He hoped that was a good thing for soup to be, and it apparently satisfied Challoner, who took another spoonful from his own bowl.

"It's completely home grown," Challoner said. "Well, there's a bit of bacon in it... we raised the pig, but we had to buy the salt. But the potatoes, and the onion, and there's a few other root vegetables in there for variety." He stopped talking, then frowned at his bowl. "You were in custody the whole time? From the hotel until now? At the security center?"

Remy didn't know quite how to play that one so he went with the truth. "Yes." And because he really didn't feel like making a return trip anytime soon, he added, "I appreciate the excellent job they do to keep us safe. And it's wonderful that they were able to save you from the shuttle explosions. Our security service deserves our full cooperation, and I was happy to help with their investigations."

Challoner frowned at him, and Remy tried to fight back the panic. He remembered the lawyer and the interrogator: friendly and relaxed one moment, hurling accusations the next. Had Remy said something wrong? He'd been afraid it might sound sarcastic if he'd been more effusive, but maybe that's what Challoner was looking for. Damn it, what did this man want from him?

But Challoner eventually relaxed back into his chair. "You were in a cell?" he asked, and Remy finally got an idea of what this might all be about.

"I was in an interrogation room," he said, and he let his eyes widen. "They just kept asking me questions, over and over." Should he sound like a whipped puppy, or a brave lion? He cast his mind back over the research he'd seen on Challoner, but couldn't make it fit. And the rest of the scene didn't work too well, either. If Challoner wanted to chain him up and interrogate him, what the hell was the point of the soup? Still, it was all he had, so he said, "It was frightening. But it was a little exciting too." He cast shy eyes up at Challoner to see the effect of his confession.

And the son of a bitch was laughing at him. "I don't want to play prisoner with you, David." Then he got more serious, suddenly, as if something had occurred to him. "It's not all about sex all the time. Sometimes people just want to be nice to each other."

"I'm sure that's true, Mr. Challoner. But I know how much you're paying to have me here." Or at least, he assumed it must be a lot of money. Surely this wasn't another one of Baryman's freebies. "So it's really not about 'being nice'. If that's all you want, there are a lot of much more deserving people out there, and you wouldn't have to pay a small fortune for the privilege of helping them out."

Challoner didn't say anything for a while. Then he said, "At the hotel, after the explosion, I was escorted to a private hospital for observation. They found a scratch"—he lifted his forearm to show a shallow graze on the inside of his wrist—"and disinfected it, and asked whether I wanted to consult with a plastic surgeon immediately or wait and see how it healed on its own." He smiled as if inviting Remy to join him in his amusement, so Remy obligingly returned the expression. Challoner immediately grew serious again. "Then I was taken home, in a fleet of shuttles, all armed and armored. I've had a call from the President asking whether I'm okay. I've had follow-up medical care in my own home, and my staff has been even more solicitous than usual, checking on me at every opportunity." He must have seen Remy's curious look around the room because he snorted a laugh and said, "I sent them home. All of them. Gave them the weekend off, just so I could have some peace."

"And some privacy," Remy suggested. Was he really supposed to think it was a coincidence that he was there for two days, and the staff were gone for two days?

"Some *peace*," Challoner softly insisted. "And you've spent the past three days in an interrogation room." His grin arrived quickly and left just as fast, but his eyes danced as he added, "Being *excited*. But also being afraid, and not getting much sleep. You actually look a lot better than I expected you to."

That was close enough to a compliment for Remy to take it as a victory. "I'm resilient," he said.

"You're drugged," Challoner corrected. "Right?"

"Nothing serious. Caffeine, essentially."

"It's caffeine that's got your pupils that dilated?"

"Arousal, maybe." Remy used his soft, husky voice even though he was pretty sure he didn't have a prayer.

"Or the arousal is from drugs too," Challoner said. "You're here for me this weekend, right? To do what *I* want. Right? To respond to my needs, and my wishes?"

That was more like it. "Absolutely, Mr. Challoner."

"Adam."

It took a moment for Remy to realize that it was a name, not some sort of coded instruction. He really was off his game. "Adam," he repeated obediently.

"And you're David." Challoner looked at him. "Is that your real name?"

"Yes," Remy said. "Unless you want it to be something else."

Challoner snorted again. "No, I just want it to be real. The name your parents gave you."

Remy pushed the tray carefully aside and stretched, long and languorous. He watched Challoner's gaze follow the movement and then said, "My parents gave me this *body*. How about we spend a little time talking about it? All the things it can do for you...."

"I already know what I want." Challoner's voice was calm and matter-of-fact. "I want you to go to one of my guest rooms... I'll show you which one." He stood up and gestured for Remy to follow him. "I want you to brush your teeth using the toothbrush and toothpaste in the bathroom, and wash your face or do whatever you would do before going to bed at home. You with me so far?"

Remy nodded. It wasn't one of the world's more interesting kinks, but he could manage it, at least what he'd heard to that point.

"Then I want you to change into the pajamas that are laid out on the bed. They're my pajamas, so they might be a little big for you, but I...." He frowned as if realizing something. "I like the idea of you wearing my pajamas." He glanced at Remy to see his reaction, then looked away from Remy's encouraging smile. "Then I want you to go to bed. I want you to sleep, for real. That's part of it, okay? I want you to be really asleep when I come in." He squinted doubtfully. "Can you do that, with the drugs?"

Remy considered it. The stim was there, all right, a constant, jittering presence, but so was the fatigue. "I think so." If he couldn't, he could certainly fake it well enough to fool a rookie like Challoner.

"Okay. That's what I want. You just sleep in that bed until I come in. You can do that?"

"Yeah, sure. And, when you come in... do you want that part to be a surprise, or do you want to tell me what I should be doing then?"

Challoner's smile was a mix of sweet and wicked. "I want it to be a surprise, absolutely."

"Okay."

They'd been moving through the mansion, Remy halfheartedly trying to keep track of where they were going in case he was later called on to retrace his steps, and now Challoner stopped in front of an antique wooden door. "You've got it? Get ready for bed, put on the PJs, and sleep until I come for you. It's clear?"

"Crystal." Remy stepped past Challoner, brushing just a little too close, and turned to smile at the man. "I'll see you soon?"

"When I'm ready," Challoner replied. "And you stay asleep until I decide otherwise."

Remy nodded, half shut the door for mystery without making it seem unwelcoming, and headed for the bathroom. There was a wide array of toiletries in small bottles and tubes, and he did what he could to repair the damage of the past few days. Then he went into the main room, changed into the soft flannel pajamas, and climbed into bed. His brain was still jangling, but as soon as he saw the pillows he knew he'd be able to sleep. He arranged himself in an appealing pose, flat on his back with one arm thrown up over his head, and let himself drift away.

He woke to sunlight. That couldn't be right. It had barely been dark when he'd gone to bed, and the winter nights were long. Where the hell was Challoner? Then Remy heard a sound from the hallway, and realized that it was a repetition of the noise that had woken him up. There was a gentle knock on the still half-open door, and then Challoner poked his head into the room. "Ready for breakfast?" he asked.

"Breakfast?" Remy was still groggy, but he struggled to pull himself together. "I'm ready for whatever you want. You didn't... you didn't come last night."

"Oh, I did," Challoner said sincerely. "I spent a few hours just watching you sleep, jerked off a few times... very degenerate, that's me." He saw Remy's look and grinned. "Seriously, you'd be happier if that were true? You'd rather have some old sicko perving on you in your sleep than accept that someone saw you looking tired and wanted to help out?"

"How much did that cost you?" Remy demanded, then he remembered to whom he was speaking. "I mean... it's your money, obviously. I can do whatever you want me to do." And this was far from the strangest thing he'd been a part of. But somehow, it felt wrong. "But this is supposed to be about *you*. It's supposed to be about what *you* want. I mean, if this is your thing, if you get off on bringing home tired whores and putting them to bed... that's cool. That's great, I can use the sleep. But it's not your thing, is it?"

Remy frowned and pushed the blankets away from his body. He hitched forward onto his knees and brought his hands to the lapels of the flannel pajamas. "I've seen you looking. You want this body. You want to touch it, enjoy it. And you're paying for the privilege. So why the hell are you playing nursemaid instead?"

"Because I'm an adult, David." Challoner sounded a little impatient. "Because I can want things, and realize that I won't be happy with myself if I take them." He gestured at the cart he'd rolled in, and pulled a silver lid off a tray of freshly cooked bacon. "I *want* to eat that whole plate of bacon, and eggs and toast and pancakes as well, but I know that if I eat like that, I'll get fat, and I don't want to be fat, so I don't eat like that." He waited for Remy to draw the connection.

"I'm calorie-free, Mr. Challoner. Hell, I can give you a damned workout, if you let me."

Another snort. "I'm sure you could, David, but that's not what I want. Not in the long run. And I'm the client, and the client is always right. Right?"

"Yes."

Challoner looked like he wasn't sure he trusted Remy's answer, but he nodded anyway. "Okay. So. I want you to sit up, and eat some breakfast. And I want you to stop with the 'Mr. Challoner'. Call me Adam, please."

"I normally only use the first names of people with whom I'm intimate," Remy said primly, and he tried not to smile when Challoner laughed. They set the tray up so Remy could eat in bed, and Challoner sank into the armchair by the nightstand and watched Remy have breakfast. It was a bit weird, but Remy could handle it.

He hadn't realized how hungry he was, and it seemed to make Challoner happy to see him enjoy the meal, so he didn't hold back. He'd be back on starvation rations when he returned to the stable, but one big meal wouldn't hurt too much, he hoped. Finally, he took one last bite of toast and sank back into the pillows. He really had to pee, but he wanted to hold out for just a little bit longer. Challoner was watching him, looking like he wanted Remy to say something, and so Remy did. "What's the bad thing that would happen, if you had sex with me?" he asked. "If you ate too much, you'd get fat. If you had sex with me, you'd...."

"I'd be an asshole," Challoner said firmly. He stood up. "Okay. There's clothes on the dresser, there. Get cleaned up, get dressed, and come downstairs. I'll be in my office... turn left at the bottom of the stairs, then the first door on the right."

"Yes, sir," Remy said. He swung his legs over the side of the bed and headed for the bathroom. He was pretty sure Challoner was watching him, but he didn't even try to tease the man. Challoner didn't want to be an asshole. Remy didn't understand the reasoning there, but he respected the general principle, and he'd stop trying to seduce his way past Challoner's barriers. At least, he'd stop for a little while.

CHAPTER FIVE

REMY did as he was told. After all, he was a good whore, even if he wasn't being asked to do any actual whoring. He put on the clothes Challoner had left for him, and was pretty sure that they were from the man's own closet again; the length was about right, but they were loose on Remy's lean frame. Pure cotton jeans and a flannel shirt. Remy wondered whether the rich actually preferred natural fabrics or just liked how much they cost.

He found his way down the stairs and followed the directions to the open door of Challoner's office. The room was large, furnished with the same quiet, understated elegance as the rest of the house. There was nothing shabby here, but nothing opulent either. It felt like the house of a man who liked nice things but wasn't trying to impress anyone.

"You live alone?" Remy asked. It was inappropriately personal, but he didn't think Challoner would mind.

"I do. Well, there's usually staff here, during the day. But most of them live off-site, and there's a cottage for the housekeeper and another for the security guys." He stood up. "I thought we might go for a walk. I could show you the property."

Remy thought about his too large boots, with the stiff plastic already chafing against his heels and toes. "Sounds great," he said. "You raise a lot of your own food here? That's interesting."

"It's just a hobby, really," Challoner said, coming out from behind his desk and walking toward Remy. "But it's reassuring too. You know. If things go wrong, I can still feed me and mine."

"I thought there was no 'mine'. Didn't you say you live alone?" Remy followed Challoner down the hall in a direction he hadn't yet been.

"The staff," Challoner clarified. "I mean, I'd need their labor anyway... there's no way I could run the place all on my own. But I'd be able to keep them fed. Try to keep them safe."

Remy wondered what Baryman would do if there were some sort of economic crisis and the food supply dried up. It was probably a good thing that Remy didn't have a lot of meat on his bones, because he was pretty sure Baryman would *eat* his employees before he worried about feeding them.

"You can borrow one of those jackets, there." Challoner gestured to a tidy row of garments arrayed on wall hooks. "And there's gloves and hats on those shelves. It's pretty cold out." Challoner pulled on his own outerwear, and Remy followed his example. Then he caught sight of the row of rubber boots lined up by the door. They looked like they were assorted sizes, and they looked softer than Remy's cheap footwear.

"Is it... would it be okay if I borrowed boots, as well?" he asked. His body was his livelihood, after all. Pain he could handle, but he had several clients who were pretty damned fond of his high arches and pedicured toes and they wouldn't appreciate any damage.

Challoner looked down at Remy's feet. "They're just rubber boots. They won't be warm. Are yours not warm?"

"Uh, not too warm, no. And they don't fit all that well." But Remy couldn't antagonize a current client in order to protect future clients that he might not even see until the blisters healed. "But they'll be fine. It's not a problem. Sorry."

Challoner seemed to ignore the second part of Remy's answer. "I can get you some extra socks, I guess. That'd help keep you warm. And you can probably find a pair that fit you fairly well, and we can add or remove socks as needed. But we don't have to go for a walk at all, if you'd rather not. I didn't really think about footwear."

"No, it's fine. I'd like to go. But, in the future... well, you know, if there's a future. With me, or with anybody else. You can specify if you need us to be dressed a certain way. Like if you have a specific activity in mind."

"I didn't really think of going for a walk as being a special request."

"It's not exactly what we're used to," Remy said. "Traditionally, I'm taking clothes off, not putting them on."

Challoner nodded. "Yeah. I guess that makes sense. Okay, well, I'll go grab a few pairs of socks and you look for some boots that fit just a bit loose, okay? And then if your feet get sore, let me know, and we can come back." He stopped and frowned at Remy. "That's an order, or whatever you want to call it. It's my thing. You're here to do what I want, and what I want is for you to tell me if your feet get sore. Clear?"

Remy nodded. "Yes, sir."

"You haven't called me 'Adam' yet today." Challoner didn't sound angry, but he was waiting for a response.

"Sorry, Adam," Remy obediently replied. It felt strange to use a client's first name without purring it or gasping it. Just saying his name, like a normal word. "Adam," Remy repeated thoughtfully.

"David," Challoner replied, and Remy found himself wishing that he'd given the man his real name. Challoner headed for the door. "Okay. I'll be right back."

And he was, before Remy had even found the right pair of boots. Remy hurried, but Challoner stood patiently, and when Remy sat down to pull the socks on, Challoner knelt at his feet as if ready to serve. Again, it was nothing Remy hadn't experienced before; he'd had clients who wanted to serve him. He'd had clients who paid good money to have him yell at them, abuse them, and one who'd wanted to be pelted with frozen peas, for God's sake. But this, somehow, felt different. Remy didn't like it. He took the socks out of Challoner's unresisting hands and pulled a few pairs on top of each other before stuffing his feet into the boots he'd selected. "Sorry for the nuisance," he said, standing up as if reporting for duty.

Challoner apparently picked up on the military theme. "What are your orders for this walk?"

"Tell you if my feet hurt. But they won't... that is some serious cushioning we've given them. They're like little foot-babies, all wrapped up and warm."

"Foot-babies, huh?" Challoner smiled. "Okay, a new order is to let me know if their diapers need to be changed."

"Yes, sir."

Challoner rested his hand gently on Remy's shoulder and guided him toward the door. The cold air outside almost took Remy's breath away and he was glad of the borrowed clothes. He fell in at Challoner's side, about half a step behind, and Challoner scowled at him. "I've finally convinced my own staff not to do that. Will you walk beside me, please?"

Remy obligingly moved forward. The proper way of walking was ingrained deeply enough that he didn't need to worry about messing up the next time he was around a more traditional client, and it didn't matter if walking this way made Remy feel uncomfortable. He was there to serve.

They walked down a long, carefully shoveled and salted path, and then across a sort of yard that was probably a lawn in the summer. "Vegetable garden," Challoner said, gesturing to a fenced rectangle. "We try to keep it organic, but we're not totally pure. And that's the orchard, over there."

"Apples?" Remy guessed. "We're too far north for peaches, aren't we? Do you have cherries?"

Challoner looked a little surprised. "Yeah, too cold for peaches.

We might be able to baby them along, if we tried, but that doesn't really fit the philosophy, you know? I mean, if this is supposed to be a self-sustaining operation, then we should be focusing on efficiency, not exotic possibilities." He looked out over the landscape as if envisioning it during the growing season. "You're right, there's apples and cherries. Plums, pears, and grapes. Nuts, and berries. Quite a variety, really. Beautiful in the spring, when they blossom."

Remy nodded. "How do you keep them? Like, freezing, or canning, or drying...?"

Challoner squinted at him. "You know a bit about growing fruit. Where'd that come from?"

Remy ignored the sudden churning in his stomach and forced his voice to be light. "I pick these things up. You aren't the only rich guy who wants to pretend he's a farmer." And then he braced for the reaction to those words, because they had been far too disrespectful. He'd let himself get distracted and now it was all falling apart.

But Challoner didn't seem upset. "I guess not. Maybe you should introduce me to the others and we could have a little club."

Was this a test? Remy tried to pull his scattered thoughts back together. "I wish I could," he said. "But, of course, client confidentiality makes that impossible."

"You don't discuss your clients with other clients."

"I don't discuss my clients with anybody. This is your business, but nobody else's."

"Except for Mr. Baryman," Challoner prompted. "You report back to him, or to his minions."

"Only as required to improve the client's experience," Remy lied. He didn't like where this conversation was going. "For example, I might let them know that the next person who comes out here should bring hiking boots and warm clothes."

"But you didn't tell Baryman about the other night? About

what happened at the hotel? Between you and me, I mean, not the bombing."

"No, I didn't."

Challoner gave him a look. "Because you haven't seen him yet. Because you came straight here from the security center."

"I was taken somewhere to get cleaned up. If anyone cared what happened between you and me, they could have asked me then. And I could have told them... well, actually, I don't know. We never got around to talking about that." Now it was Remy's turn to give a questioning look. "It seemed like maybe you *wanted* Baryman to know about the other night. What little there was to know. So if you'd said that you wanted me to tell him, I'd have told him."

"He doesn't have the rooms bugged? That's his hotel... I thought he might have it wired."

"I'm sure he wouldn't violate his clients' privacy like that." Remy tried to sound scandalized, but it was such an obvious lie that he didn't know why he bothered.

"This house is clean," Challoner said abruptly. "The property too. I have it swept regularly. I have monitors and blockers... everything. Anything that's said here, stays here."

There was no way Remy was going to have this conversation, not with a member of the upper class, not with anybody. "I'm sure that if people were listening, they wouldn't hear anything to alarm them. And of course I wouldn't question your decisions on the matter, but I know that I'm comforted when things are monitored. I'm confident of my own loyalty, and know that I won't say anything that could get me into trouble."

"So how come you were taken into custody after the hotel?" Challoner stopped walking and turned to face Remy. "If you're so pure, why did they think you were worth interrogating? I checked, and the other... the other people who were working on that floor weren't detained for more than routine questioning. So why did the investigators spend so much time with you?"

Remy should have been prepared for this question. There was no way he could mention Dar, or Colony Seventeen. And he couldn't think of any other compelling reason for the interest in him. "I don't know," he said as calmly as he could. "I imagine that with such a dramatic attack, they were casting the net more widely than they usually would. I was just a little fish who got hung up with the sharks, I suppose. They were thorough, and once they were satisfied of my innocence, they released me. I was pleased to be of service."

"You 'appreciate the excellent job they do to keep us safe,'" Challoner said dryly.

"Yes."

"And you never resent the limitations on your freedom?"

Remy didn't have to fake his shocked expression. "Of course not," he spluttered. What was Challoner trying to get him to say? Maybe the man had been telling the truth and there really were no listening devices on the property, but that didn't really matter. Challoner's word against Remy's wasn't even a contest. If Challoner said Remy could fly, Remy would be expected to lift off.

He searched his panicking mind for the words. They should be second nature to him, after all the repetition on the holos. "We need to make small sacrifices in order to preserve the larger good," he managed.

Challoner watched him a moment longer, then nodded sadly. "Of course," he finally said. He looked out over the frozen land and took a deep breath, as if drawing strength. After a moment, he said, "We have over three hundred hectares in crops—wheat, canola, and corn, mostly. Another hundred hectares in hay and forage for the livestock. And almost eighty hectares of carefully managed hardwood forest. We get maple syrup from that, but mostly we're looking for the lumber." He started walking, and this time didn't object when Remy fell in half a step behind. "The livestock barns are this way. Would you like to see the animals?"

"Of course," Remy said. He felt like he was back on solid ground, but he had no confidence that it wouldn't shake beneath his feet at any moment. He thought of his worst-case scenario from the shuttle the night before and almost laughed out loud. He'd thought it was tough when Hesterman wanted to pretend to be boyfriends? He'd been naïve. Being a pretend lover was easy compared to being a pretend *friend*.

Chaper Six

Remy managed to avoid saying anything too knowledgeable about the livestock. And it wasn't that difficult, because he hadn't been around animals like these in a long time. Some of his clients had high-strung horses, and many had dogs or cats, but none kept pigs or cattle or goats. The smell of manure made Remy's stomach churn, and he put his hand over his nose to try to block it out.

"A bit strong," Challoner said apologetically, and Remy let him believe that. Better to have him consider Remy a prissy city boy than to try to explain the physical symptoms of something Remy could only interpret as homesickness. "The chickens smell too, in the winter," Challoner continued as he led the way through the large barn. "In the summer, they're outside as much as possible, but in the cold weather, we keep them in most of the time."

Chickens. Remy braced himself. Feeding the flock, easing his small hands under the hens to gather their eggs, trying not to cry when they pecked at his tender young skin... and running to his mother for comfort when the hurt was too much. Chickens had been his job.

He thought about claiming his feet were sore. Challoner would take him back to the house, he was sure of it. But there was something drawing him on, some part of him that *wanted* to be reminded of the pain.

There was a chicken-wired enclosure ahead of them, with a woman standing just inside. She nodded at their approach.

"Adam," she said. "I'm glad I ran into you. I've got the brooder set up, but the temperatures are still low. We may need to buy another one." Her skin was a medium color, just like Remy's, and he assumed this meant that, despite her casual tone, she worked for Challoner. The upper class was proud of its racial purity. Whether white, black, or Asian, they obsessively traced their lineage and glorified their own race. It was the lower class, the people like Remy, whose ancestors had mixed with each other and averaged out to a warm brown tone.

"Damn," Challoner said. He turned to Remy. "David, this is Wendy. She's in charge of the animals. Wendy, David's visiting for the weekend." She nodded a polite greeting and Challoner said, "The brooders are hard to get hold of, for farms this size. We're hunting for antiques, mostly. Is it okay if I take a look at that? You're okay on your own for a second?"

"Of course," Remy said. He wished Challoner hadn't asked; the charade made Remy feel foolish, especially in front of a stranger. He stepped forward into the space Challoner left as he went to take care of his business.

There were about forty chickens. That was more than they'd had on the colony, but that made sense; the colony planet was so far from Earth that it would have been far too expensive to ship something as fragile and spoilable as eggs or meat. The colonies focused on wheat and other grain crops for export, but tried to be self-sufficient with other foods. Remy's chickens had just been for his family; Challoner's were apparently intended to feed a small community. An estate the size of this one would have a considerable staff, and if this was Challoner's hobby, he probably wanted food to serve to his guests as well. Remy thought about the eggs he'd eaten that morning and looked down at the chickens busily pecking at the floor of the barn. "Thanks, guys," he said.

He used to do that. Talk to the chickens. He'd had friends, of course, but they'd all lived on their own farms. They saw each other at school and on holidays, but Remy had been on his own at home.

"You all like it here?" he asked. One of the hens looked up at him and cocked her head as if trying to understand. "I think you should. Seems like a pretty good place. They feed you, keep you warm, and you get to go outside in the summer. That's pretty good, right?" The hen tilted her head in the opposite direction.

Remy nodded at her. "Yeah, okay, there's a downside. They steal your eggs, and they probably kill you eventually. But everybody's got to die, right? Sooner or later. At least you guys have it easy up until it happens. It's not like you'd do very well outside on your own." He thought about Dar, raving about freedom, and shook his head at the hen. "It's a cold world out there. Dangerous. This is the spot for you. Warm and safe."

The hen gave him a long look from her beady eyes, then resumed pecking with the others. Remy crouched down and watched her through the wire fence. He wished she'd come back, but she flapped into a crowd of birds squabbling over something or another, and he wasn't even sure which one she was anymore.

"You ready to go?" Challoner asked, and Remy jerked in surprise. His cheeks were cold, he realized. Wet. Damn it. He stood up but kept his head turned toward the chickens long enough to give his face a quick rub. Then he turned and smiled at Challoner.

"I think I'm a little allergic. My eyes are watering like crazy."

"Let's get you into the fresh air, then." Challoner's voice was easy, but there was something about the way he laid his hand on Remy's shoulder that made it seem like maybe he wasn't fooled.

They headed back to the house, Challoner making easy conversation, Remy responding with as much charm as he could muster. They were by the garden gate when Challoner said, "We had a few chickens go feral last year. In the summer. They made it out of the yard, roosted in the forest, and refused to come back. We lured them with treats, tried to scare them in, but they wouldn't come."

"What happened to them?" Remy wasn't sure he wanted to

hear the answer.

"Flew south for the winter," Challoner said.

"No, seriously." Remy stopped walking and Challoner turned to face him. "They died, right? Did a fox or something catch them? Or did they freeze to death?"

Challoner stepped closer. "David. I saw them flying, and they were heading south. That's the last I saw of them."

"They're *chickens*. How far could they get?"

"They got a hell of a lot farther than the rest of the flock ever did," Challoner said firmly. He started walking again, and Remy fell in beside him. He remembered not to hang back.

They made it into the house, stripped down, and returned to their chairs by the fire. There was a book next to Challoner's seat, an old-fashioned paper kind. "Do you read?" he asked, laying his hand on the book. He touched it respectfully, almost lovingly.

"I *can* read," Remy replied, "if you want me to."

"What about swimming? There's an indoor pool, if you want."

"Okay. I can swim if you want me to."

"David...," Challoner started, then caught himself and started over in a more patient voice. "What do you normally do in your free time?"

"Uh... I exercise. Swimming is good exercise. Would you like me to swim?"

"Exercising isn't really free time, though, right? I mean, you exercise for your job. To stay looking good. What do you do with *your* time?" Challoner seemed to be losing his patience again. "Holos? There's a holo room, if you want to play games, or you can just watch a show up there."

"Which would you prefer?" Remy was starting to get just as frustrated with this conversation as Challoner seemed to be, although he was trying harder not to show it. "Or...." He didn't want to offend with his persistence, but he had a specialty, and it wasn't playing holo games. "You could reconsider your decision on sex. I've already pleased you one way, and I don't think it's done irreparable harm to your character, has it? I can do that again, if you like, or whatever else you'd prefer."

"Jesus, David," Challoner said. He sounded pained. "No. That's not going to happen. At the hotel, that was... well, that was complicated, but it was a one-time thing."

"If the attack hadn't happened," David asked, "were you going to come and visit me, in the bedroom?" *Were you going to fuck me?* It would be so much easier to ask it straight out, but some clients were prudish about that, and David really couldn't get a firm grip on Challoner's sexual mores.

"If I had, I would have regretted it," Challoner said slowly. "I'm glad it didn't happen. I'm sorry that... you know. I'm sorry that anything happened."

Remy was suddenly exhausted. It didn't make sense, because the night before should surely have left him well-rested, but he just didn't have the energy for this. "Fine," he said. "But I'm here now, and you're paying for the privilege of my services whether you take advantage of them or not. Why don't you save us some time and just tell me what you want me to do? No sex. So... do you want me to swim, read, play holo games, or watch holo shows? Or something else, if you want. But just because you're pretending that this isn't business doesn't mean I'm pretending the same thing. I work for you. What work would you like me to do?"

Challoner squinted. "If you work for me, then maybe you'd better get a little better at pretending to be who I want you to be. And I want you to be someone who's enjoying himself."

Remy only paused for a moment. Then he said, "Holo games sound like fun!" He kept the sarcasm out of his tone; he didn't need it. "Do you have *Swamp Warrior Seven*? I heard it's excellent. You get to kill alligators with sonic grenades!"

Challoner shook his head in defeat. "I don't know if I have it. If I don't, feel free to download. The games room is down the far hall, past the staircase, on the right."

"Great! You don't want to join me? There's probably team play, or we could face off against each other." Remy kept his voice light and excited and practically bounced to his feet.

"No. I think I'll do some work."

"That's too bad. But, thanks, Adam! This whole weekend's been just what I needed, and getting to blow up some alligators—that's going to be the icing on the cake!" Remy was pretty sure his laugh would sound genuine even to someone looking for the lie. "But let me know if you need anything, okay? I think I'm maybe going to get a little carried away with this game, if I'm not careful."

Challoner stood up and looked closely at Remy. "You really are a piece of work, David."

"Thanks!" Remy said with a happy smile, and he practically skipped out of the room. He kept the energy going as he headed down the hallway and found the games room, but once he was inside and out of sight, he let himself flop onto the plush sofa. Damn. It wasn't even noon on Saturday, yet. He had a hell of a lot of time to spend with this no-sex, happy-farmer son of a bitch. He really wasn't sure how he was going to handle it.

"You want some lunch?" Challoner's voice came from the open doorway, and Remy paused the stupid holo game. He should concentrate on the *real* game he was playing; it was much more challenging, and much more important.

"Oh, I'm sorry! I could have made that for you! I mean, I'm not a great cook, but I could have helped, at least." His smile was apologetic.

"No, it's fine." Challoner stepped cautiously into the room as Remy turned around. "Damn, you really have been blowing up alligators."

"Game off," Remy said, and the holographic alligator remains disappeared, along with the corpses of the villainous rebels he'd been dealing with. He stepped out of the sensor area. "It was kill or be killed."

"Of course. So, ready for lunch?"

"Absolutely. Is it home grown as well? I don't think I mentioned how delicious the eggs were this morning. I could really taste the freshness."

Challoner squinted at him as if trying to judge his sincerity. "Thanks," he said cautiously, and he started walking, Remy trailing behind. "And, no, not really home grown this time. Well, parts are, but the greenhouse isn't going to be built until the spring, so the salad is imported. And we're still selling our grain instead of milling it on site. So the bread is homemade, but not with our ingredients. The cheese is ours."

"Wow, you have a dairy? That must be fascinating!"

"Okay," Challoner said, and he stopped and turned to face Remy. "I'm sorry. It was obnoxious of me to try to pull rank on you, and you've absolutely proved your point. Can we go back to argumentative David now?"

"I can argue if you like, Adam. But you were right. I *do* work for you. I'm here to please you, in whatever way you wish. If having a happy houseguest is your thing, then I can and will be a happy houseguest."

"How old are you?" Challoner raised his hand to stop Remy from speaking. "And don't you dare ask how old I want you to be. Just... tell me the actual number."

"Eighteen," Remy said.

Challoner squinted at him. "Bullshit." He stepped closer and peered at Remy's face, then down his torso. "You take good care of yourself, but you're older than eighteen."

"How old do I look?" This was actually a useful conversation. It would help Remy determine how much longer he could hope to work for Baryman, and let him know how desperately he should be searching for his post-whoring career.

Challoner looked him over, top to bottom, then said, "Twenty-four."

Remy smiled. "Damn, you're good." Challoner had only underestimated by a couple years.

"So why'd you say eighteen? I specifically asked you to tell me the truth, and you lied. Why?"

Well, that was an awkward question. But Challoner seemed more curious than angry, so Remy decided to try the truth. "It's the age I *should* be," he said. "I don't know your tastes, but eighteen is a pretty safe bet for everyone to be okay with. Young enough that I still seem fresh, but old enough to not make more conservative clients feel uncomfortable."

Challoner started walking again, and gestured impatiently for Remy to walk beside him instead of behind. "You were doing this already, when you were eighteen?"

Now it was Remy's turn to stop walking. "Mr. Challoner. Sorry, Adam. Adam, if you want me to tell you the truth, you should stop asking questions where a true answer may upset you. I don't want to upset you."

Challoner's voice was quiet. "You were doing this before you were eighteen."

Remy didn't speak. He started walking again, and after a moment's hesitation, Challoner fell in beside him. They had made it through the doorway to the large, warm kitchen when Challoner stopped again. "No. I want to know. I want the truth, even if it's 'upsetting'." He gripped Remy's shoulder and gently turned him until they were facing each other. "How old were you when you started with this?"

Remy knew he should lie. Challoner was a client, and clients didn't get to see the inner workings of the Baryman empire. So he was going to lie, but somehow, when his mouth opened, it told the truth. "Nine," he said. Challoner's hand loosened on his shoulder, and Remy took that as permission to turn away.

There were plates and bowls full of food set up at a long wooden table, and Remy walked in that direction, painfully aware that Challoner was not following him. "Do you care where I sit?" he asked.

Challoner didn't answer immediately but eventually said, "No, it doesn't matter. Wherever you like."

Remy stood behind the wooden chair and waited for Challoner to make his way to the table. When he finally arrived, he sank into his chair and frowned at the food laid out before him.

"The bread's homemade?" Remy said. "I've never seen that done. Is it difficult?"

Challoner shifted his frown from the food to Remy's face. "Not really," he said. "Please, serve yourself."

Remy obliged, and ate quietly, leaving Challoner with his thoughts. Remy wondered whether he was about to be sent away. Someone like Challoner, with his ridiculous ideas about respect, about not having sex with prostitutes... someone like Challoner didn't want to be in the presence of a person who'd been whoring since he was a child. Remy had let this strange situation make him careless, and he hoped the punishment wouldn't be too severe. If Challoner was kind, he would just tell Baryman's people that something had come up and he couldn't use Remy's services after all. But if he wasn't kind... if he told the truth... Remy tried not to think about what would happen if Challoner told the truth.

"My father died," Challoner said abruptly. He looked up and saw Remy's expression. "About a year ago," he clarified. "And I inherited his fortune. I'm an only child."

"I'm sorry for your loss." Remy had no idea where this conversation was supposed to be going, but at least it didn't seem likely to lead to his immediate removal from the premises.

"I'd been living in Europe. I moved over there when...."

Challoner caught himself, and laughed, although he didn't really sound amused. "I was going to say I moved over there when I was just a kid. But I was twenty years old. That's not a kid."

He looked at Remy as if waiting for confirmation, but Remy just shrugged. He was hardly an authority on childhood. "What part of Europe were you in?" That seemed like a safe topic.

"I moved around. I went over to go to school, and I just stayed."

"What did you study?" Ask the client questions about himself, but nothing too personal. Be interested, but not nosy. Remy was getting back in the swing of things.

"Nothing, really. Well, everything, but nothing with any intensity." Challoner jabbed his fork into a piece of cucumber. "I was a typical trust-fund brat, bumming around and wallowing in angst." He looked at Remy. "Twenty-two years ago. You were... two?"

Well, there didn't really seem to be any point in dragging that out any longer. "Five," Remy clarified, and waited while Challoner double-checked his math.

"Can you *never* just tell the truth from the start?"

"I like to make you work for it," Remy said, and he made his voice husky and low.

"Yeah, I noticed." Challoner seemed amused, but then sobered. "What I meant, with all the Europe stuff... I didn't realize how bad it had gotten here." He frowned thoughtfully. "No, that's not quite right. I didn't let myself acknowledge how bad it was here. I shut my eyes and acted like it wasn't there. That's closer to the truth."

"There's no reason you should have done differently," Remy said. "And it's not that bad here, really. Is it? I mean, not for me. I've got food and a warm bed. That's more than a lot of people can say. I get taken care of. I'm valuable. I don't have a problem with that."

"You've been prostituting yourself since you were *nine years old*." Challoner seemed to think he'd proved something.

"Other kids were working in factories at the same age. I've never worked in a factory, but the numbers say that the jobs are dangerous. And they barely pay at all. So those kids put in a long day's dangerous work and go home to sleep in an overcrowded apartment and eat half-rotten food. And if they get sick, that's it for them. I do *my* job and go back to my private room, where I eat healthy food and have access to quality health care." Remy shrugged. "I could quit anytime I wanted, but I don't. I'd rather do this than do that, for sure."

"Those are the only two choices." Challoner's words were halfway between a question and a statement.

"No. Those are the *best* two choices. The other options... I could not work at all, and beg for food on street corners, sleep under a bridge and freeze my feet off in the winter. Or I could join the army and go be cannon fodder for quarters and food no better than if I worked in a factory. No thanks." Remy stretched luxuriously, then reached out and pulled a stray piece of cheese off one of the plates on the table. He put it in his mouth and chewed slowly. "Delicious," he said.

"The system's broken, David." Challoner sounded sad.

Remy just shrugged again and looked around the room. "Looks like it's working pretty well for you." He grinned and looked for more cheese. "And it's working okay for me too. No complaints here."

"I can't decide whether you're in total denial or absolutely insane," Challoner said. "Or maybe just lying your ass off. Again."

"So, could we say that makes me 'mysterious'? Some guys find 'mysterious' very appealing, you know."

Challoner smiled. "I'm not going to have sex with you, David. I don't care how appealing you are."

"That is very sad, Adam. For you, I mean. I think you are really missing out on a good thing."

"I think I probably am," Challoner agreed. He took a bite of his sandwich, and when he was done chewing, he asked, "Do you play chess?"

"I know the basics. But I'm not much good."

"Let's play chess this afternoon. I'll help you get better."

"Your wish is my command, Master."

Challoner rolled his eyes. "Yeah, right." He popped the last bite of sandwich into his mouth. "You had enough?" At Remy's nod, Challoner stood up. "Grab your plate, and whatever else you can carry. You were busy killing alligators while I was slaving away making all this, but you can help clean up."

"Yes, Master."

"Stop that," Challoner said, but he sounded amused, and Remy was pretty sure he could push it a little farther.

It was actually sort of amazing how far Remy seemed to be able to go with this client. And amazing how far he himself seemed *willing* to go. He was walking on treacherous ground, and he knew it. But somehow, he seemed to believe that if he stumbled into quicksand, Challoner would be there to pull him out. It was a stupid, dangerous belief, and Remy would do well to dismiss it from his mind, but he didn't seem to be doing that.

"So, this chess thing... any chance of making it *strip* chess?" he asked. "I think that might really help me keep my mind on the game."

"No," Challoner said firmly as he led the way to the kitchen's work area. Then he smiled. "It might help you pay attention, but it would be *very* distracting for me." And finally, unwillingly, his gaze took a quick trip down Remy's body before returning to his face. "*Very* distracting," he said quietly. Remy tried not to make his sense of victory too obvious.

Chapter Six

The chess was a revelation. For someone who seemed so clueless about the actual world, Challoner sure knew his way around the pretend universe of royalty, pawns, and knights. On the way back to the room with the fireplace and comfortable chairs, Remy had been wondering how well he should allow himself to play. Clients didn't like to be beaten, but they didn't like to be bored, either. But after only a few minutes of play, he realized he'd have to give the game his full effort just to avoid total humiliation.

Challoner was an excellent teacher, for the most part. He got a little testy about Remy's insistence on hiding his queen—"There's no point in having her if you don't *use* her"—but was otherwise patient. They played for a few hours, until Remy's third yawn in as many moves.

"You're still catching up on your sleep," Challoner said kindly. "Why don't you have a nap? I'll wake you in time for dinner."

"I should help you make dinner. Besides, we're in the middle of a game, here."

"We're three moves from checkmate. The game's over."

"What?" Remy stared at the board. "No, my queen's going to... well, never mind what she's going to do. She's going to earn her keep, though, just like you said."

"She's going to take the knight? Really?" Challoner leaned back in his chair and smiled. "I take it back, then. We're *two* moves from checkmate."

"What?" Remy stared some more. It was hard to visualize it all. "Oh. If I took the knight, you'd... no, wait, what would you do? Oh, shit, I see it. Damn it!" Remy had seen a holo once that had a man playing cards, getting frustrated, and knocking the whole table over. He wondered what Challoner would do if Remy pulled a stunt like that. Probably nothing. But it wasn't worth the risk. The risk of being punished, but also, strangely, the risk of disappointing Challoner. "I'm no good at this game. I'm really sorry."

"You're doing fine, and you've come a long way just this afternoon. I've been playing for years." Challoner seemed genuine.

"You're a good teacher," Remy said. He was just deciding whether to turn the statement into a sexual innuendo by suggesting that Challoner could teach Remy a few other things, or to turn it into a sexual innuendo by suggesting that it was Remy's turn to do a little teaching, when a chime sounded. A digitized female voice announced, "Visitors at the front door, Mr. Challoner."

Challoner frowned. "I'm not expecting anyone. I sold my place in the city because people were dropping by all the time and now they're coming out here too?"

"I think you were right about that nap," Remy said. "I'm more tired than I thought. Is it okay if I go upstairs for a while?"

"Of course," Challoner said automatically, but then he gave Remy a sharp look. "Except you're actually hiding, right?"

"I was thinking of it as a tactful withdrawal."

"No, David. You're an invited guest. Whoever's on the doorstep—"

"Is probably a friend or close acquaintance, because otherwise they wouldn't be dropping by without an invitation." Remy stood up. "And I'm not a guest, I'm an employee. I make the same amount of money whether I'm catching up on sleep or making awkward conversation with visitors who are wondering about the dark-skinned pretty boy wearing their friend's clothes." He saw Challoner's doubtful look. "You don't need the complications. And I *could* use the sleep. I work for you and I'll do as I'm told, but if it's my choice, I'd like to go upstairs."

Challoner was stuck on that one, as Remy had known he would be. Now that Remy was getting him figured out, Challoner wasn't hard to manipulate. "I don't want you to be uncomfortable," Challoner said doubtfully.

Remy tried not to laugh. Compared to the humiliations some clients delighted in inflicting on him, an awkward visit with curious friends was nothing. But Challoner didn't need to know that. "I think I would be," he said. "But I can stay if you like."

"No, of course not." The chime sounded again, a gentle reminder, and Challoner grimaced. "I'll try to get rid of whoever it is."

"No hurry," Remy assured him, heading for the hall. "I'll be asleep, remember?" And then, just so Challoner wouldn't have to worry about Remy wandering in partway through his visit, he added, "I'll stay up there until you come get me." He waggled his eyebrows suggestively. "You cheated me out of my surprise last night, but that doesn't mean I don't still want it...."

Challoner just shook his head, then turned and headed for the door.

It felt strange going up to the bedroom alone. Remy was tempted to snoop around a little, see what was going on in the rest of the house, but he resisted the urge. A good whore didn't go beyond the boundaries, and Remy had already pushed far too many limits this weekend.

He found the guest bedroom and flopped down on his unmade bed. He closed his eyes against the light coming in through the huge windows. They must face south, he decided, because he remembered the light coming through them that morning, as well. And that was the last thought he had until he woke up to a gentle hand tousling his hair.

"Dinner's ready," Challoner said softly. "You can go right back to bed afterward, if you want, but you should eat something, first, or you'll wake up in the middle of the night, starving."

"Go right back to bed alone?" Remy asked. "Or can you think of something that might sweeten the deal for me?"

"You wake up fast," Challoner said with a chuckle. "Or else you're trying to seduce me even in your sleep. Get up, now. I made a good dinner."

"I was supposed to help with that."

"Nah. I like cooking for people. It's my *thing*."

"I thought people telling you about sore feet was your thing," Remy said, obediently swinging his legs over the side of the bed and then standing up.

"I only get one? That seems pretty restrictive, David. I would expect you to be a little more open to my needs. A little more appreciative of my *things*."

"I'll appreciate as many of your things as I can get my hands on, if you'll let me." Remy headed for the door. "Your visitors are gone?"

"Yeah. A while ago. It was my neighbors... they spend most of their time in the city and they have another couple country places they visit, so I don't see much of them. But I guess they're nice enough. And out in the country, neighbors are important."

"Of course," Remy agreed. The social niceties were important to the rich. "And you still had time to make dinner?"

"You've been asleep for over four hours, David. I had time to do quite a bit." They were at the staircase now, and Challoner hesitated before starting down. "I called the... the agency? Is that what you call it? I called Baryman's people."

Remy froze. "Oh?" he said, fighting to sound casual.

Challoner didn't seem to notice anything; he was too wrapped up in his own thoughts. "I wanted to see if you could stay another night. I originally... booked you, I guess? Is that how you say it? I asked for you to be here until midafternoon on Sunday. I thought that would be time for you to get rested up, I guess. I don't know. I don't really know what I was thinking at all, to be honest."

Remy let himself breathe. "And now you think you'd like me to stay longer?"

"I would. I thought we could go for a drive, maybe. There's a few places around here that I've been wanting to visit, and I thought maybe you'd want to go with me. You know, if you were interested."

"Of course I'd be interested," Remy said.

"Yeah, but... they said you couldn't do it. They said you needed to stick to the original schedule. You're needed back in the city." Challoner's tone was a strange mix of tension and sadness. He turned and started down the stairs, and Remy followed him.

"For Sunday dinner," Remy said.

Challoner turned to look at him. "What?"

"Yeah, it's weird, but... I don't know, I can't explain it. Mr. Baryman's not religious, as far as I've ever seen, but he has this thing about Sunday dinner. All the—" Remy caught himself. "All of us, we all get together and help cook, and get caught up with each other. It's pretty hectic through the week, so it's great to just have a chance to talk and visit. And eat. It's pretty much a feast." Remy knew he needed to stop before he said that Santa came and gave them all presents or something equally crazy. "So, yeah, that's why. Sunday dinner. Sorry."

Challoner nodded slowly, then smiled. "Oh. That sounds kind of nice, really. I was thinking... you know. That you were booked elsewhere."

"Not on Sunday night," Remy said solemnly. "So it'd be good if tonight's dinner was pretty big too. That way I can start getting my stomach stretched out. What have you got for me?" He followed Challoner into the kitchen and let himself enjoy the aromas. "Is that chicken? Oh, no, is it one of yours? But not one that I saw this morning, right? Those guys are still all fine. Right?" Let Challoner distract himself with assuring Remy about livestock; it would mean he wasn't thinking about what Remy would be doing the next evening.

It wasn't entirely clear to him how this had happened, how Remy had gone from being contemptuous of Challoner's naiveté to being an active party in preserving it, but apparently there was something about the man that inspired such decisions. He seemed so pure, so sweet, and Remy wanted to remember him that way, after the weekend was over.

Challoner had decided to give him a chance to recover, and he'd absolutely done that. It should have made Remy strong, but somehow, he ended up feeling weak. He thought about whatever Baryman had booked for him the next night. To go from this to... well, to go from this to pretty much anything else would be miserable. But he had no choice in the matter, so he forced his mind back to the smells coming from the kitchen. "Is that corn too?" he asked. "Corn's my favorite." He didn't have all that much longer in this sanctuary, but he'd damn well enjoy the time he did have.

THERE was more chess after dinner. Remy knew he still wasn't providing much of a challenge, but there were a few times when he at least made Challoner slow down and think, so that was encouraging. He made his token seduction attempt at bedtime, accepted rejection gracefully, and retired to the guest room. It was a little strange to spend two nights in the same bed, and certainly strange to spend two nights alone. He counted back over the days since he'd last had sex; first the security center, then Challoner's House of Chastity... Remy didn't think he'd ever had such a long break, not even when he'd had pneumonia when he was seventeen. Apparently, in the cornucopia of sexual interests among Baryman's clientele, there were men who found chest-rattling coughs and general weakness to be irresistible. Remy hadn't been sorry to regain his health and lose a few clients.

He slept well, woke up with the sun, and found his way downstairs to the kitchen. There was a woman standing in front of the counter. She looked stout, maybe middle-aged, and from what he could see, her skin was the same medium tone as his. Her back was to him, and he froze in his tracks. He could have sworn he hadn't made a sound, but without turning around, the woman said, "Breakfast will be ready in a few minutes."

He wondered if she thought he was someone else. "I'm David," he said tentatively.

"Adam said you'd be down eventually." She turned toward him and he saw her eyes, staring blankly at some spot over his shoulder. "I'm Carralina. I work here. Adam asked if I could come up this morning and take care of you."

She had no apparatus, no tools of the sorts Remy had seen on others who'd lost the use of their natural eyes. Did that mean she actually couldn't see him? "Oh," he said. Not very useful. "I mean… is Adam around? I don't need breakfast, really."

She turned her body back to the stove but kept her head turned a little toward him. He supposed that was the advantage of having learned to do things without using her eyes. "He had to go out. Some sort of livestock emergency." Even without the visual cue, he could hear the eye roll in her voice. "As if there isn't one of *those* every other day."

"Okay," Remy said. "I can just go back upstairs. Or wherever. I can just wait for him." Or for the shuttle to arrive. He tried to suppress his totally irrational feeling of disappointment. He had come to the house to serve; if his services were not needed, that shouldn't mean anything to him.

"Adam said to tell you that the oats were grown on the

property," Carralina said.

Remy paused, waiting for that to make sense. "What oats?" he finally asked.

"The ones in your porridge. And it has dried berries and nuts, also grown here." She lifted a pot from the counter and put it on the stove. "Front burner, level six," she said in the clear voice that most people seemed to reserve for speaking to electronics. Her voice was softer when she said, "Maple syrup and goat's milk too. He seemed to think you'd want to know that the ingredients were all from this property."

"What about salt?" Remy asked. "Did you put any salt in it? That's not from around here, right?"

She smiled. "It always comes down to the salt. You caught us." She waved a hand in the general direction of a row of comfortable stools in front of one of the counters. "You can sit and chat, if you like. It'll be about ten minutes for the porridge."

Remy wasn't used to friendly staff. Usually, servants treated him with contemptuous, cautious distance; they couldn't ignore the relationship he had with their masters, but they were too puritanical to accept his presence. He wondered whether Carralina knew why he was at the house. Then he wondered whether he really knew why he was at the house, himself.

He deliberately shuffled his feet as he walked across the kitchen so she would know that he was moving. Then he remembered how easily she'd sensed he was in the doorway and felt foolish. There were metal feet on the wooden stools, and the noise of them dragging across the tile floor suddenly seemed deafening. Remy perched on the stool and tried to sit completely still, not even rustling his clothing.

Carralina seemed oblivious to it all. She obviously knew the kitchen well, moving confidently from one tool to the next as she added ingredients to her large mixing bowl.

"What are you making?" Remy asked. "Do you need any help?"

"Bread. And, no, thanks. I have a system. You'd get in my way."

"Or move something and forget to put it back in the right place," he admitted.

Her smile was quick, and somehow familiar. "That's right. That's exactly what would happen." She turned back to her work, leaving Remy with a nagging ghost of a memory. Who did she look like?

He'd never met a blind cook, he was sure of that. He'd never met a blind person without an apparatus, as far as he could remember. So he obviously didn't know her. There were lots of people he'd come across in his years of service, and she probably just reminded him of one of them.

"I had some bread here yesterday. Sandwiches. It was delicious." He wasn't sure why he was trying to keep this conversation going, but she'd said sit and chat, not just sit, so he felt like he should try to earn his keep.

"Thank you. Adam does like things to be homemade. It took a little getting used to, but now I enjoy the challenge."

"Have you worked here long? I guess Adam just came back from Europe fairly recently... did you work for his father?"

"No, not long," she said, and that was it. Possibly the "chat" portion of the invitation wasn't too important to her after all.

So he sat quietly and watched her work. When she turned the heat off the little pot of porridge and reached for a bowl, he stood up and moved closer. The least he could do was help with his own meal. But she raised a hand to hold him back, dished up the porridge, added a spoon, and then finally extended the bowl in his direction. "You'll want to add milk and maple syrup, probably, but I don't know your tastes in that. So you can do *that* much yourself. Milk's in the fridge, syrup's in the cupboard to the left."

Remy was tempted, but he skipped the syrup. This client apparently wanted him to eat, but the other clients wanted him lean. He needed to do his best to keep everyone happy. He let himself add a little milk, though.

He returned to his stool and ate his breakfast, and then brought the bowl over to the sink and excused himself. None of this was new, of course. His clients were busy, important people. He was often left to his own devices while in their homes, or their hotel suites. He was there to satisfy one set of needs, not all of them.

But somehow, it felt different that it had happened in *this* house. And that, he realized as he made his way back up the stairs to the guest room, was a problem. He'd let himself get sucked in. He should have known better. He *had* known better, *did* know better, but he'd let it happen anyway. Challoner was a client, not a friend. Challoner might be confused about the difference, but Remy shouldn't be.

So he showered and primped, got dressed in the clothes he'd arrived in, and made himself look as fuckable as possible. Then he pulled three different envelopes out of the pocket of his ripped jeans. Alertness, arousal, and orgasm. He couldn't just swallow them. There was no way to delay the effects of the pills, so Remy couldn't take them before he was sure they'd be needed, not unless he wanted to parade in front of the client with an unwanted erection. He shook a few of each into the toilet and flushed it. If he'd returned them all to Sasha, it would be clear he hadn't been working very hard. Too late, he hoped that Challoner's home had a good chemical filtration system on the wastewater system; he didn't want the fishes downstream to have an unnatural party in his honor.

And then he waited. He thought about going back down to the games room, but he hoped that wasn't necessary. Instead, he lifted the in-room comm screen off the bedside table. "Activate," he said. Then, "Search 'chess instruction'."

That kept him busy for several hours. He thought about contacting his handlers to get his own information about when the shuttle would arrive for him. Most clients seemed to prefer to handle the transportation details themselves. It made it clearer that they were in control. Remy wasn't leaving of his own accord, he was being returned because his clients were done with him. But that didn't mean that Remy wouldn't be the one held responsible for holding up the shuttle schedule if he wasn't ready to go when it arrived.

He had the comm screen set to contact the agency when he heard heavy steps in the hallway outside. He quickly switched the screen back to chess, then set the device aside as Challoner knocked on the open door and came into the room.

"Sorry," he said. "Sick cow."

It was good that Carralina had given Remy the story already, because Challoner wasn't filling in details. "Will she be okay?"

"Probably. We ran the diagnostic program, and it gave her some drugs. But I try to be on hand when these things happen. I want to learn as much as I can, myself, so that if the system shuts down, or we can't connect to it for some reason, we'll still have lots of knowledge right on the property."

"You really think that's ever going to happen? Losing access to the system?" Remy had seen holos about the idea, nightmare scenarios of anarchy and destruction, but he couldn't imagine it ever actually happening.

Challoner shrugged. "Probably not. It's just a hobby." He stepped closer to Remy's bed. "So maybe I shouldn't have gone, this morning. I'm sorry for abandoning you."

"No, it's fine. I had a wonderful breakfast, and then did some reading. Very relaxing."

Challoner looked at his watch. "But you need to leave in just a couple hours. And you should have lunch first."

Remy shrugged. "I had a big breakfast, and there's always snacks on the shuttle." And maybe it was time for one last attempt to get this weekend on track. He swung his legs off the side of the bed and stood up, straight and tall, then stretched his arms above his head, leaning back to make his shirt ride up and expose his flat, toned stomach. He brought his arms back down and said, "And I can absolutely think of better ways to spend our last couple hours."

Challoner didn't say anything, and his eyes were locked on Remy's. Damn. Was this finally a crack in Challoner's wall of discipline? Remy hadn't taken a pill, and didn't have the caplets in place; he was surprised to realize that he'd been expecting Challoner to refuse him again. But maybe he could manage to put on a good act without the chemicals. He'd had several days off, after all. He stepped forward, slow and cautious, and Challoner said nothing to stop him.

"David," he murmured when Remy was close enough to feel his breath on his face. Remy didn't answer, just laid his hands gently on Challoner's waistband and brought his face in a little closer. He had to be careful not to spook the client, had to make himself completely available without going over the edge and giving Challoner a reason to run. And then he just had to wait. He closed his eyes.

When it happened, it happened fast. Challoner gripped the back of Remy's head, pulling him that tiny bit forward until their lips met in a hard, demanding kiss. Challoner pushed his tongue against Remy's lips for access, and Remy opened his mouth and brought his own tongue forward for a complicated, slippery embrace.

Challoner was everywhere, dominating and possessing as he lined up their bodies. Remy relaxed underneath him and instinctively began cataloguing Challoner's technique. His legs were stronger than Remy's, demanding that Remy's spread and wrap around him; his cock was hard and insistent even through the layers of fabric, finding its spot in the crease of Remy's hip and making itself at home; his chest was broader, heavier, crushing Remy into the mattress and holding him almost motionless. His lips demanded as well, his tongue roamed confidently and aggressively inside Remy's mouth, down his neck, across his jawline—wherever Challoner wanted. And his hands. One controlled, moving Remy's head or his arms, while the other explored, searching under Remy's shirt, around his back, and finally, dangerously, down to Remy's torn jeans.

Remy needed to make himself a bit more active, now, because he knew Challoner wouldn't like what he found if he reached Remy's cock. Challoner's actions should have produced a totally natural reaction in Remy, but they hadn't. And it wasn't Challoner's fault, not at all. This was good, Remy was pretty sure. If Challoner was dealing with someone who liked sex, who got turned on naturally... Remy was pretty sure that Challoner was making all the right moves. Even with Remy, there'd been enough friction to get a bit of a reaction, and that was saying something. But Challoner wasn't the sort of man who was going to be happy with a half-hard partner, and that was all he was going to be getting, here.

Remy needed to get one of the pills out of his pocket, and then he needed to find a way to get it in his mouth unnoticed, and then he needed to slow all this down long enough for the pill to take effect.

He needed to take charge, and he didn't think Challoner wanted that to happen. But he'd *let* it happen, Remy was pretty sure, because Challoner wanted to be a good guy. So Remy heaved a little, started the roll, and as expected, Challoner allowed it, let himself be pushed over so that he was the one on his back and Remy was sitting up, straddling him. A few hip rolls had Challoner's attention, his wide pupils directed away from Remy's face. Remy ran one hand up over his chest, putting on a little show while he reached around with his other hand and fumbled in his back pocket. He felt for the familiar pill shape, and found a stim tab as well; the combination would speed up the drug-processing time. This was going to work. He leaned forward, down so his chest was lined up with Challoner's, and gently, teasingly kissed Challoner's lips before working his way across to Challoner's ear, then down to his neck. He brought his hand to his mouth, dry-swallowed the pills, and grinned. Another victory for superwhore.

He rolled back over, pulling Challoner with him, and gave his best lust-soaked look. But something was wrong. Challoner was still there, still tight in against Remy's body, but he wasn't really moving. His eyes were still dark with desire, but they weren't staring anymore. No. Had the son of a bitch gotten his self-discipline back that quickly?

Challoner wanted to be in control. That was his kink, his style, whatever. But his conscience wouldn't let him *take* control. He wanted everything to be safe and consensual and respectful. It was a conundrum, and not one that Remy had frequently encountered, but he wasn't ready to give up, not yet. Not when he could already feel the chemicals working through his body, getting him into condition to be everything Challoner wanted.

"Adam," he breathed, with just a hint of a whimper. "Please, Adam. More. Keep going." He stretched up enough for his lips to find the underside of Challoner's jaw, and he kissed and nipped in his best submissive-but-horny manner. He was tempted to go for Challoner's lips, but he was pretty sure that would scare the man right off.

With a similar cautious attitude, he made his fingers tease along Challoner's ribs, his shoulders, instead of diving right down for his cock. Challoner was still there; he hadn't pulled away entirely. He still wanted this. He was still wrestling with the decision, and Remy could absolutely make it work. He damn well *would* make it work.

He pulled his face away enough to get a good look at Challoner, to gauge his current state and plan the next move. And Remy froze. Challoner looked miserable. Pained, almost. He was breathing fast, a condition Remy had taken as part of his general arousal, and maybe that was part of it. A big part, maybe. But Challoner looked like a man who was having something torn out of him, something he cared about and really, really wanted to keep.

They lay there, both frozen, and Remy remembered Challoner's words from the first night in the house. If he slept with Remy, he'd be an asshole. Remy didn't believe it, but Challoner obviously did. And Remy was in the house to serve the client.

"Adam," Remy said softly. Challoner didn't respond. Remy pushed for Challoner to roll over again. Challoner was heavier, less willing this time, but he eventually went along with it. But this time, Remy didn't roll with him. Instead, he lay on his back, stared at the ceiling, and took a deep breath. He wasn't superwhore. He wasn't going to win this one. And he'd just have to accept that.

"I'll wait for the shuttle on the roof," Remy said quietly. "Thanks for the weekend. And the chess." He waited for an answer, and when it seemed that none was coming, pulled himself to his feet.

He was halfway to the door when Challoner said, "David."

Remy stopped, but didn't turn around.

"Thank you," Challoner said.

And that was nice, maybe. "Mr. Challoner," Remy said. "If you don't want to fuck a whore, you shouldn't *hire* a whore. You know? It just leads to complications."

Challoner's groan was only a little melodramatic. Remy could hear the man's body flop back onto the soft bed. "Yeah," he finally admitted. "That's good advice. Thank you for that too."

"It was nice to meet you, Mr. Challoner," Remy said, and he headed up to the roof to wait for the shuttle alone.

CHAPTER SEVEN

THE shuttle arrived, as Challoner had said it would, a couple hours later. Remy refused to turn and look out the window as the craft lifted off and started back toward the city. This had just been another job, nothing more, and Remy didn't reminisce about his work. He didn't waste time wishing that things were different. There was no point to any of that.

There was no one else on the shuttle, no one but the pilot, who was, of course, far too elevated to even consider talking to whores. Well, he'd talk to them, according to the girls, but only to proposition them for freebies and make leering comments. Remy and the other boys he ignored completely. He was just making a cargo run.

But Remy needed to know where he was going, and what he was expected to do when he got there. Well, the "do" would probably be pretty clear, but there were always details. He called up the agency on the comm and was greeted with a cheerful, "David, on shuttle, reporting for duty!"

Ah. Marlene was working. She could never just say what he needed to hear, and normally he liked her playfulness. So he should try not to ruin her fun just because he was in a bad mood. "This is Marlene, at HQ, with all the information you need," he replied.

"Oh, great. It's good to talk to you, Marlene. You are beautiful and lovely beyond description, and it brightens my day every time

I hear your voice." Damn, she was cheerful. Or possibly setting him up for something.

He decided to get it over with. "David, you've got a job to go to right away. I'll tell you the details now." He waited, and finally she responded in a less manic voice.

"Yeah. David, you've got a job to go to right away."

"There's no wardrobe in the shuttle. Am I fine as I am? Retro rent-boy, I think Sasha called it."

"Wardrobe will be provided at the function," Marlene said neutrally. Then, quietly, "Mr. Baryman is having a party."

Remy should have felt well-rested. He should have felt prepared for anything, even one of Baryman's parties. But all he wanted to do was go home, crawl into his narrow bed, and burrow down under the covers. He was pretty sure he wanted to stay in bed forever. He took a deep breath. "Okay. Thanks, Marlene." He didn't need any more information from her; the whole team would be at the house or at whatever venue Baryman had found, and they'd get Remy set up just as they wanted him. He flipped the comm switch and sank back onto the padded bench seat. He wasn't sure how long the trip out to Challoner's house had taken, but it must have been at least an hour or two. So it would take that long to get back. He had that much time to compose himself and get rid of the ridiculous ideas he'd let himself pick up in the country.

By the time the shuttle touched down, he was ready. He waited for the door to open for him and then strode down the ramp, tossing a casual, "Thanks, Jeeves," back over his shoulder at the pilot. They were at Baryman's city house, an ostentatiously palatial building that gave Remy the shivers every time he thought of it. But there was no time for shivering now, and he strode purposefully over to the door Sasha was holding open for him.

Sasha gave him a critical once-over. "Here," he ordered, and he pulled out his kit. Eyeliner and lip gloss, then Sasha said, "Mr. Baryman would like to see you in his office."

"Wait." A Baryman party was much different from a personal summons to Baryman's office, and Remy had been prepared for the first, not the second.

Sasha smiled tightly. "The party is later. We're setting up downstairs—the usual rooms. You'll come find us when you're able."

That was open-ended, which was appropriate given the circumstances. Mr. Baryman came by the house to inspect his whores fairly regularly, but a private audience was not usual. And almost certainly not good.

"He was pleased with me, you said. We took the good shuttle to the country because he was pleased with me." Remy tried to fight down the panic.

"It seemed that he was," Sasha admitted. "And he may still be. I think that he has a special interest in this weekend's client. He may just wish to hear your report in person."

Remy's nod was jerky. Sasha prodded him gently in the shoulder, and he started walking. He knew the way, and defiance was... it was impossible. The house wasn't just a palace, it was also a fortress. There was no escape. And even if Remy made it outside, where could he hide that Baryman wouldn't find him? His mind flashed to the huge chairs by the fire in Challoner's home. That was ridiculous. There was no way to get there, and no reason to expect help from Challoner even if Remy did make it. The faster Remy got thoughts like that out of his head, the better.

He reached the huge wooden doors of Baryman's office and made the requisite knock before speaking into the comm panel. "David Stone to see Mr. Baryman," he said. His voice sounded a little tight, but not terrible.

The door buzzed and swung open, and Remy stepped inside.

Mr. Baryman was sitting behind his desk, an imposing piece of furniture that had always reminded Remy of a coffin. Baryman himself was a large man, mostly fat but with enough muscle to do damage when that was what he wanted. And it was what he wanted quite often. His skin tone made it clear that, for all his wealth, he was not one of the pureblooded aristocrats like Challoner, and Remy had seen Baryman beat a man almost to death for pointing that fact out. Several of his associates were sitting in front of the desk, apparently having a meeting, but no one was talking as Remy approached them.

Mr. Baryman just stared at him.

"I'm sorry for interrupting, Mr. Baryman, but I was told you wanted to see me?" Remy kept his gaze somewhere around Mr. Baryman's right shoulder.

"I did," Baryman said, leaning back in his chair. "I do."

There was no real answer to that, so Remy didn't know why Baryman had stopped talking. The whole setup, Remy was pretty sure, was designed to make people nervous and crazy. But even knowing that it was deliberate didn't do much to neutralize the effect of it all, at least not for Remy.

Finally, Baryman said, "You were at the hotel when the bombs went off. You were questioned extensively about that. Why?"

Baryman would have seen the security team reports as soon as they were composed. More likely, he'd had access to the live feed of the interrogation-room proceedings. "I may have known one of the bombers. Long ago, when I was a boy. And I've seen him a few times since then, just... around. But our security forces determined that I had no connection to the bombing. That's why they released me."

"They released you because I paid them a healthy bribe," Baryman corrected, and he waited again.

"Thank you, Mr. Baryman."

"Twelve highly respected citizens died in that bomb attack. Some of them were my friends. My clients. I am taking a personal interest in finding the people responsible, David." Mr. Baryman's voice was harder when he added, "Or should I call you Remy?"

Another question with no right answer, but Remy was clearly expected to say something. "Sir, of course you can call me whatever you wish. But if you mean that... that I might have some loyalty issues, because of who I used to be before you rescued me... I was a child, sir. I didn't know about any of it. And I've always been grateful for the assistance you gave me, and I've always been loyal to you, sir, and loyal to our government. I have no knowledge of the bombing, but of course I'd be honored to help your investigations in any way, if you think I could be useful. Just as I was honored to assist the security services, although I don't believe they found me to be much use."

Baryman didn't speak right away. He looked at one of his colleagues as if silently asking for an opinion, and when the man shrugged, Baryman returned the gesture, then brought his attention back to Remy. "Adam Challoner," he said. "You were doing well with him, in the hotel."

So they had been listening. Not a surprise. "Thank you. I was pleased with my work there."

"And he specifically requested you for the weekend. Insisted, really." Mr. Baryman's smile was oily. "If it hadn't been for him, I'd have left you to fester quite a bit longer in that interrogation room. I don't like hearing that one of my whores has been friends with a terrorist since they were children."

"I had no idea he was a terrorist," Remy protested. He'd probably get in trouble for talking back, but he'd be in more trouble if Baryman actually believed that Remy had been in any way involved in the attack. "And I haven't seen him for years. Just when we were kids, and then he'd pop up to say hello every now and then. I never sought him out." No, Remy had never looked up his only surviving friend, had never made any effort to stay in contact with him or help him out. Not Remy. It wouldn't have made Mr. Baryman happy if Remy had done anything like that.

Baryman waved a hand dismissively. "I'm interested in Challoner now," he said. "He fucked you? At his house? More blowjobs? What happened? What's his game?"

"He...." Remy had to be careful, not only for Challoner's sake, but for his own. Challoner had said that he didn't want Baryman to be suspicious of him, and Remy didn't want to contribute to anything like that. He also didn't want Baryman to think that Remy had wasted almost two whole days and hadn't been able to seduce a man who'd admitted several times that Remy was just his type. But it would be suicide to lie straight out. Too many chances to be caught. "He's confusing. No fucking. No blowjobs. He... he said he jerked off, watching me sleep." That was true, technically. Challoner *had* said that. "I think... he's got a hang-up about whores. And he really likes control." Baryman was looking interested, and Remy wanted to laugh, or maybe cry. If he told the truth, if he said that Challoner was a decent human being trying not to become an asshole, Baryman would think he was lying. So he'd have to lie in order to make Baryman think it was the truth.

"He says that he doesn't want to sleep with whores because it's disrespectful, or something." Baryman would have heard that much over the hotel microphones. "But really... like I said, he's into control. We messed around some and he was... not rough, but... yeah, controlling. I think maybe the real reason he doesn't like whores is actually that they *do* consent, you know? I think he doesn't just want to control, he wants to *make* the other person do things. I tried to pretend that he was forcing me, but... he's smart enough to know he wasn't. I think that's what ruined it for him." Remy had taken Challoner's decent, if misguided, actions and turned them into something dirty and cruel; he was pretty sure Baryman would approve.

And the man was nodding thoughtfully. "So he's not some virtuous puritan, after all. He's not a reformer, just another fucking pervert, deeper in denial than some of the rest of them." He stared at Remy. "Is that what you're telling me?"

"I'm just a whore, sir. I can't say any of that for sure. That's the feeling I got. That's all."

Baryman looked at one of the men sitting in front of the desk. "He's just another fucking pervert," he repeated, and the man nodded his agreement. "Use that. The bastard thinks he can fuck with me? He thinks he can refuse to sell land that I need? I'm trying to build a fucking *landmark*, a full block development. I'm just about to make some serious money, and he's just getting in the fucking way. I own every other property I need except for that one chunk he's holding on to. He thinks it should be a fucking *park*? He thinks he's better than me, with his old family money and his fancy education? Fuck him." Baryman frowned at Remy as if deciding whether to blame him for Challoner's misdeeds. Remy managed to keep from moving or showing any tension, but his mind was chaotic, far too close to panic. He'd been punished several times when he was younger, but he'd learned his lessons and been safe for years. Nothing any client had ever devised compared to Baryman's techniques.

"So you spent the last two days just 'messing around some' and the three days before that sitting on your expensive ass in a damned interrogation room." Baryman waved one of his fat fingers in Remy's direction. "You had better make up for all that tonight."

Remy felt his whole body relax, although he tried not to move a muscle. If Baryman still expected Remy to be working the party, he wasn't planning a session. After being punished by Baryman, or even by his assistants, it would be days before anyone could be expected to function again. "Of course, sir. I always work hard for you, but I'll absolutely take advantage of how well-rested I am tonight."

Baryman nodded, then waved a hand in dismissal. Remy forced himself to walk rather than run to the door, but he froze when Baryman spoke again. "David." His voice was quiet. Remy turned around and waited respectfully. "You use your head. I like that." Baryman nodded. "You're not as young and pretty as you used to be. Clients have started to notice; there's some that don't want you anymore. You're okay for a while, but we were starting to think we'd be cutting you loose soon."

It wasn't a surprise, but it was frightening to hear it being discussed so casually. Remy managed to nod his understanding.

"But maybe there's a job for you somewhere else in the organization." Remy thought about Sasha, working his magic, then going home to sleep in his own bed, free of the restrictions that were placed on members of Baryman's stable. Sasha had all of the benefits of one of Baryman's whores, without being treated like an animal. And he liked Remy well enough. Maybe Remy could be his apprentice or something.... But Baryman wasn't quite done talking.

"Maybe we should transition you to female clients." Remy was glad he hadn't shown any emotion in response to Baryman's first statement. "You've worked with women, right?"

"In shows, mostly," Remy said. "Not female clients. Well, wives, sometimes. But not *just* women."

"No, women don't want to be fucked by skinny little pretty boys," Baryman said dismissively. "But you're filling out. Nothing to be done about it; starving you bastards only keeps it off for so long." He nodded as if the decision was made. "Keep up the good work, keep thinking, and reporting back, and we'll see about getting you some training, and changing your look, and maybe we'll try you with the women clients. It's a niche market, but it's a career with some serious longevity. We've got guys in their forties still fucking women for a living."

In his forties. Doing this for another fifteen or twenty years. Remy tried to smile. "Thank you, sir. I appreciate your concern for me. I'll be pleased to serve in any way you think best."

"So get your ass out to the party, then," Baryman ordered. "We'll worry about the rest of it later. In the meantime, show a little hustle. I'm watching you."

"Yes, sir. Thank you." Remy made it out the door that time, and kept walking. He wondered if he could do it, if he could bluff his way out the front door just by looking busy, saying he was running an errand for Sasha, saying... Jesus, saying whatever it took. But there was nowhere for him to go once he got outside.

He had no idea what his problem was. He'd worked Baryman's parties before; they were never pleasant, but he'd always survived. But this time he felt like his skin had been peeled off his body, as if every touch, every look, even, would be agony for his raw flesh. He was practically vibrating with anxiety, and there wasn't a damn thing he could do about it. Then he saw Sasha, bustling over to direct some underling on the proper way to anchor a St. Andrew's Cross. Sasha. Sasha could fix this, at least temporarily.

"Sasha!" Remy called, and his voice cracked partway through the name. Damn it. He tried to control himself as he walked across the wide hallway. "Sasha," he tried again, in a more reasonable voice.

Sasha grabbed his arm and spoke quietly but urgently. "David, what's wrong with you? You look terrible. Are you working tonight? Did Baryman...." He caught himself. "Were you disciplined?"

"No. I'm working. I will. I can." *I must.* "I just... can you give me something?" Some of the other whores were drugged daily; there were times when Remy thought he might be the only one doing his job without chemical assistance. Well, without assistance for his mind. He'd always been proud that he was tough enough not to need it, but today.... "I don't know what I want. Something to calm me down. Shut me off. You know? Something to let me get through it. Please." There were more words that wanted to pour out of Remy's mouth, but he managed to stop when he realized that the next syllable would come out as a sob.

Sasha frowned in concern. "What did he *do* to you? Your weekend client. He's the one who did this to you, right?"

And there was no point in hiding from that fact. "Yeah," Remy croaked. "He did it to me. Now... get me back to normal. Okay?"

Sasha's hand was warm against David's cold cheek. "Okay, baby," he said gently. "We'll make it better." He leaned over to rummage through his bag, and David felt himself practically sagging with relief. Sasha was going to give him something. Sasha was going to make it better.

Please. Please. "I just need to get through it," he said.

"I know, baby," Sasha said, and he pulled the short sleeve of Remy's T-shirt up and jabbed something into his bicep. "That's for now. For tonight. If we go long, I'll come find you and give you another dose. And then, tomorrow, we'll talk, and we'll figure out whether you need something longer term."

"Okay," Remy agreed. He could feel the injection already working. Everything was receding. The world was still terrible, but Remy wasn't really *in* it anymore, and that was the best he could ask for. "Okay," he said again.

"Yeah, it is, baby," Sasha said. "Now, you get yourself up to the first bedroom on the left for costuming." He grimaced. "It's cowboy night again."

Great. Spurs and ropes and whips. But it didn't matter. That was all going to happen down here, on Earth. Remy was floating off into the distance of space. He was back where he belonged. He was in space, floating back to the place he'd lived as a boy, the last place he'd felt safe. He was going home.

Chapter Eight

Remy made it through the party. He was detached from his body, floating above and watching as it was bent and tortured, penetrated and defiled. A few times he felt sorry for the poor creature being subjected to it all, but that was about the only emotional connection he experienced. Just when the body started to tug at him, trying to call him back, Sasha was there, with a murmured word and a quick injection, and Remy was free again.

He wondered, absently, how long he could continue that way. Maybe forever. Or for as long as it took for the body to stop fighting, stop trying to survive. That would be all it took, really. Maybe Remy could talk to Sasha the next time they were both on the same plane of existence and make arrangements for a little extra medicine. Enough to finish all this nonsense forever, to send Remy away on a permanent trip to the stars.

Would Sasha allow that? Would Remy, really? Well, he would as long as he was floating away up there. But in order to talk to Sasha, he'd have to go back to his body, and once he was back in it, he figured he'd probably have trouble giving up. He'd have trouble admitting that he'd lost, was really what it was.

He managed to drift right from the drugged stars to the sleepy clouds, and when he finally came back to himself, it was morning. His body was stiff and sore and cold, curled up half on a bearskin rug that probably cost a fortune, and half on the hard tile floor. He managed to stumble away from the rug, at least, before he puked up the little that was left of Challoner's oatmeal into a potted plant. He was naked, without even a hint of a costume, and he looked around the room to find other whores in similar condition. Mr. Baryman wouldn't want to wake up to this mess, Remy knew, but he was in no condition to organize the cleanup. Instead, he wandered toward the bathroom, stuck his head under the tap and gulped huge mouthfuls of water, threw that up into the toilet, and then went back to the sink and tried to drink with a little less greed. Apparently Sasha's drugs had a dark side, but Remy was still glad he'd had them.

He ran the water as hot as he could stand and tried to warm up by submerging various body parts in the filled sink, but he was still shivering uncontrollably when the door opened and Sasha looked in at him. "Oh, baby," Sasha said. "You look almost as bad as you did last night." He burrowed into his bag and pulled out a few capsules. "See if you can keep these down. And come out to the main room. We're doling out clothes and arranging transport back to the house."

"I'm c-cold," Remy said.

"I know. And the clothes aren't going to help a whole lot, baby. You just have to ride it out. But we need to get this show on the road. It's almost noon, and you're booked for three o'clock this afternoon." Sasha gripped Remy's jaw and forced his face up. "You got some sleep, at least, after it all." His gaze ran down Remy's body. "But you've got a *lot* of bruising, baby." He shook his head. "The less it hurts, the more they hurt you." He looked as if he were almost overwhelmed by the paradox, and Remy wondered whether Sasha had been self-medicating a little. Either now, or normally, and he'd allowed things to wear off somehow.

But he pulled himself together and gave Remy a quick, sharp slap on each cheek. "Let's go, David! Clothes, lunch, shower and wardrobe, then work! It's Mr. Olivieri this afternoon, and you and he always have fun, right?"

"He's very nice," Remy said automatically. "I look forward to spending time with him."

That answer shouldn't have made Sasha look like he was going to cry. He pulled Remy forward into a quick, awkward embrace, kissed him on the forehead, and said, "Excellent. Everything's fine. Let's get going."

So the show went on. Mr. Olivieri that afternoon: lots of gasps and moans to cover for the fact that Olivieri was a three-pump chump. Two new clients that night: a couple from somewhere in Africa who seemed to consider Remy's existing bruises a challenge for them to outdo. Painful hours in the clinic on Tuesday: the bruises were drained by leeches and then the damage repaired with subcutaneous lasers. Which got Remy ready for Tuesday night: dinner with Mr. Hesterman and his friends. Hesterman's hand, proprietary and sweaty on Remy's thigh, his shoulder. Hesterman's leering, his suggestive comments that were supposed to make Remy blush like a virgin. And then back to Hesterman's home, his lips wet and rubbery on Remy's face, his body, and all Remy could think about was Challoner's strong, confident kiss. Wednesday afternoon: Remy was scheduled to work a show with a couple other whores, and in the shuttle on the way to the venue, he sat beside Sasha and said, "I need another shot. To get through it."

Sasha looked down at his bag, then looked over at Remy. "David... one time is one time. But if you want it again now, for a job you've done a hundred times before... that's not one time anymore. It's a pattern. A regular thing. The drugs aren't physically addictive. But mentally, once you get in the habit of taking them, they become part of your life." It was all said very matter-of-factly. Sasha was just giving him some information. "Is that what you want? For it to be a regular thing?"

The words made no sense. What Remy *wanted*. What he *wanted*. Remy turned them over in his head, tried to figure them out, but finally abandoned the effort. "I need to get through it," he said.

Sasha nodded sadly. "Yeah," he agreed. "You hit the wall."

"What wall?"

"Not a real wall. Just... when it's all too much. Almost everyone gets that way, eventually. You're still young, but you've been doing this for a long time. It wears you down." He rummaged through his bag and pulled out a small bottle. It was blue glass, and the shape of it was curiously, unnecessarily beautiful. Sasha ran his fingers lovingly over the curves and spoke in a way that made it seem as if he was talking mostly to himself. "Some of us see it coming. We slide into it gradually. Others...." He raised his eyebrow at Remy and smiled. "Others, it sneaks up on. They're fine, they're fine, they're fine, and then they're not." He handed the bottle to Remy and spoke in a more businesslike tone. "Try these. They're not quite as strong as the shot, and they take longer to work. But you can take them on your own, when I'm not around, and the comedown isn't quite so harsh. They might be enough."

"I just take one?"

Sasha nodded, then turned to gaze out the window. "One to take the edge off. Two if you want to be totally out of it." He turned back to Remy. "More than that and you could be out of it permanently." He looked down at the bottle and then back out the window. "Too many might make you throw up before the medicine got where it needed to be. I've always thought five would be a good number. *Maybe* six." He sounded almost dreamy.

Five or six. Remy nodded slowly. That was good information. Sasha was a good friend. The pills were good friends. Remy was lucky.

He guessed Sasha was right; he'd hit the wall. Maybe it was just coincidence that it had happened right after the Challoner job. Or maybe that weekend had just provided the final few bricks that made an existing wall totally impassable.

He made it through the next couple of weeks by taking a pill before every job. The first few times, the clients noticed, but they didn't seem too upset about it. After that, Remy either got better at hiding it or the clients just stopped expecting any different from him.

Hesterman actually seemed to prefer Remy when he was stoned. "You're having fun, now, sweetheart! That's right, put your head on my shoulder. We're very happy together, aren't we? I've got a big dinner tonight. You just sit there and look pretty, and you don't even have to worry about talking to any of them. I'll tell them you're shy. You just smile at me and show how much you adore me, and it'll be wonderful."

Remy could do that. With the pills, it was easy. He'd make himself be in his body just long enough to set an expression on his face, and then he'd let himself drift. He practiced, giving Hesterman an adoring smile right there in the shuttle, and Hesterman rewarded him with a sloppy, drooling kiss. And apparently was so taken with the new Remy that a kiss wasn't quite enough.

He pushed Remy backward so he was reclining on the bench seat, rolled on top and grinded in. Remy's cock was ready to get hard because of the arousal pill, and apparently Remy's consumption of the other pill created a similar response in Hesterman's groin. The man was gasping now, dry-humping furiously, and the whole situation was just too ridiculous.

"Sweetheart," Remy whispered. Then, a little louder, "Sweetheart! You don't want to mess up your pants, do you? Before the big dinner?"

Hesterman stilled, but didn't climb off Remy. Possibly he was just trying to get his breath back.

"Let me take care of you, sweetheart," Remy said. He remembered this. He remembered being a good whore, and maybe he could be that again. He could take a little pride in his work, and look after his clients when they were clearly unable to do it themselves. The drugs offered to take him away, to let him retreat from all this nonsense and go back up to the stars, but this time, he resisted the invitation. "Roll off me, sweetheart, and I'll use my mouth. Okay? Would you like that?"

Hesterman's grunt wasn't exactly clear, but it was certainly enthusiastic, and he shifted his weight obligingly. It wasn't graceful, but Remy managed to get the bulky man stretched out on his back on the bench seat, with Remy kneeling on the floor beside him. "Do it, sweetheart," Hesterman moaned, waving vaguely in the direction of his crotch.

Remy obliged. He didn't tease or go for any finesse. He'd felt the shuttle touch down and knew that they were at their destination. He knew the pilot was watching them, getting either turned on or disgusted or maybe both, but that didn't matter. It couldn't matter; if Remy started getting worried about things like that, he'd never survive. So he slurped away at Hesterman's cock, used all his tricks right off, and had barely gotten started before he heard Hesterman groan. He shoved his cock further back in Remy's throat right before he came and Remy sputtered, working to swallow from that angle. He was still choking a little when Hesterman pushed his head away and started straightening his clothes.

"Let's go, sweetheart," Hesterman said, impatient now. "There are people to meet out there. A few of them could be very important for my business interests, so be on your best behavior."

Remy straightened obligingly. Hesterman looked a bit of a mess, but Remy had a feeling that the client didn't really care about that. His suspicion was confirmed when Hesterman opened the shuttle door and looked out at the crowd of people waiting for his appearance. "Sorry for the delay," he said loudly and joyfully. "My sweetheart just had a little present to give me." He adjusted himself lewdly and grinned in Remy's direction.

The crowd laughed, mostly, and a few of the men shouted their approval and congratulations. These were the people Hesterman surrounded himself with. Remy fixed an adoring smile on his face and let himself drift away. Hesterman was greeting his audience, one arm wrapped firmly around Remy's shoulders, and Remy was flying, up almost to the roofline, looking down at the teeming crowd and not caring what happened to any of them. Not even caring what happened to the one they called David. But there was another group of people down there, a few steps away from the crowd, and they caught Remy's attention. Were they another party who just happened to be eating at the same restaurant, or were they some of the new people Hesterman had been talking about, the ones that might be good for his business? Whoever they were, they'd seen Hesterman's little show, and they didn't look impressed.

Remy looked at them a little more closely, trying to blink his way through the fog. There was one of them, turned away, looking at the ground... then turning back, his broad shoulders shifting to reveal his strong chest and his sad, disappointed face.

Challoner saw that Remy had seen him, and he looked back with some expression that Remy could not read. Could not, and would not. Remy transferred his attention back to Hesterman and tried to control his racing pulse. He fished around in his pocket and found the pill. He remembered Sasha's instructions. *Two if you want to be totally out of it.* That sounded just about right. He'd already taken the first pill, but now he downed the second. He thought about the rest of Sasha's speech. The blue bottle was safe back at the house, only a few pills left in it. If they'd been there, in Remy's pocket right then... five or six, Sasha had said. Five or six. Remy needed to remember that.

THE pill took effect quickly. By the time they were inside the restaurant, Remy was floating. With one pill, he could fight it. He could stay with his body if he wanted to. With two pills, there was no choice to be made. He was floating, flying, gone. His body seemed to be working just fine on autopilot, though. Remy could see himself sitting next to Hesterman, smiling at him, even eating the occasional mouthful of food and sipping at his glass of wine. But he couldn't see anything else at the table, couldn't see *anybody* else, and that was perfect.

He lost track of time. At some point, the meal was over, and Hesterman stood up, so Remy stood up too. But Hesterman put his hand on Remy's arm. "I've got to go take care of some business, sweetheart. You stay here. You're okay here." So Remy sank back into his seat.

With Hesterman gone, there was no point in the rest of the guests playing the game, so they just ignored Remy. That was nice. He propped his hand under his chin and let his eyes close. He was jerked awake when a rough hand seized his shoulder and pulled him to his feet. Remy stumbled but kept his balance, and then Hesterman pulled him in tight. One hand was on Remy's ass, tight and possessive, and the other tilted Remy's head back for a deep, angry kiss. Remy could hear more cheers from the crowd, but Hesterman didn't seem to be enjoying them this time. Instead, he pulled away from Remy just long enough to snarl, "Get your ass in the shuttle. Now." Then another bruising kiss before turning Remy around and shoving him toward the exit.

Remy went. He had no idea what was going on but the instructions had been clear. He was three-quarters of the way to the door when another hand shot out and caught his elbow. Jesus, he was too stoned for all this random grabbing.

This time, there was no kiss. Just Challoner, his face and voice tight. "Don't go with him, David. I pissed him off, and I think he might take it out on you. I'm sorry. Stay here, and I'll take care of you."

That was against more rules than Remy could count. He wrenched his arm free. "I came with Mr. Hesterman. I'm with him tonight." He made it one stumbling step toward the shuttle before Challoner had his arm again.

"Did you hear what I said, David? He's angry. He may be violent."

"I'll be fine," Remy said. "He's nothing. Nothing compared to what Baryman would do if I stayed with you." He hadn't meant to say that last part. But at least it startled Challoner into letting go of his arm.

Remy was almost to the shuttle when Challoner's hand fell on his shoulder again. It wasn't tight, wasn't really trying to control him, just asking that he stop. One of Hesterman's bodyguards stepped forward, but Remy held up a hand and turned to face Challoner. Mentally, he was too far away for any of this to matter, but even from a distance, he didn't think he wanted to see poor, naïve Challoner getting roughed up.

"It's fine, Mr. Challoner," Remy said. He got distracted for a second, staring at the way Challoner's face was flushed, the way the rosy glow crept down until it ended at his crisp white shirt collar. Like a sunset on a winter's day. But Remy needed to stay in his body for just a little bit longer. "Go back to your farm, Mr. Challoner. That's a good place for you." He swayed a little, steadied himself by gripping the railing of the ramp to the shuttle's door, and smiled. "I like thinking about you out there. Sometimes. Sometimes I think about it, and I can't stand it." But that wasn't helpful at all. None of that was going to get Challoner off the shuttle pad. "I'm going with Mr. Hesterman. And if he sees you out here and gets mad... it'll be worse than it has to be."

That was the best Remy could do. He turned, dragged his leaden feet up the ramp, and then he was inside the shuttle with the door sliding shut behind him.

He collapsed onto the bench seat and let himself float away. The cold, wet splash in his face woke him. He licked his lips. Red wine. He must look like he'd been in a bloody accident. He struggled to sit up and focus on Hesterman's livid face.

"Have you been cheating on me, David?" Hesterman's voice was high and tight. "Have you been seeing... have you been *fucking* other men?"

Remy was *way* too stoned for this. He saw Hesterman maybe once a month, or once a week more recently, but the man knew he was a whore. There was no lie, there, not even in Hesterman's fantasies. Not usually. Remy had no idea what the right answer was, so he stayed silent. Hesterman was obviously looking for something else, and the slap he delivered knocked Remy sideways on the seat. He pushed himself back upright, and Hesterman hit him again, with a closed fist this time.

It didn't really hurt, not with Remy so far away from his body. But he'd rather not go through too much more bruise-reduction therapy, so he slid down onto the floor of the shuttle and tucked his knees under his chin, putting his hands up to cover his head. He was counting on Hesterman being too fat to want to bend over that far for more hitting. Hesterman kicked him a couple times, but it was hard to stand on one foot in a moving shuttle, and he wasn't able to get much power going. Remy heard him swear, and peeked out to see him staggering over to sit in one of the bucket seats.

Remy cautiously uncovered his head. He wanted to be quiet, to let this blow over, but it wasn't a very long ride back to the stable, if that was where Hesterman was taking him. It would not go well for Remy if he was kicked out of the shuttle of an angry client, so he needed to get this problem solved fast. He tried to collect his scattering thoughts. Hesterman. It was Hesterman. What did Hesterman like?

"Sweetheart, I'm so sorry I made you angry. I never wanted to do that."

"No, you didn't want to make me *angry*. You just wanted to make me look like a fool. Like I'm the only one who doesn't know about your whoring around. You fucking slut."

It was a strange conversation, and Remy couldn't see a way to get it back to normal. He couldn't see much, if he was being honest. Sasha hadn't been lying about the effects of two pills. Maybe fewer words would help.

He crawled forward, supplicant and pleading, and Hesterman didn't push him away. Remy laid his head on Hesterman's thigh and said, "I'm sorry, sweetheart. I'm so sorry." And then he zoned out for a while, but when he came back to himself, Hesterman was running his fingers through Remy's hair, so things seemed to have gotten better.

"You just can't help it, David. I should have known that. I should have known you weren't strong enough to be good, not without me keeping an eye on you. Poor little baby. You must have been so scared. That Challoner son of a bitch, talking to me like he knows you, or something. Like *he* knows what you need."

Remy wondered whether he'd have wanted to hear that conversation. Probably not. Neither Challoner nor Hesterman would have had a fucking clue. "I just need *you*, sweetheart."

"I know. And I neglected you. That wasn't nice of me, was it? I'm going to make it up to you. I'm going to take you inside and fuck you so hard you won't be able to *think* about another dick, let alone take one. Does that sound good, sweetheart?"

Remy moaned and rubbed his cheek against Hesterman's thigh. Like a cat. They'd had a cat, when Remy was younger. His parents had joked that it was there to catch mice, but of course that was silly. They hadn't brought any mice with them to the colony. The cat was a pet. Remy smiled, thinking about its soft fur, and he rubbed his cheek against Hesterman's thigh again.

Hesterman chuckled deep in his throat. "You can hardly wait, you little slut. You need it so bad, don't you?" He gripped Remy's jaw and tilted his head around. The angle was awkward, but Remy's smile didn't fade. Cats had flexible necks. The grip on Remy's jaw didn't relax but Hesterman was clearly speaking to the pilot when he barked out, "What the fuck is taking so long? Why aren't we home yet?"

"I'm sorry, sir. There's a security cordon in sectors three and seven; I'm in a holding pattern waiting to see if we'll be allowed to pass or have to detour."

"Fucking terrorist scum!" Hesterman growled. He looked down at Remy. "You can't wait, can you, sweetheart? You need it right now. I can see it in your face. You'll explode if we have to wait."

Remy moaned in agreement and did a little more face-rubbing. Hesterman seemed pretty damned fond of that. And he was developing an annoying taste for exhibitionism too, it seemed.

"Take off your clothes, sweetheart. Let me see that beautiful body."

Remy tried to focus his eyes and figure out the best response. "But the pilot," he protested. "I want *you* to see me. Only you."

"*Fuck* the pilot," Hesterman growled. "If he turns around, I'll have his eyes cut out. You hear that, you fucking pervert? Don't turn around!"

Neither Remy nor the pilot bothered to point out that the cockpit had a screen showing shots from all angles of the interior and exterior of the shuttle. It wasn't like Remy actually cared what the bastard saw. He didn't care about much of anything, and he started slowly taking his clothes off, piece by piece.

But apparently Hesterman wasn't interested in taking things slow. He already had his fly open and his pants shoved down, and he grabbed at Remy, pulling at his clothes in a frenzy. Remy tried to speed things up, but it wasn't easy when he was feeling so distant from it all.

Finally, they managed to get him naked and Hesterman pulled him forward. Even stoned, Remy knew the right moves; he was pretty sure that the years of repetition had burned them into his DNA forever.

Climb onto the client's lap, not too much weight on the client's legs, then gracefully arch your back as you rise up to hover for a moment of sweet anticipation. Remy could hear Hesterman's guttural breathing speed up in anticipation. *Give a deep, satisfied moan with just a trace of a whimper when you sink down and accept the intrusion into your body. Show some of the pain on your face, but not too much.* With Hesterman's current mood, Remy went a bit heavy on the pain. *Keep your eyes closed, because it's just too wonderful to be treated to a close-up view of some sweaty, greedy face and you can't bear that level of happiness.* It was too bad he couldn't shut his ears as well so he wouldn't have to hear

Hesterman's grunting. *Let the client set the rhythm but don't expect him to do too much of the work; be sure to make lots of noise, an appreciative gasp or moan with each thrust.* A bit of a whimper mixed in, this time, to go with the pained expression. *And, of course, pace your simulated orgasm to his genuine one. Flick the capsule out from behind your molar, keep it in your cheek, and make sure that your noises grow a bit more frenzied, then more and more. By the time the client finally comes, you should be sounding like a litter of possessed puppies, yipping and howling and gasping for air. Crush the capsule, inhale sharply and then swallow the plastic casing as your body reacts and does its job, and then collapse, totally spent and overwhelmed with ecstasy. Repeat as many times as the job requires. Don't think about any of it.* How many times had Remy done this in his lifetime? But, no, better not to think about that, either.

He nuzzled into Hesterman's neck. He tried to remember whether Hesterman had any pets. "So good, sweetheart. You're so good to me."

"You just can't get enough, can you, sweetheart? God, you really love me, don't you?"

Well, that was a new one. But the right answer was pretty damned clear. "Oh, sweetheart!" Remy cast his eyes shyly up to Hesterman's face, then back down to his sweaty chest. "I can't help it. I just... I do. I love you so much."

"It must be hard for you when I'm not around. You must get lonely."

"I try to be brave." Remy smiled softly. The gray hair on Hesterman's chest was swirling like long grass in a windstorm, and Remy was pretty sure he could see a little family of mice running around underneath the cover. He reached out and batted at a few with his paw, but they ran away.

Hesterman giggled and caught Remy's hand before it tickled any more. "I'll see what I can do, sweetheart. I'll see what I can do."

Remy couldn't even remember what the guy was talking about. He let himself be shifted to the side, and eventually, slowly, he started pulling his clothes back on. It was hard to get much done with all the distractions in the shuttle; every flash of light was something that might be hunted, every rustling movement of fabric could actually be the scratching of little rodent claws. Finally, though, he had most of his clothes on, and he returned his head to Hesterman's lap, where it received a few absentminded strokes. Remy liked being a cat. He wondered how long he'd be able to keep it up.

CHAPTER NINE

REMY had always been a bit contemptuous of the group of whores who hung around in Sasha's office. They weren't bad, exactly; bad whores were not tolerated in the Baryman enterprise. But they weren't trying very hard to be good. They didn't have the same dedication to excellence that Remy had always prided himself on.

Since the weekend at Challoner's, since the pills, they'd become his best friends. He'd hit the wall, and they could tell, and they didn't seem to care. They actually seemed to welcome it.

"You hung on for a long time, little Remy," they said. They always called him by his real name, and once he got used to it, he liked it. "You did your best. You tried to play their game, but you forgot that the deck is stacked against us. You can't beat the odds, little Remy." It was strange, how they all seemed to be able to speak without opening their mouths. How they all seemed to share one warm, loving voice.

He was sitting on the floor, watching Sasha sort pills out into different packages. Sasha was so careful, so meticulous. It was hypnotic. Remy hadn't had a client since Hesterman the night before, but he'd taken a pill anyway. He was pretty sure Sasha had an endless supply, and apparently Remy had an endless appetite. An endless need.

The door opened without warning, the corner of it jamming into Remy's shin, but it didn't hurt. Nothing hurt. But even through the haze, Remy noticed the sudden tension among the other whores, and he turned his head to see Baryman himself standing in the doorway.

Baryman raised an eyebrow at the assemblage, then directed his attention to Sasha. "None of them have jobs?"

"They're almost all booked this afternoon," Sasha replied quickly. "And this evening. But mornings are slow."

Which Baryman knew perfectly well. He looked down at Remy. "You. What the hell have you been up to, David?"

That was not a question Remy felt at all prepared to answer. Sasha had green pills and blue pills and orange pills and clear pills and yellow pills and big white pills. Remy could talk about that. The rest of it....

"He's been here with me since he got back from his job last night," Sasha said. "We didn't hear anything from Mr. Hesterman... was there a problem?"

Baryman ignored him and nudged Remy's thigh with his toe. "I asked *you*, David. What have you been up to?"

Remy frowned thoughtfully. He thought about sharing his cat experiences, but decided against it. "He likes doing stuff in public now. Well, just in front of the pilot. I said I loved him; I think that's what he wanted me to say. Mr. Challoner wasn't involved."

Baryman looked disgusted. "Jesus, Sasha. Why the fuck is he stoned at 10:00 a.m. without a job in sight? I supply the drugs to keep them working, not to give them something to fucking do." But he didn't seem all that angry. "Unless this is what Hesterman likes about him... he usually has that edge, doesn't he? That sense that he could actually be a little dangerous? That's fucking *gone*. He's a fucking kitten now."

Remy blinked in amazement. Had the transformation somehow become visible to others?

"I can cut him back, if you want, Mr. Baryman. I gave him a supply, but I can ration it out more carefully, if you think that's wise."

"I don't fucking care. Not right now. He's off active duty for a couple days. Tell dispatch to reschedule his jobs."

Sasha looked as confused as Remy felt. "Of course, Mr. Baryman."

Baryman crouched down and reached out to grip the hair on the back of Remy's head. He tilted Remy's face this way and that. "You look about the same as you always have, you pretty little whore. So what the fuck has got everyone panting over you now? Did you learn some new tricks somewhere?"

Baryman waited for an answer, and when he didn't get one, he tightened his grip and pulled Remy's head back awkwardly. "What's fucking different, David?"

"I don't know," Remy managed to say. His brain wanted to float away, but he fought to stay with his body. If he zoned out now, if he pissed off Baryman, the punishment would be something that no quantity of narcotics could erase. "I don't understand what you mean."

Baryman released his grip so suddenly that Remy's head bobbed on his neck. "Stand up," Baryman ordered as he straightened his own body.

Remy obliged. He wasn't dizzy, which was nice, but it was a little hard to stand totally straight. Baryman seemed to notice, but not care. He walked around Remy in a slow circle, inspecting. "I've been contacted by two different lawyers this morning, David. Both of them offering to buy your contract from me. What the fuck do you think of that?"

Remy had no idea what he thought. He was aware of these sorts of sales, of course. They were rare, but not unheard of. Clients who became obsessed with a particular whore, clients with more money than they knew what to do with, would sometimes decide that they wanted to make things exclusive. But Baryman wouldn't sell Remy unless the price was right, and Remy was pretty sure that he was still making a lot of money for the stable. "Were they fair offers?" he asked.

Baryman seemed surprised. "You don't want to know who they're from?"

"There were two?" Given Hesterman's possessiveness the night before, he seemed like an obvious candidate. The other... Remy shook his head. "Challoner? Hesterman and Challoner?"

"How the fuck do you spend one weekend with the man, one weekend with no fucking *fucking*, and get him to make an offer for your contract? And, yeah, it was a fair fucking offer."

"It's him and Hesterman," Remy explained. "They were doing some... I don't know. Some possessive thing last night." Remy made himself stop talking. He had no idea why he still felt this strange loyalty to Challoner, but there was something in him that didn't want to see the man hurt. Remy should be careful with his words. "I don't know what happened. I was at the table. But Hesterman was mad when he came back. And then Challoner tried to keep me from going with Hesterman."

"And Hesterman didn't like that, I'll bet." Baryman sounded positively gleeful.

"I don't know. He was angry when he got in the shuttle."

"But he didn't stay angry...."

"No. I apologized." And acted like a cat. Remy's brain was still trying to convince him to let go of his body, and it was harder and harder to refuse the invitation.

"And he fucked you in front of the pilot."

"Yes."

"And now he wants to buy your fucking contract." Baryman shook his head, and smiled. "This is good, David. I mean... Hesterman, who the fuck cares? If he's got the money, he can have you. But Challoner... I'm going to make that fucker *cry*! He wants to put a fucking *park* in the middle of a complex I want to build.

I'm trying to build a fucking *palace*, luxury accommodations for people who fucking matter. And he's getting in my fucking way just to be a pain in the ass. But now, I've got something *he* wants." Baryman had been practically vibrating with enthusiasm, but then he stilled and frowned. "Why does *he* want you? Just to piss Hesterman off?"

To rescue me. But Remy wouldn't say that. It was too ridiculous to put into words. And Baryman would never understand. "Yeah, I guess, to piss off Hesterman. And maybe... maybe he thinks I don't want to be bought. So if he bought me, then it would be like he *was* forcing me into something... I don't know. Maybe." Remy pretended to be distracted by Baryman's shoes, and then actually *was* distracted by them. They were so shiny, with the light glinting off them. They looked almost like plastic, but Baryman would never wear something so cheap.

Baryman was talking to Sasha, now, and Remy only heard some of the conversation. "Keep him stoned, if that's what they like," he heard. And, "Gonna play that fucker for all he's worth." Then Remy's hair was being pulled again, his head tilted back, and Baryman was peering at him from far too close. "You keep yourself pretty, David. Get lots of sleep, or not enough sleep, or whatever the fuck it is that these assholes like about you." He shook Remy from side to side like a man would wrestle with a dog's head, and it would have been loving except that he was pulling Remy's hair, hard. "You're a good boy," he said, and then he was gone.

Remy sank back down to his spot on the floor. He waited for Sasha to start counting pills again, but he didn't. Instead, he slid down onto the floor in front of Remy, and one by one, the other whores slipped off the couches to join him.

They didn't say much, but this time, they were all talking with their own mouths and their own voices. "Chrissy got bought out," one of them said.

"Never heard from her after that. But I bet she's doing good."

"Or she's dead. Once you're bought, nobody cares if you live or die."

"Like anybody cares about that now."

"Fuck, yeah, they do. You're not making them any money if you're dead."

"*You're* not making them much money anyway, you dried-up old queen."

"Fuck you, you whore."

They lapsed back into silence, and Sasha reached out and took Remy's hands in his. "Hesterman would be okay, right? You don't talk about Challoner. The weekend with him... it was bad?"

Remy nodded slowly. He remembered the chess, and the chickens, and the goddamn soup by the fire. "It was bad," he echoed. He thought about the big, warm bed, and the morning light streaming in through the window. He thought about Challoner the night before, offering to protect Remy as if that was actually something that was possible, and he curled up on the floor and put his head on Sasha's lap. He didn't want to think about Challoner. He didn't want to think about anything. He closed his eyes and let himself float away.

CHAPTER TEN

REMY stayed stoned. There was no reason to avoid the pills, and many, many reasons to seek them out. Remy tried to remember Challoner's words: *I shut my eyes and acted like it wasn't there.* But Challoner had come back from Europe, and he'd opened his eyes. Opened Remy's eyes too, unfortunately.

How had one weekend done this to him? How had one man, one stupid, naïve, ridiculous man, forced Remy to see all the things he'd gotten so good at ignoring? Remy was tempted to blame the chickens. Possibly that one chicken in particular, the one who'd listened to him; that little bitch had been making a damn point, with her head cocking and her unblinking gaze. Remy thought about that chicken a lot. He bet she'd be the one to go feral next. She'd flap out to some tree and roost out there, keeping her eggs to herself. She wouldn't know that they weren't fertilized and would never hatch, and maybe she wouldn't even care. No, not that chicken! She'd be *glad* if they didn't hatch. Babies would just slow her down. They'd get in the way of her workout regimen, get in the way of her planning. That chicken was going to fly south, next fall, and she wasn't going to let anything get in her way.

Possibly he was spending too much time thinking about chickens. And too much time thinking about Challoner, with his quiet smiles and his insistence on trying to be decent. *The system's broken, Remy.* Of course, Challoner hadn't said "Remy." He'd said "David." Because the system wasn't the only thing that was broken.

He was lying in bed, drifting in and out of restless sleep, when he heard the sound at his window. He'd gotten used to hearing strange sounds lately, things that nobody else seemed to hear or care about. When he wasn't under the effect of Sasha's pills, he classified the sounds as auditory hallucinations; when he *was* under the effect, he didn't give a damn what the hell they were. But this one was persistent: an annoying knocking, not loud enough to get anyone else's attention but not quiet enough to let Remy sleep. Finally he stood up. It had been quite a while since he'd taken a pill, he realized, so maybe there was actually something to investigate.

He peered out into the darkness and saw a human shape in the shadows; the building had a metal balcony that technically served as a fire escape, and it wasn't unusual for people to sit out there during the day. But this was the middle of the night. Remy pushed his face a little closer to the glass, and the shape outside crouched down to get closer to him.

It was Dar. He looked frightened, maybe, but mostly he looked alive in a way that Remy could barely remember ever having felt. But that didn't begin to explain what the hell he was doing on Remy's fire escape.

Dar gestured frantically, the two-fingers-to-his-eyes movement that everyone knew meant the government security cameras. Then Dar drew a hand across his own throat. Death. Dar would die if the security cameras caught him? Then it was already too late, because Remy knew that the outside of the building was well covered. But Dar should know that too, and he didn't look worried. He grinned, and pointed to the sky, then drew the hand across his throat again.

The cameras were dead? That was impossible. Remy looked up to the corner of his room, searched for the blinking red light that let him know he was being watched. Being protected. But the light was gone, and Remy felt a surge of something powerful, something exhilarating and terrifying. He looked back out at Dar, and he knew his eyes were wide.

Dar pointed to the ground below, gestured with his fingers to show people walking, then drawing guns, and then Dar pointed to himself and made that same death gesture again. If the security patrols found Dar, they'd kill him. That seemed pretty damned likely. Dar pointed to the handle of the window. He wanted in.

Remy shook his head. The window was welded shut. None of the whores had windows that opened; if they wanted to leave the building, they were supposed to go out through the main doors and give the guards a good explanation for the excursion.

For the first time, Dar looked desperate. He glanced down at the street, then back at Remy. It was Dar. Laughing Dar, racing through the forest, his young body as vibrant as his pure soul. Remy shook his head, then gestured back to Dar. Three fingers, tap the glass, point to the left. Dar was moving before Remy had even stepped back from the window.

The hallway was quiet. Everyone else was sleeping, and Remy wanted to wake them up so they could share this experience, this strange holiday from observation. But he tiptoed down the hall instead, pushed open the door of Sasha's room, and headed for the window. Sasha had gone home that night, as he did most nights; his private apartment was a rare privilege, and he liked to take advantage of it. This room was just for late nights, and for working and visiting. And only a few days earlier, Remy had seen Sasha push his window open in order to throw out the dregs of a cold cup of tea.

Remy hadn't remembered the creak the window made, but he would just have to hope it wasn't loud enough to wake anyone. He pushed it open as far as it would go, and Dar climbed through gracefully. Remy was reaching to close the window when he saw a second shape on the fire escape, and he stepped back in surprise as another man, bulkier than Dar, eased his way inside and stood staring at Remy.

"David?" Challoner said, the surprise clear in his voice.

Dar pushed between them and reached for the window. "Don't

worry about his name," he ordered Challoner. "You don't need to know him. He's not part of this."

Remy jerked his gaze away from Challoner in order to stare at Dar. His shock at seeing a client climbing around with a terrorist would have to wait for a while, because Remy needed to figure out more immediate issues. "Not part of it? You're kidding, right? You think they'll believe that, when they catch you here?"

Dar shook his head. "They won't catch us. I hope." His smile was as charmingly wild as always. "There's tunnels beneath this building, right? I have a contact who told me they used to send whores to their jobs through the tunnels, back before it was legal. She said the tunnels ran clear into the next sector, and connected to every hotel and apartment building on the way."

"How did you know which window was mine?" Remy wasn't sure what part of this to try to understand first. "And what the hell are you doing with *him*?" He looked back toward Challoner, then looked away quickly.

Dar didn't even try to look sheepish. "I heard about the tunnels, I knew you lived here... so I watched the windows. I need to know things, Remy. It's what keeps me alive." He glanced at Challoner, who was frowning at the use of Remy's real name. "Do you two know each other?" Dar demanded.

"No," Remy and Challoner said in unison.

The lie was obvious, and Dar frowned. "That's not good." He turned to Challoner. "He knows your real name?"

Challoner nodded slowly.

"Fuck," Dar said. He shook his head as if trying to clear it. "Okay. We'll worry about that later. First thing, we need to get out of here before the cameras come back on."

"Why are they off? What's going on?"

"Less you know, the better," Dar said. Then he paused. "But maybe it's time people started talking. Maybe it's time they realized that we're fighting back, and we're not fucking powerless.

This was just a test run, but we know that it works now. We'll do it again, bigger next time, and it won't be long until it's permanent. The cameras will be dead, and freedom will be reborn!"

"You're one of *them*?" Remy asked Challoner. "A terrorist? You're part of this insanity?"

Challoner was still staring at Remy, but he finally managed to say, "I'm involved, yes. I'm working for freedom. I'm trying to make things better."

Remy knew exactly what he should do. What he had to do. Whatever these two were up to, they were working against the government, and that meant they were the enemy. And the enemy had to be turned in. Remy needed to step into the hallway, yell for the guards, and let them take over. They would do what had to be done, and he could step away from the whole situation. He could take another pill and crawl back into bed and try to forget all about it. But it would take more than one pill to forget Dar, and more than two to forget Challoner. Remy would need to take the five or six that Sasha had recommended if he ever wanted any peace after betraying either of these men. And he found he wasn't quite ready for that yet.

"Fuck," he said quietly. Then he squinted at Challoner. "The hotel bombing. You knew about that? You were part of it?"

"No time for that, Remy," Dar said. "The tunnels. Can you get us to them?"

Remy wanted to slow this down. Everything was spinning too quickly, changing too fast, and he didn't really understand any of it. Could he get them to the tunnels? "Yes," he said. "But there's locked doors. At least one."

"Shit," Dar said, but Remy was already moving. The tunnels were old and rarely used, but they weren't completely out of service. He reached into the top drawer of Sasha's desk and pulled out the key ring.

"I don't know which one will fit," he said. "But there aren't many. Most of the doors are on keypads. They just never bothered to run the system down to the tunnels."

"The system's not down there at all?" Dar sounded excited. "Like, no cameras? No listening?"

"I don't know for sure. But I don't think so."

"That could be useful. Incredibly useful. They stretch right across the sector line?"

"Yeah." Remy had been escorted through the system several times, going to assignations that were, for one reason or another, more secret than usual.

"That is excellent news," Dar said with his cocky grin. "Give us the keys, tell us how to get to the tunnel entrance, and go back to sleep. How come you're not working tonight?"

And that was definitely time for another look at Challoner. "Some crazy men are trying to buy my contract. I'm on vacation until it gets settled."

"Wow," Dar said. "That's a lot of money, right? I mean, your master doesn't sell his slaves for cheap, does he?"

"I'm not a slave. I could leave anytime I wanted."

"But not work for anyone else." Challoner's voice was deep and steady. "At all. Most prostitution contracts state that you can't work for anyone else in the field, but yours is worse than that. You can't work for anyone else, doing anything. That line you fed me about not wanting to work in a factory and not wanting to join the army... that was bullshit. You *can't* work in a factory or join the army. This is the only job you're allowed to have, and you're only allowed to work for Baryman." He stared at Remy, his face a mix of frustration and sorrow. "I did some research."

Dar shook his head. Remy had always glossed over the details of his working life when speaking to Dar. The man was the closest thing to family Remy had left, and sometimes it was just easier to pretend that things were going well. There was nothing Dar could do about any of it, after all. "Seriously? Jesus, Remy, why would you sign a contract like that? Were you drugged?"

"He was *nine*." Challoner said. "Nine years old, and they signed him to a lifetime contract."

"Do you guys want to find that tunnel or not?" Remy started for the door. "How long are the cameras off for?"

"An hour, maybe. Best estimate. We're already at least fifteen minutes in." Dar stepped toward Remy. "Depends how long it takes them to figure out what we did. But you shouldn't come with us. I wasn't joking about you going back to bed."

"You need the key, and I don't know which one it is."

"Just give us all of them."

"Sasha would notice if the whole key chain was missing. He'd have to report it, and with the hotel bombing so recent, they'd drag me in for questioning, for sure." Remy put his hand on the doorknob and tried to ignore the crawling tendrils of fear at the thought of an interrogation. "I'll get you to the first door, we'll figure out which key works, and you can take just that one. Hopefully Sasha won't see that it's gone, at least for a while." The others didn't object, so Remy started moving.

He opened the door as casually as he could, took a quick look outside, then gestured for Challoner and Dar to follow him. A quick scurry down the hallway to the staircase, a nervous look to be sure the red light on the camera was still absent, and then down four flights of stairs to the basement.

"The lights are still on," Remy said. "You guys didn't kill the power, you just killed the cameras?"

"The lights are simple electricity. The cameras are hooked up to a data network. We went after the network." Dar sounded smug.

"And got yourselves trapped in the process?"

"It was a test run. Things didn't go as smoothly as we might have hoped." Challoner, at least, sounded a little sheepish.

Remy rested his hand on the basement door. He didn't think there was any point in trying to seem casual anymore; anyone who saw him down there would know he was up to something. "We need to move fast. I don't think they patrol down here, usually, but if they know something's going on with the cameras, they could be stepping things up."

Dar nodded, and Remy opened the door, took a quick look for any observers, and then started off at a jog. They were in a large storage room, crates of clothes and alcohol stacked on one side, unused furniture and miscellaneous items on the other. Remy had played down there, when he'd been younger, and he knew the space well. But the tunnels had been forbidden; he supposed he'd been too valuable to risk in an unsecured environment.

Still, he knew the way. Through another unlocked door, then down a short hallway to another room, and he was pretty sure they were already out from beneath the main building. Another staircase, this one steeper than the others, with rough stone walls and air that was beginning to feel damp. "I've only been in the tunnels a few times. The best one, I think...." He tried to think it through. He hadn't been paying too much attention to his surroundings on past trips; he'd either been trying to get ready for where he was going, or trying to recover from where he'd been. But he called back the basic memories, at least. "If you take the main tunnel, it ends at the Roosevelt Theater. That's pretty far, but it's still in this sector. But there's a side branch, off to the left, at an angle... maybe forty-five degrees left of the direction you'll have been traveling in... and it takes you to the Landman Hotel." He was working through the keys on the ring as he spoke, trying to find the one that would open the heavy wood door.

"The Landman?" Dar sounded excited. "That place is a dive. Hardly any cameras at all."

"And it backs on the ravine. Trees and lots of homeless people—you should be able to get lost there, if anywhere." Another couple keys, but still none that turned.

"That's excellent, Dav—" Challoner stopped. "Remy." He shook his head. "They called you David in the contract. David Stone."

"Remy Stone," Dar said firmly. "Hey, does that mean the contract could be voided?"

"You still believe in the law being on our side, Dar? I thought you were a cynical freedom fighter." Remy shook his head, then looked his old friend in the eyes. "You want to keep using the tunnels, so you don't want a body found down here. But you'll be coming for me, right? You can't afford to leave me alive."

Challoner jerked his head in surprise, but Dar returned Remy's gaze levelly. "I don't know, Remy. I'm going to really try to find a way out of it. You're a friend."

"What the hell are you talking about?" Challoner didn't seem to know whether to stare at Remy or at Dar. "Why would you hurt him? If he wanted to turn us in, he could have done it well before now. When we were on the fire escape, or any time in the hallways."

"It's not about what I want," Remy said quietly. "It's... it's the interrogators. After the hotel, they didn't really think I'd been involved, so they didn't come at me very hard. But I've seen what they do to people who are actually suspected of something. Truth drugs, absolutely, but also anything else they can think of. Everyone talks. I'd talk."

"And he knows your name," Dar said sadly. "It wouldn't matter if he gave *me* up; I'm already a fugitive. But you... you're important, Adam." He looked shiftily at Remy and added, "I mean, you're useful yourself, but your money... we can't afford to lose access to your money." He looked at Remy again. "If I'd known you knew him, I never would have come to your window. I swear."

Remy nodded. That was something. Then he reached into his pocket and pulled out the little envelope that he'd started carrying with him like a lucky charm. "I have pills. Enough to kill me. I could take them if I knew the security forces were coming...."

"But you *won't* know they're coming," Dar said, and Remy just nodded.

"No. Nobody's taking pills, and nobody's being interrogated, and sure as hell nobody is being killed just because he recognizes me. That is...." Challoner looked fiercely at Dar. "That is not acceptable. I will not be a part of anything like that. Innocent people being killed—"

"What about the pilots?" Remy asked quietly. "At the hotel. Twelve upstanding citizens killed... that's what all the news reports talk about. But three shuttles exploded. That's three pilots, and probably some security guards, some assistants... who knows how many other people." Challoner looked sick, but Remy kept talking. "Innocent people have already been killed. You sat there in your hotel suite and waited, knowing it was going to happen? And then you went up on the roof and hung back so you wouldn't be on one of the shuttles?" It was the only thing that made sense, even if it was hard to reconcile that level of duplicity with sweet, innocent Challoner. "And if people have figured out that the cameras are off tonight, probably some more innocent people have died, because the cameras don't *just* catch terrorists, they also catch criminals. There could be rioting in the streets, for all we know." There were only a few keys left untried, and Dar impatiently pulled the ring out of Remy's hands and started working on the lock himself.

Challoner seemed to have lost interest in the entire process, focusing on Remy with almost frightening intensity. "So what are you saying? We should do nothing? Just sit back and let them win? Should I have... was I wrong to be part of the shuttle explosions? Yes, I was part of it. And...." He nodded as if his neck had stiffened in resistance and he had to force the muscles to comply. "It wasn't my idea, but I knew it was going to happen. I knew people were going to die. It was important to the cause. We needed a distraction, and we needed to make people pay attention. But... was I wrong? Could we have found another way?" He asked the questions like he really wanted to hear the answers.

But Remy didn't have much more to say. "I have no idea what you should do. No idea what anyone should do. I'm just saying... I don't know. I guess I'm saying you should be honest about what you're doing. You can do the big strategy stuff if you want, and maybe you need to sacrifice some pawns. I guess I'm saying that you should at least *remember* the pawns. We're people too."

"I know you are," Challoner protested. "I'm the one who was saying you had to be kept safe."

"But at the house, you told me that there's no point in having a queen if I don't *use* her. And I'm nowhere near as powerful as a queen. I'm just a pawn, if that. So you should use me if you need to."

"Okay, you guys are getting really hard to follow, and we need to *move*." Dar made a satisfied noise as he turned a key in the lock and yanked the door partway open. He peered cautiously into the space beyond and was apparently satisfied by what he saw. He pulled the key off the ring and handed the extras back to Remy. "It's the same one that opens the door at the other end?"

"The other end wasn't even locked, last time I was there. It's just an old door in an old store room. But if you can't get out that way and have to use a different exit, yeah, I think that key will work."

But Challoner was still distracted. "I'll increase my bid. I'll go as high as I have to. If you're free of the contract, we can hide you. Get you out of the country, even."

Remy thought about Baryman's wild glee at the thought of holding out on Challoner. "You can't go too high. It'll be suspicious. And Baryman won't sell me at a reasonable price. He hates you. Some real estate deal you're blocking? That's what he says, but really he just... he doesn't like people who think they're better than him. He wants you to lose."

"Let's *go*, Adam," Dar said, and he stepped through the doorway. Challoner followed him reluctantly, and then they were gone. No parting words, no brave smiles. Remy pushed the door shut behind them and heard the lock click. That was it. He was on one side of the door, and they were on the other. And he had no idea how much longer he had before the cameras came back online. He turned and started back. He'd never been more reluctant to go to his small, safe room.

Chapter Eleven

Remy wasn't too surprised when he received the summons the next day. Baryman wanted to see him. At least it wasn't the security forces. Baryman punished, but he didn't usually interrogate during the process, so hopefully Challoner's secret was safe.

Remy thought about taking the pills anyway. Five or six, and it would all be over. No more worries, no more fear. He could practically see that bitch of a chicken staring at him, waiting to see what he was going to do. Prepared to judge him if he took the easy way out.

So he shoved the envelope down deep in his pocket and obediently headed for the shuttle pad. Mr. Baryman didn't like to be kept waiting.

A short shuttle hop, the long hallway to the office, and Remy forced himself to lift his hand and knock. "David Stone to see Mr. Baryman," he said, and his voice was level.

It was the usual group of men in front of the desk, but Remy didn't acknowledge them. "I'm sorry to interrupt, Mr. Baryman, but I was told you wanted to see me."

"Always so polite, David. So fucking careful. I trained you well." Baryman stood up and stalked around the desk. The men hurriedly moved their chairs out of the way. Baryman had been one of them, a goon serving a big man, until his brutality and cunning had made him the big man himself. They knew what he was and respected him for it. Baryman ignored them, his gaze still locked on Remy's. He stopped when he was only inches away and ran the back of his hand over Remy's cheekbones. It would have felt loving if Remy hadn't been staring into Baryman's cold eyes.

"Challoner wants to walk away," Baryman finally said. "I got the message this morning, from his lawyers. He says I'm asking too much, and he's losing interest anyway." He turned his hand around so that it gripped Remy's jaw. Still gently, for now, but the strength and the threat was clear. "I'm not pleased about that."

"I'm sorry, Mr. Baryman. Is there anything I can do?"

"You could have done a better job in the first fucking place," Baryman snarled, and his grip turned into a hard, angry push against Remy's chin.

Remy had good balance, and he hadn't taken a pill since the previous afternoon; he could have caught himself if he'd tried. But he fell instead, sprawled on the floor and tried to look defenseless. "I'm sorry," he said again.

He expected the kick. Hard and sharp, but to the muscle of his thigh instead of some more vulnerable part; Baryman was still in control of himself, willing to cause pain but not exploding into the rage that could cause serious damage. "I want him to *want* you," Baryman growled, and he found the same spot on Remy's leg with another kick, and another. Remy's thigh muscles spasmed and screamed in protest but he didn't try to get away.

Baryman stopped kicking and stared down at Remy. "I've got people on the comm with him right now. Persuasive people. They're going to convince him to let you go out for another visit." Baryman drew his leg back as if building up for a savage kick, and Remy forced his muscles to relax so they wouldn't be torn by the impact. Baryman put his whole body into the swing, but jerked to a halt a breath away from Remy's thigh and merely nudged him with his toe. "You need to make him want you."

He crouched down and grabbed Remy's jaw again, pulling him up so their faces were aligned. "Can you do that, David?" He squeezed his fingers tight. "Because I've decided not to sell you. Hesterman's gone off the deep end, raving and ranting but not coming up with enough fucking cash, and Challoner... I'd set you on fire before I gave that bastard the satisfaction of getting what he wants. So you're staying with me. Do you understand?" He ran his fingers gently down Remy's neck. "You're mine, and you're staying that way for the rest of your fucking life, if I want you to. So you need to make me happy. Understood?"

"Of course, Mr. Baryman. I always do my best for you."

"But sometimes you need a little help, don't you, David?"

"I... I don't know, Mr. Baryman." That was true enough. Remy had no idea what Baryman was talking about.

"Sometimes Sasha helps you," Baryman prompted. "He finds the right clothes for you to wear; he makes you look pretty. Right?"

"Yes, sir," Remy said cautiously.

"And sometimes other whores help you. If you're putting on a show, or if the client wants something special. Right?"

"Yes, sir."

"And sometimes... well, sometimes, for special clients, you need special help." Baryman smiled. "I think, for Mr. Challoner, you need a little help from my boys." He stepped back, as if Remy were dirty and he didn't want to be contaminated. "I think that motherfucker needs to be reminded that if he doesn't buy you, then other people get to have fun with you. And sometimes their fun leaves marks." He smiled, then directed his attention to one of the men. "I want a lot of bruises, but no permanent damage. Nothing on his face; keep that pretty. The rest of him—I want Challoner to see a fucking rainbow when he unwraps this boy. Don't fuck him, though... use his mouth, if you want. Clear?"

"Yes, sir." The same words that had come out of Remy's mouth, but said with so much more conviction from the hulking man Baryman had been speaking to. He turned to Remy. "David... this way, please." His voice was clipped and distinct, not the brutish mumble Remy would have expected from a man who looked like this one did. The man was undoing his jacket as he spoke, and he pulled it right off as Remy trailed after him. Getting ready for work. "I think we'll do this in the bathroom. Easier to clean up. Make sense?"

Remy couldn't seem to make a sound. He was pretty sure that if he managed to push anything out it would be a string of obscenities that would get him beaten even harder, so he allowed himself to stay silent.

The goon didn't seem to be offended. "I'm going to go get a few things," he said, still pleasant. "You go in there and strip down." Another businesslike smile, and the goon headed off down the hall.

Remy looked longingly toward the staircase. Down there, out the front door, and free forever. Dar was managing to live off the grid, somehow. Maybe Remy could too.

Of course, his plan was flawed. Mr. Baryman's doors were guarded, and they'd have been warned that there was a whore in the building who might be desperate enough to make a break for it. Remy had nowhere to go, and no way to get there. He took a deep breath, pushed the bathroom door open, and started to undress. He hung his shirt tidily on the hook that was meant for towels, running his fingers along the collar to make sure that it was smooth. He didn't want it to get wrinkled. Mr. Baryman wanted the bruises to be a surprise; he wanted Remy to look good until he was undressed. And it was important to give Mr. Baryman what he wanted. Remy lined his shoes up under the shirt and unbuckled his pants. He'd been through worse, he reminded himself. Much worse. He stepped out of the pants and hung them over the towel rack, the crease carefully maintained.

Then the goon was back, carrying a duffel bag that looked as if it had been prepacked with whatever tools the man needed. Remy supposed they'd been used many times before.

"Good, you're being sensible about this," the man said when

he saw Remy's undressed state. "You would be surprised by some of the nonsense your colleagues can come up with." He looked around the room thoughtfully. "Let's do your front first," he decided. "Stand over there, your back against that wall. If you have to puke, aim for the toilet; I'm not cleaning up after you, and you'll be too sore to want to do it yourself."

Remy did as he was told. He had no choice.

"Ready?" the goon asked pleasantly.

Remy made himself nod; he still didn't trust himself to speak. The man had a sack in his hand, and it looked like there were balls of some sort inside it. Remy closed his eyes and made himself stretch up out of his body. It would have been easier with the drugs, but he'd been able to do this by himself before Sasha's chemical intervention and he could do it by himself now, too.

There was a body in the bathroom, and a man was hitting it, over and over. He used different tools from the bag he'd brought, and when the body collapsed onto the floor, he kicked it a few times, then rolled it over and started working on its back and shoulders. Bruises there, welts raised on the ass and thighs, and a few more bruises down on the calves. The man was very thorough. Remy could feel the pain, but he managed it. He accepted it as stimuli, as his body telling him something it thought was important, but there was nothing Remy could do about it, so he tried to disregard the message. It was just pain.

Then the goon bent over and laced his fingers through Remy's hair, pulling his head back to see his face. "Okay, I think that should do it," he said. He was out of breath. He frowned and slapped Remy's face sharply. "Hey! Pay attention! I'm talking to you!" For the first time, there was a trace of irritation in his voice, and Remy didn't like to think about where that might lead. He tried to focus his eyes, and he gave the goon his best apologetic smile.

"Sorry," he managed to croak.

"Get cleaned up," the goon ordered. "You're all sweaty. No

blood, though... I did a good job with that. Then get dressed and go up to the shuttle. They'll take you where you're supposed to go." He checked his watch. "Fifteen minutes," he said. "I'll tell the shuttle you'll be ready to go by then."

He rebuttoned his cuffs and pulled his jacket down off the hook. "You were a good boy," he said. "I'll tell Mr. Baryman." And then he was gone, closing the door behind him.

Remy lay still for a few breaths, then rolled awkwardly to his feet. Everything hurt, but the goon was right; he'd done a good job, and nothing was actually damaged beyond functioning. Remy splashed some water onto his face and ran a washcloth over the rest of his body. He didn't have time for a shower, not moving in slow motion like he was.

He reached for his pants, then stopped. Instead of putting them on, he reached into the pocket and pulled out the envelope of pills. There were six in there—Remy's emergency escape packet. But Dar had said Remy wouldn't have time to take them because he wouldn't know the security forces were coming for him, and Dar was right. The forces were trained to keep suspects from escaping in *any* manner. So the pills were just for Remy. They were just for if he decided to give up.

He took a long look at the envelope, then shook the pills out into the palm of his hand. Before he could change his mind, he turned his hand over and let the pills fall into the water of the toilet. He paused for a moment, let the desperate need to reach into the water and rescue the pills peak and then ebb away, and then he flushed. He wasn't going to give up. He didn't even know what he was fighting *against*, but that didn't matter, not right then. He was going to fight. Somehow.

He pulled his pants and shirt on, trying to ignore the desperate complaints of his body, and headed for the staircase. For the first time, he wondered what Challoner was up to, backing out of the purchase agreement. He wondered whether Baryman's persuaders had managed to convince Challoner to allow a visit.

And he wondered how he would possibly stand it, if he had to go out to the farm again and then return to his life in the city.

THE pilot didn't tell Remy where they were going, but after about twenty minutes in the shuttle, he figured it was a sure thing. There was nowhere in the city that took that long to reach, not unless they got stuck in a security blockade or something.

So he was going back to Challoner's farm. He looked out the window at the snowy landscape below. Mostly industrial properties for the first while, but then some agriculture too. Finally, he saw forest and hills and knew that the shuttle was approaching the nature enclave where so many of his clients kept homes. Challoner's place was on the far side, just on the edge. His neighbors never would have let him play farmer if he'd had to cut down their precious trees in order to do it.

Remy stood up before the shuttle landed and tried to compose himself. His bruises had stiffened while he'd been sitting still, and now they roared into aching, complaining life. He tried to ignore them; he had no idea what he was walking into, and he couldn't afford the distraction.

He thought about Dar. He'd said he'd try to find a way around killing Remy, and he'd seemed sincere. But maybe he hadn't come up with anything. Maybe he'd persuaded Challoner to protect himself, and Remy was making a one-way trip out here. If Remy disappeared, no one would look too hard for him. Baryman would be the only person with power who'd even notice Remy's absence, and he would certainly agree to take a payoff rather than lose money by seeking justice.

But Remy couldn't believe that Challoner would do it. He had no idea where his faith in the man came from, but it was there. Dar... Dar was an old friend, but he was a realist, as well. He always had been. He'd do what needed to be done, if Challoner let him. But what if Challoner couldn't stop him? With any other two people, Remy would have had no doubt that the man with the money was the man with the power, but Challoner seemed strangely reluctant to use his wealth to his advantage. And Dar had never been much for accepting *any* authority other than his own. Remy had to face the possibility that Challoner wouldn't be able to stop Dar from doing what he had to do.

So when Remy found his way in off the empty roof and the first person he saw was Dar, he wasn't exactly reassured. He instinctively turned and looked back toward the shuttle pad; he wasn't sure if he was looking for an escape route to protect himself or checking to be sure that the pilot was gone in order to protect Dar. When Dar stepped forward, a smile on his face and a hand extended, Remy let himself relax a little. Dar was hard, but he wasn't duplicitous. He wouldn't smile at Remy if he didn't mean it. False smiles and feigned affection—those were Remy's specialties, not Dar's.

"You made it," Dar said. "Adam said he could do it. I guess it's easy to manipulate people who hate someone as much as your boss hates Adam." He shook Remy's hand vigorously, and the movement sent pain up Remy's arm and across his chest.

"Why am I here?" Remy asked. "Is something going on?"

"Hell, yeah something's going on. I'm calling it Operation Remy Escape."

"Escape from what? What are you talking about?"

A new voice, deep and familiar, said, "Come on downstairs, and we'll explain." Challoner looked tired, but still strong, standing at the top of the staircase and waiting for them.

Remy obeyed. He still didn't know what was going on, but he knew that it was his job to follow a client's orders. And his instinct to follow Challoner's requests.

The house was quiet, just as it had been on Remy's previous visit, but there was something different about it this time. There was Dar's energy, certainly. The man bounced along next to Remy like a puppy going for its first walk rather than a jaded terrorist. But Remy could sense something else as well. Challoner seemed more purposeful than usual, striding confidently down his hall to the formal living room rather than the cozier office. There was a man in there, sitting comfortably on a leather sofa. He was blond and blue-eyed, and Remy bet the man could trace his heritage back to the damn Vikings, or at least pretend to. Meeting a new member of the upper class, in this setting, made Remy's skin crawl with apprehension, but neither Dar nor Challoner seemed nervous. And Remy was good at looking comfortable even when he wasn't, so he kept his shoulders loose as he let Challoner lead him a few steps further into the room.

"Alfred, this is Remy Stone. Remy...." Challoner smiled at him like only the two of them were there. "I like that name. Suits you a lot better than 'David'." But then he turned back to the Viking. "Alfred's going to help us get you out of here. We're thinking Europe, at least initially, but after that we'll try to get you settled wherever you want to be."

Remy gave that a moment to make sense, but it was no use. "What do you mean? Did Mr. Baryman agree to sell my contract? He really...." Remy thought back to the man's expression only a few hours earlier. "He *really* didn't seem to be interested in doing that, last I heard."

"No, I was the one to back out of the negotiations." Challoner looked pleased with himself. "While the contract was on the table, he wasn't letting you out of the house, and we need to get moving on this, so I told him I wasn't interested, and let him talk me into having a visit."

"Yeah, but he was never planning on actually selling. He was just jerking you around, trying to make you crazy. He just wants you to *want* me, so he can have the fun of saying you can't have me."

Challoner's frown was only temporary. "Okay, well, that's interesting, but the main thing is that we're getting you out of the country, now. He can come after me for the value of your contract, if he wants, but once you're gone, there's no way to get you back."

"But... where do you think I'm going?"

Challoner seemed to have been expecting a different reaction, and he spoke slowly, as if Remy were a confused child. "We've made arrangements to get you to Europe. You don't have travel documents—I already checked on that." He smiled. "It was one of the reasons I gave for backing out of the contract. And if we try to *get* you documents, it'll take a long time, and people will know what's up. You'd have to do the standard pre-exit interview too, and we'd rather you didn't go through that, all things considered. So we're sending you through a back door."

"Why?"

"So we don't have to kill you." It was Dar, now, and for once, he wasn't smiling. "It was an accident, but you know too much. We can't leave you somewhere as vulnerable as the whore house."

Remy saw the Viking wince at the word "whore," and it made something tighten in his chest. "So how much is this costing you? And what the hell am I supposed to do in Europe? Do I just get dumped over there? I'm pretty old for a good organization to be interested in me. And I don't even know how things operate there. Would I even *work* through an agency, or are all their whores independents? What are the rules, the laws? I don't know any of that stuff."

Alfred stood up then and crossed the floor to extend his hand to Remy. "That's where I come in, Remy. I work for SWR, helping ex-prostitutes get started in new careers. That's what we envision for you."

"What's SWR?" The detail probably wasn't important, but Remy needed to give himself time to catch up. "And what the hell kind of career do you think I'm qualified for?"

"Sex Worker Rescue," the man said. "I'm surprised you haven't heard of us. We've been doing a lot of outreach down in Sector

Three—"

"I'm not a fucking streetwalker," Remy said defensively. Maybe he would be, once he got too old for his current clients, but not yet, and he needed to cling to that as long as he could. "I work for the Baryman Agency."

"As a sex worker," Alfred said, his enunciation overly clear.

"As a whore, yeah. But trust me, you doing outreach to a bunch of overage addicts isn't going to get your name in front of me or anyone I work with."

"I was under the impression that there was a drug-use issue in your case, as well," Alfred said, looking to Challoner for verification.

"There's all *kinds* of issues in my case, darlin'." Remy gave Alfred a good shot of seduction eyes to go along with the husky drawl.

"Okay," Challoner interjected. "So, the main point is, we've got people set up to help you out with your new life." He turned his head enough to make it feel like he was talking just to Remy again. "And I'm happy to help, as well. If you want to go to school, I can provide a scholarship program, or whatever's needed for that. We can work out the details later."

"Later? Like, after you get killed while running around pretending to be a freedom fighter? 'Cause that's where you're heading, and you're not going to be a whole lot of help to me then."

"I'll set up a trust fund," Challoner said stiffly. He didn't look too pleased with Remy's reaction so far.

Remy knew he should care. Challoner was his only ticket out of this mess. Keeping Challoner happy was important. It was Remy's job, no matter who his actual employer was. He forced a calm, peaceful smile onto his face. "I'm sorry. I'm just a little overwhelmed, I guess. Is it okay if I go visit the bathroom? I'll be back in a couple minutes with a much better attitude, I promise."

There was no way for Challoner to deny that request without being the asshole he was trying so hard not to be, so Remy turned and headed for the door as soon as he was done speaking. He wasn't prepared for the firm hand on his shoulder, wasn't prepared for the pressure on the bruise just over his collarbone, and he gasped in spite of himself.

Challoner lifted his hand immediately, and Remy just kept walking. He was out the door and halfway down the hall when he heard Challoner call his name and jog toward him. Remy reluctantly stopped walking and half turned, pressing his back against the wood-paneled wall as he waited.

Challoner stood in front of him with a frown on his face. "Are you injured, Remy?"

"No." That was true enough, really. An injury was something that would keep him from doing his job. He was just hurt.

But Challoner didn't seem convinced. He stared at Remy's face, then slowly lifted his hands to the buttons of Remy's shirt. They hovered there for a moment, then he lowered them. "It seemed like it hurt, when I touched your shoulder. Why?"

"You hit a bruise. It's not a big deal."

"Where'd you get a bruise? You've been off work for several days, haven't you?"

"Even nonwhores get bruises now and then. It's not from a client."

"So what's it from?" Challoner's voice was still quiet, but he didn't seem inclined to let this go.

Remy smiled. "I said this the last time I was out here: you shouldn't ask questions when you don't really want to hear the answers."

"And my response is the same as it was last time. I *do* want to know." Challoner's hand was gentle on the side of Remy's face, asking but not telling him to lift his head. "Remy, what's your bruise from?"

Remy managed to look Challoner in the eye for a moment, then found a spot over his shoulder to focus on. "Baryman wanted to send a message. He wanted to remind you that if I don't work for you, then I'll work for other people, and they might not be gentle."

"So it *was* from a client?"

"No. Just one of Baryman's goons."

Challoner nodded slowly, then said, "It's your body, Remy. I don't... I don't want you to feel that you *have* to show me. But if Baryman's using you to send me a message, then maybe I should see the whole message."

That was hard to argue with. Remy kept his eyes fixed on the spot over Challoner's shoulder, but he raised his hands and started on the buttons of his shirt. He undid them all, then shrugged the shirt off his shoulders and let Challoner look.

"Turn around," Challoner said, his expression unreadable. Remy complied. It was nice to be able to close his eyes. He felt Challoner's fingertips, so gentle that they were more like a little breath of air, tracing over the marks on his skin. "Remy...," Challoner started, and it sounded like he was about to cry. He stopped, and when he spoke again, his voice was stronger. "The same on your legs? Under your pants?"

Remy shrugged. "Yeah. It looks worse than it is. The guy was a pro. Like I said, it's a message, not an actual punishment."

Challoner didn't say anything. He lifted the collar of Remy's shirt from where it was gathered around his waist, and slowly, gently, lifted it back up to rest on his shoulders. Then he leaned forward a little. He still wasn't touching Remy, but he braced his hands on the wall Remy was facing, circled his arms around him like a protective cocoon, and finally, so softly that Remy wasn't sure it was real, he kissed the back of Remy's head. "It's over, Remy. It has to be over. We'll find something else for you. You never have to go back there. I can't... you can't go back there."

"Yeah, that's the message he wanted you to get, all right." Remy forced himself to push through Challoner's near embrace, and he started down the hall again. "Bathroom," he said, and Challoner didn't stop him.

Remy made it to the bathroom and locked the door behind him. He looked in the mirror and splashed some cold water on his face. Then he sat down on the toilet seat, and he waited until he finally stopped shaking. It took a long time.

CHAPTER TWELVE

REMY got sick of sitting in the bathroom before he felt like he was ready to go back to the living room. He didn't want to impose on Challoner's hospitality, didn't want to snoop, but he had to move. So he headed down the hall to the back of the house. He'd been allowed in the kitchen on his last visit, so hopefully he wasn't being rude by returning.

Carralina was sitting at the wooden table, her hands wrapped around a mug, her back straight and strong as she stared at nothing. She turned her head in his direction and smiled, and Remy felt physically dizzy, as if his memory had actually transported him somehow, quickly and without warning. He took a step closer, but he didn't need to. He knew why he'd thought she looked familiar on his last visit. He knew why he'd recognized her smile.

"Mrs. Wright," he said softly, and her smile faded only a little before returning.

"Remy," she replied. "Dar told me you were coming. I'm sorry I didn't recognize you on your last visit."

"You didn't... well, no. How could you have? But I didn't recognize you, either. Mrs. Wright...." His chest felt tight, and the dizziness wasn't going away. He took a few steps and pulled out a chair at the table. Manners might require that he wait to be invited, but he was beyond worrying about such things. He had to ask, even though he knew the answer, even though there was no way to even hope for anything other than what he'd seen with his own eyes. "Mrs. Wright...."

She shook her head sadly. "No, Remy. I'm sorry. Only me. Your parents didn't make it."

Remy tried not to react. He'd seen them killed right in front of him, their deaths gruesome and final. But Dar's mother had been listed among the dead as well, and somehow, here she was.

"Mrs. Wright, I don't understand. They told us you were dead." Even through his own nightmarish pain he could remember Dar sobbing, screaming in fear and loneliness. There was no way that had been a feigned reaction.

"They told everyone that," Carralina said quietly. "And for a long time, I wished I was." She touched her face, and from this close, Remy could see the faint scars around her temples. "I was unconscious for almost a year. My parents bought my way out of the prison hospital, put me in an excellent long-term care facility, and then disowned me when I had the bad manners to wake up."

Remy nodded. He'd known, vaguely, that Dar's grandparents were wealthy. Carralina's brown skin and vaguely Asian features made it clear they weren't from the very top level, the ones who considered themselves pure, but they'd had enough money to be comfortable on this planet. Carralina's decision to start a new life on a colony must have been inexplicable to them. "They didn't help Dar?"

"They refused to acknowledge that he existed. After all, if they had no daughter, they couldn't very well have a grandson."

Remy could understand that. He was beginning to feel a bit more balanced again. "Your sight can't be repaired? I thought they had an apparatus to fix everything these days."

"I have one," she said. "It works. But I won't wear it. Not when so many people lost so much more than their sight. Not when every time I put it on I just see more ugliness, more cruelty and injustice." She smiled. "I'd like to wear it, someday. I'd like to see the flowers in the spring, and I'd like to see Dar's face. And the face of my grandchild."

"Your grandchild? Dar has a kid?"

She beamed like any proud grandmother. "Livia. She's three. Dar and her mother aren't really together, but Breanne works here now... Adam helped get them out of the city and gave her a job. It's so much safer for Livia. Adam's been a godsend."

"How did that happen? You working for Challoner. Did he know Dar first, or you first?" It was probably nosy, but this whole thing was confusing, and Remy wanted some details to help his mind settle.

"Me first. I had a job in the city, but the factory closed, and Adam was hiring. I think he chose me out of pity, at first, but I do well without my eyes. I'm good at my job. He met Dar through me, and then... I honestly don't know why Dar took the risk of approaching him about the resistance. They'd had some conversations, certainly, but only Dar would try to recruit a member of the ruling class into an organization devoted to overthrowing that class!" She sipped from her mug, then smiled again. "But enough about that! What about you? Dar said you were working in the city, but he didn't say what you were doing. Something pretty important, I guess, if you're meeting people like Adam and flying around in shuttles and such."

Remy had lies all ready for occasions like this. He even had a set of identification cards that showed him working as a Social Coordinator, planning parties for the well-to-do and events for the large corporations. He thought of the Scandinavian and his Sex Worker Rescue organization, and he said, "I'm a whore."

She didn't say anything for a while, then she nodded slowly. "Oh. I guess that makes sense. I couldn't figure out how you'd have managed to get any education, not without family to back you up." She reached her hand out in Remy's direction, and he let her find his fingers and grip them tight.

He wished she'd been outraged. It would have been a lot easier if she'd ordered him out of her kitchen and screamed at him for disgracing his family. He knew what to do in the face of cruelty, but this... this was as bad as Challoner letting Remy decide whether to show his bruises or not.

When Carralina spoke again, she sounded like she was trying to be confident, but wasn't completely without doubts. "Adam doesn't... you don't work for Adam. Not that way."

"No. Not that way."

"Is he going to help you? Are you looking for a different line of work?"

Remy didn't think he'd get into the contractual issues. "He wants to, yeah. I'm thinking about it. Trying to figure it all out."

"He's a good man, Remy. He really cares about people. Individuals, and people as a whole. You should let him help."

"Yeah," Remy said quietly. Then even more softly, he said, "Do you ever wish you hadn't gone to the colony? Or... you know. Do you wish you'd gone, but not been part of the revolt? You could have been safe, if you'd stayed here."

"I wonder about that sometimes," she admitted. "Not because of myself, but because of the others. The people at that colony were the most beautiful human beings I've ever encountered, and I don't mean on the outside. For them to have been destroyed like they were, for no good reason, and so brutally...." She stopped and gave Remy an apologetic look, as if she thought he couldn't remember the agony of his parents' death without her prompting. She shrugged and smiled sadly. "It was terrible. But I can't say I'd take back any of the decisions that brought me there, no. To have experienced that one brilliant flash of freedom... how could I ever give that up?" She leaned forward and tightened her fingers around Remy's. "For seven perfect, glorious months, between our declaration of independence and the arrival of the military... for seven months, we lived the way humans are meant to live. For me, and, I really believe, even for those who lost their lives, it was worth it. Absolutely."

He nodded slowly. "Even the way it ended? That didn't destroy the memory of the time before?"

"It made the memory stronger. And not just with me. You should talk to Adam about it. He thinks of this place as carrying on the ideals of Colony Seventeen. Self-sufficiency, respect for all, harmony with nature...." Her smile was quick and bright. "I don't tell him what a pale imitation this is of the real place. But I think he knows. He's still working on it."

"I never thought of it that way. I guess I try not to think about it at all."

"That would be truly tragic, Remy. If one of the people who was there forgot about it? No, don't let that happen."

"It makes it kind of hard to live *here*, though. You know?"

She nodded slowly. "I suppose. For me, when I was working in the factory, the memories were all that got me through. I'd imagine myself in a big, open field, or walking through the forest, with those crazy trees that were almost but not quite like the ones on Earth. And I'd imagine going home to have dinner with my husband and my son and all my dear friends."

Remy didn't know how to respond. He didn't know how to tell her that he was trying to save the memories for something special, trying to keep from getting them dirty with his everyday life. So he smiled politely, realized that she couldn't see the expression, and cleared his throat instead. "I should get back in there, I guess," he said. "I told them I'd be gone for a couple minutes... must be a half hour ago by now."

He stood up, and wasn't sure what to do next. Well, he should go back to the living room, obviously, but he wasn't sure how to say good-bye to this woman. He had no idea where he was going or whether he'd ever see her again, and it seemed strange to just walk away so soon after having found her. He looked around the kitchen and saw the organized tools on the counter, the collection of vegetables by the sink waiting to be washed... the evidence that she had found a home for herself, a place where she fit. He didn't think he wanted to go all the way back to his memories of the colony, but this could be something for him to think about when he needed to imagine something pleasant. Carralina could picture herself going back to her friends and family on Colony Seventeen; Remy would use this place, the warmth and acceptance he'd felt from Challoner and Carralina herself. It wasn't the same, he supposed. But it was something.

REMY walked quietly on his way back to the living room. If he could just sneak in, sit down, and just be unnoticed for a while, he'd be okay. But as soon as he appeared in the doorway, Challoner stood up. Dar and Alfred stared at him from their seats.

"Are you okay, Remy?" Challoner asked.

"I stopped by the kitchen," he said, looking straight at Dar. "Ran into an old friend." He stepped a little closer. "I guess you've got more to protect than just Challoner's money, huh?"

Dar looked like he wanted to argue, but then reluctantly admitted, "Yeah. A lot more."

"I sympathize. But I'm not going to Europe."

"Remy—" Dar started, but he stopped when Remy raised his hand.

"No. I'm not running away. And you can ease off on the death threats, killer, because you know a hell of a lot more than I do and that hasn't made it necessary for you to kill *yourself*. So obviously you're used to a bit of risk."

"Because I'm making a contribution," Dar insisted. "Because I'm being useful."

"So I'll make a contribution too." Remy felt strangely calm about it all. But Dar wasn't the only person in the room, and Remy's nerves returned when he turned to face Challoner. "I can be useful. This is my country. The people you're trying to help...

they're my people." He glanced over at Dar, then back to Challoner. It was Challoner he needed to convince. It was Challoner who thought Remy was just useless, damaged decoration. "This government butchered my family, my entire colony, for daring to stand up for themselves in a totally nonviolent way. Now you're telling me that it's too dangerous for me to fight back? I'm a drugged-up whore, Challoner, whether you like it or not. My life is nothing. I'm not even... I'm not even a pawn. I'm a square on the damn chessboard, just background to the actual fight. I want to be a pawn, Challoner. A pawn isn't powerful, but they can be dangerous."

That was the best Remy had, but Challoner still looked unconvinced.

"The chickens that flew south... that's great, for them, but they're still just chickens when they get there. They left all their chicken buddies behind, worked their asses off to get somewhere warm, and they're still just... just chickens."

"You're no longer making even a little bit of sense," Dar interrupted. "I was kind of with you for the pawn part, but I don't understand the chickens at all."

"Challoner does," Remy said. He inched closer. "Right? You know about doing the right thing instead of the safe thing. Your involvement in all this is proof of that. And you know about trying to make things better, trying to build things and grow things. That's what I want to do. I want to make things better." He turned back to Dar. "The Colony Seventeen Rebellion isn't over. Not yet. And I've been out of the fight for too long."

"Remy, no," Challoner said. "It's too dangerous for you here. Europe is much safer. It's a much better option for you."

"It's not an option at all, because I'm not going to Europe." Remy shook his head. "You won't open my shirt without permission, but you think it's okay for you to decide my whole future?"

"You don't need to do this, Remy. You've already been through enough. Colony Seventeen... Baryman buying and selling you at such a young age... everything you go through every time you're with a client... the shit they did to you today...." Challoner shook his head. "No. It's already too much. Far too much."

"Or flip it around," Remy said. He smiled at Challoner. "I've already taken the punishment—now it's time to do the damn crime."

"That's right," Dar said triumphantly. Remy had known that a little bravado was the way to Dar's heart. "That's my boy!"

"I can help, Challoner." Remy stepped closer. He wasn't sure what he'd do if Challoner refused. Wasn't sure whether he'd be able to convince Dar to let him in without Challoner's agreement, but also wasn't sure whether he would be able to ignore the man's wishes himself. He needed Challoner to approve. This was about more than taking part in a social movement—it was about Remy's self-respect. He needed Challoner to see him as a person, not a cause. "I want to contribute. I want to be something more than just a whore."

"You already are," Challoner said softly.

But Remy wouldn't let himself be lied to, not anymore. "I'm not. But I could be. I will be. If you won't let me help, I guess I'll have to go back to Baryman's. I'll find a pill that's faster acting... maybe you guys could give me one of those, if you have them. And then the next time it looks like I'm going to get taken in, I'll swallow the pill. So I won't give away your secrets, but it'll be for nothing." He ignored the Viking but looked long and hard at Dar and Challoner, trying to make them understand how serious he was. "I've thought about dying. Lots of times. I'm not afraid of it. But if I could *use* it somehow, if I could make my death mean something... I'd like that." He looked at Dar now. "My parents, your father... they got to have that. I want it too."

Dar nodded, and Challoner said, "Damn it, Remy." He shook his head reluctantly, then slowly turned to Alfred. "I want the travel plans kept in place. If things get hot over here, if something happens to me, I want Remy to be able to get the hell out of this mess." He looked back at Remy. "And I'll set up that trust fund. If you want to go to school, if you want to start a business... whatever you decide to do, you'll be able to do it. If things go bad here, you'll still have somewhere to run to, okay?"

Remy was pretty sure they both knew that if things went bad, there'd be no escape for any of them. But it seemed to make Challoner feel better, so he nodded. "Yeah, okay. Hey, put lots of money in the fund, okay? I think I could spend some significant cash if I put my mind to it."

Challoner's smile was Remy's reward. "All right, I will. And you're not going back to Baryman's. No way. We'll tell him you ran away, we'll hide you... whatever it takes. You can't go back there."

"I should go wherever I'm useful. I'm a pawn, now, remember?"

"Don't start with all that again," Dar interjected.

"Sorry for the false alarm," Challoner said to Alfred. He'd apparently decided to wrap up that bit of business before dealing with Remy's future. "I'd still appreciate your help sorting through those contract terms and seeing if there's any room for flexibility, or for a challenge of some sort."

Alfred stood up. "I'm happy to look, but I doubt there will be. This is hardly the first employment contract Mr. Baryman has created. He's very good at what he does. Very efficient in his depravity."

Remy wasn't sure he'd ever heard a better description of Baryman. Maybe this Viking wasn't quite as clueless as he'd initially seemed.

"Do what you can," Challoner said.

"Absolutely," Alfred agreed. "The safest thing certainly would be to find a legal way out of the contract." He shook Challoner's hand, and then Remy's. "I should say the *safer* thing. Because the safest, of course, would still be for you to get out of this country, away from your pimp, and somewhere that the laws will protect *you* rather than him."

"Thanks for the advice," Remy said. "But I'm staying here."

Alfred nodded. "I see." He turned to Challoner. "Thank you for your generous donation, Adam. I'll see that it's put to good use. And I'll keep the travel set up, as you suggested." And with that, he was gone.

Challoner flopped down into an antique chair that probably cost more than Remy was worth. It creaked under his weight.

"Are you mad?" Remy asked. He felt like a little boy.

Challoner shook his head slowly. "No." He took a deep breath, then said, "But you're not part of this. You won't go to Europe... fine. You're right, I can't make you. But Remy, you can't make me put you in danger. You can't make me put you in touch with people I don't want you to be in contact with."

"But if I'm not helping, then the whole thing is pointless. I want to *do* something."

"It's not a social club, Remy." Dar shook his head. "This is the big-time. This is people who are risking their lives and the lives of their families in order to fight something they hate. Remy, for a lot of them, you're *part* of what they hate. Your nice clothes and your warm bed that you earn by sleeping with the enemy. You're a collaborator. They won't want you. They won't trust you." Dar's voice wasn't harsh, but it was firm. He wasn't judging, just stating a fact.

It hit Remy harder than it should have. He'd known all that. He'd felt the scorn of other workers all his life, from the servants in the big houses to the shuttle pilots to the tailors who came to the house to fit him with costumes. Just because he'd found the strength to make a change, that didn't mean *they* were going to change. He might feel as if his world had been torn apart and then reassembled with totally different shapes, but the alteration wasn't visible to others. He was a whore, and in some people's eyes, he always would be. He gave himself a moment, then said,

"So what can I do? How can I help?"

"You could go to Europe," Challoner said, but he immediately leaned forward and caught Remy's hand in his. "Or you could give it time. Let things get figured out. I meant it when I said you can't go back to that job. But you can't jump into something new, either. You can stay here, as my guest. You're not working for me, so it won't violate your contract, and you'll be safe here while we get things figured out."

It sounded so straightforward, so easy. But nothing was ever that clear. "Baryman will never believe it. You've been a client in the past, you've tried to buy my contract, and now I'm just going to be a guest in your home, no strings attached? He'll send the law after me. After you. He's got good lawyers."

"So do I." Challoner's voice was rock solid.

"But you're trying to keep a low profile. Trying not to look suspicious. I mean, that first night in the hotel room...." Remy glanced over at Dar, who wasn't even trying to appear uninterested. "You were there because you had to be, right? You were part of planting the bombs, somehow. But you had to have a cover, and you didn't want Baryman to be worried about you. That's why you let me stay. If I don't go back, he's going to be a hell of a lot more than worried."

"I don't care about that anymore. You're right. That night, I needed a cover, and when you arrived, I took advantage of it. Now, though, there are more important things to worry about."

"Yeah, there are, but I'm not one of them." Remy knew he was right, even though he didn't want to be. "Doing what you're doing, trying to... well, I don't know exactly what you're doing. Trying to overthrow the government? Whatever. Trying to fight back. That's more important. And if my whole reason for staying here is that I want to help with that, then it would be pretty pathetic if I ended up getting in the way of it, right? If I ended up getting you all tied up with lawyers and treated with suspicion. And Baryman's got a lot of powerful friends. Powerful clients. Not just private citizens, but government contacts. If he decides that you're trouble, he'll have them looking for any way to hurt you."

"You're not going back there, Remy." Challoner stood up, glanced at Dar as if quelling any potential input from that quarter, then turned back to Remy. "No. There's no point in fighting them if we end up being just *like* them. If we don't care about people, if we don't try to do what's right... if we don't do whatever we can to keep our friends out of dangerous, abusive situations, then what's the point of it all?"

"If you only look out for your friends and not the people as a whole, then how are you any different than they are?" Remy kept his voice as level as his gaze.

"You guys are killing me with all this damn philosophizing," Dar said with a groan. "Adam, have you learned nothing from my example? It's not about what's right, it's about what you can get away with. When in doubt... sneak around!" He smiled happily. "Remy gets back on the shuttle like a good little boy. He goes back to the house, crawls out that same window we went in through, meets me on the ground, and I smuggle him back here. Baryman's got no reason to even suspect you. Hell, you can make a new offer to buy Remy's contract the next day, or call to arrange for another appointment or something, just to make it clear you don't know he's gone."

Challoner thought about it for a moment, and then he nodded slowly. "That might work."

"'Might work'? I think that's the best odds I've heard for any of our plans so far!" Dar's enthusiasm was infectious. "This is practically a sure thing, if it gets a 'might work' from the Great Pessimist." He looked at the other two, then at the door. "So we'll talk about that tomorrow sometime. I'm going to go make some plans, get it all set up. You guys can manage without me for the evening? I think Mama-lina's got dinner started for up here, but she's going to come down and eat at the cottage with me and Liv. Breanne's got a date, I guess, so I'm on daddy duty. Give us a call if you need anything." He half turned, waggled his eyebrows so only Remy could see, and then left the room with a happy wave and an overloud, "Good night!"

Remy was embarrassed. Not for himself, but for Challoner. The man was above such crude innuendo, such sloppy matchmaking. And he hadn't wanted Remy when he was a whore, a simple fuck with no strings attached and no complications. He quite obviously wouldn't be interested in Remy now.

And he did look uncomfortable. He smiled awkwardly and said, "It's still quite a while before dinner. Can I interest you in some chess? Or would you rather teach me how to blow up alligators?"

Remy forced himself to smile naturally. "It's quite a while, you said. Maybe we have time for both."

CHAPTER THIRTEEN

AFTER several sedate games of chess, Challoner turned out to be a bit of a maniac with the holo games. The sensor area was large enough for them to really spread out, and Remy had barely turned the game on and explained the system before Challoner sprang behind a holographic boulder and shot Remy with his pulse rifle.

There was no pain, but Remy's sensors all went dead and his light over the control panel went out; he wasn't in the game anymore.

"We're on the same team, Challoner."

"You said we could play against each other."

"And then I said we'd do a round as a team so you didn't get eaten by alligators right away."

"I must have missed that part."

This soon after playing chess with the man, Remy wasn't remotely willing to believe that Challoner was stupid. But it wasn't Remy's place to argue. "Okay, fine. Game, reset. Challoner, we're on the same team. Don't—" And then Remy's sensors blinked and went dead, and Challoner was grinning at him, pulse rifle loose and ready in his hand.

Remy took a deep breath. "Okay. My mistake. We're on different teams. Have fun with the gators." He found a good-sized holographic tree to hide behind and then said, "Game, reset."

He waited. He couldn't see Challoner, couldn't hear him, so he tried to sense him. The man was patient, normally, but the game seemed to have unleashed a strange aspect of his personality. Remy was willing to bet that Challoner was already on the move. He'd be sneaking, stalking, working around the side of Remy's tree. He'd be just about at the....

"Jesus!" Challoner yelled, and the sound of pulse-rifle fire filled the room. "Alligators!" He was laughing like a little kid. "Remy, you're supposed to be on my team! Come help me with the—" Another wild laugh, and Remy saw the light above the control console blink out. Challoner was out of the game.

Remy stepped out from behind the tree and saw Challoner on the ground, still laughing, his body covered by hungry holographic gators. "Hey, boys," Remy said sweetly, and as the first creature turned its head, Remy started firing. He wasn't an expert at the game, but he'd played for several hours on his last visit, and he had the basics figured out. Head shots, especially when their jaws were open. Keep moving, circling, get them tangled up on each other. His battered muscles groaned but performed as ordered. Fire, step, step, fire, step, step, set up a rhythm, keep it going. Hell, it worked even better with Challoner in there, still drawing their attention even though he was no longer active. "They want to eat your corpse," Remy said triumphantly as he pumped a few rounds into one of the few remaining alligators. "I'm using you as bait!"

"See? I'm doing my part for the team. You should have helped me out earlier."

Remy shot the last gator and lowered his gun, but kept a cautious eye on the holo swamp. "Sorry. I was wrong to not let you shoot me a third time."

"Hey, Remy?" Challoner's voice was different somehow, and Remy let himself take his eyes off the game for a quick glance. "Nice shooting."

There was something there, a tone Remy felt like he recognized. "Game, pause," he said, and he walked slowly to Challoner, then sank down on his knees beside him. He laid his gun on the floor. "You like that?" he asked. He kept his voice playful, but let a thread of suggestion run through it. "Watching me take care of the vermin?"

"I like watching you do pretty much everything," Challoner murmured. "God, Remy. You're so beautiful it actually hurts, you know that?"

Remy had heard this nonsense from countless men, but it was somehow different coming from Challoner. He didn't think he wanted to hear any more. So he smiled rakishly. "Yeah, I can barely look in the mirror without screaming." Then he shifted quickly, off his knees and onto his side, stretched out on the floor, his front tucked in against Challoner's hip and ribs. His bruises twinged at every point of contact, but he could ignore that. "I'm still on the clock, you know. Still yours, however you want me. You want to make my last pro fuck one to remember?"

Remy had known it was the wrong thing to say even before he'd opened his mouth. Maybe he'd said it *because* it was wrong. Challoner tensed and sat up, bracing his elbows on his knees as he stared out into the holographic swamp. "No, Remy." He laughed ruefully. "If I've made it this long, I can make it a little longer. I really, really don't want to have anything to do with your 'pro fucks'."

"Your loss, man. You think this body *looks* good, you should let yourself see how it *feels*."

"You do that a lot. You say 'this body' instead of 'I'. Did you know you do that?"

"Nope, this body hadn't noticed." Remy sprang to his feet and tried to ignore the strange sting from Challoner's rejection. It didn't matter. It wasn't personal. Challoner was a good guy, and Remy liked him. If Challoner wanted to get off, Remy could help him. That was all. Remy had a skill, and he was willing to share. But if his services weren't required, that was fine too. Just fine.

"Do you want to play another round? Try not to get killed this time?" He suddenly realized just how much of Challoner's time he was taking up. "Or, you know, if you have other stuff to do, I can entertain myself. Whatever you need."

"No, another round would be—" Challoner broke off as someone knocked loudly at the door. It opened a moment later and Dar peeked inside.

He glanced around at the holo carnage and said, "I'm disappointed. I heard these high-end holo rooms had more... interesting applications." A quick waggle of his eyebrows and then more serious, and directly to Challoner, "We've got trouble. Maybe."

Challoner rolled to his feet, instantly alert. "Game off," he ordered. The holographs faded as Challoner headed for the door. "What's going on?" He seemed about to leave, about to stride purposefully down the hall with Dar, off to do whatever they had to do, but then he looked over his shoulder at Remy, still standing in the middle of the sensor area. He turned back to Dar, wordlessly consulting, and Dar shrugged.

"He already knows enough to get us both executed fifteen times over, and I don't think we're going to hear anyone else's names or identifiers."

Challoner turned back around and looked at Remy for longer than was comfortable. "You're sure?" he finally asked. "Because you don't need to earn your keep. If you want, we can find something for you to do around here, on the farm, but even that is strictly optional. You don't need to get involved in something dangerous." He shook his head regretfully. "I'd honestly really prefer that you didn't."

"Can I at least... can I listen? I don't even really understand what you're trying to do with all this. And if I already know enough to get you guys executed, then I know enough to get myself executed too. So it's hard to get more dangerous than that. I'd at least like to *know* what I know, if I'm going to pay for it anyway."

Challoner had his sad face on again. "Goddamn it, Remy," he

said. Then he turned and walked out of the room. It really didn't seem like he wanted to be followed.

Remy felt the familiar wave of panic wash toward him, and he held it back as desperately as he always did. He'd said the wrong thing. He'd offended his client. And not just his client anymore: his protector. He'd fucked up, and there would be consequences. He turned to Dar, trying to understand more than hoping to escape.

Dar was watching him closely. "He's not mad. Not at you. And if he *was* mad, you could just tell him to fuck off. He's not like the rest of them, Remy. You know that." Dar moved forward too quickly, and Remy shied away before forcing himself to stand still. It was easier to stay that way when Dar slowed down, and his hand on Remy's shoulder was lighter than it had seemed like it was going to be. "The world's fucked up, Remy, but not every single part of it. Not every person in it." His voice lost its gentleness and his face eased back into his customary grin as he added, "I, for example, am a goddamned prince among men. And I've got your back."

"You said you were going to kill me."

"Well, that was an awkward situation, Remy. Imagine how painful that was for me, with all my princely sentiments."

"It would have been a hell of a lot more awkward if you'd actually tried to do it," Remy replied. This was good. This was something he could talk about, something to distract him from the wild, fluttering tension still in his gut. "I'd pretty much decided not to go along with it."

"You think I was going to give you that choice?" Dar had his arm around Remy's shoulder, now, and he shoved him a little, got his feet moving sideways before he shifted them both forward. Dar didn't know about Remy's bruises, and Remy didn't care. "You think it would have been so easy?"

"Easy?" Remy had himself back under control, and he raised an eyebrow in Dar's direction as they walked slowly down the hall.

"I'd have had the protection of the most powerful prostitution agency in the country. If I'd changed the story just a little to make it sound like you forced me, and if I'd told the story fast enough, I'd have had the protection of the whole fucking government. And you'd have had...." Remy cast his gaze up and down Dar's frame. "You. Your raggedy ass. If I'd have turned you in."

"And you just said you were thinking about that? Right? You said you'd decided not to go along with my little plan." Dar stopped walking and turned to look Remy in the eye. His voice was still light, but there was an edge to it that hadn't been there before.

But Remy shrugged, and gave the best imitation of Dar's cocky grin that he could come up with. From Dar's response, he figured it was pretty good. "Nah. I wasn't going to just give up and go along with your plan to kill me, but I wasn't going to turn you in, either. I was just going to kick your ass."

Dar's laugh was more like a bark. "Yeah. Okay." He shoved Remy again, a little harder this time, and they continued down the hall together.

CHALLONER was already sitting with his comm when Remy and Dar came through the door. He didn't say anything, but he came out from behind the desk and gestured for them to join him in the big leather seats over by the bookcases. A wing chair each for Challoner and Dar left the couch for Remy. It felt too big for him alone, but he sat down anyway and tried to be inconspicuous.

Challoner held up his comm. "I'm reading," he said to Dar. "Getting caught up."

Dar nodded. "Has there been an update?"

"No."

Challoner went back to his comm, and Dar turned to Remy. He spoke quietly. "We have a couple people... key people... who may have been uncovered. A lot of our work involves attacking the computer systems. Viruses, worms, corruption of programs and records—however we can manage it. The shuttle bombing was a bit out of character for us, but we needed a distraction to allow us to do something else that needed to be done. We needed something big and public." He smiled in happy recollection of just how big and public the shuttles had been. "But really, the government has a lot of people. We're never going to be able to kill them all." He rolled his eyes in Challoner's direction and added, "And some of us don't want to. What makes the government so powerful is the surveillance, and the data they store. That's our main target. And the two people we're worried about are our best hackers. They're the ones who came up with the tool for killing the cameras last night. That was our test run, to see if it worked."

Remy nodded thoughtfully. That was more information than he'd expected to be given, and he had to think it all through.

Challoner tossed the comm onto the desk in disgust. "Jesus. We're just supposed to wait. Sit it out and hope it's a false alarm."

"Not much else *to* do, is there?" Dar didn't say it lightly. He sounded almost as frustrated as Challoner. "If the government's got them, that's it. And if they don't, then we're fine. If they're being looked at, though, and we do something to try to protect them...." He spread his hands in a helpless gesture. "That'd be a clear red flag. We'd do more harm than good."

"Do they know anything that would bring the security forces here?" Remy didn't want to think about it, but he wanted to know if Challoner was at risk. Maybe there was some way to persuade the man to use the same escape route he'd set up for Remy. The Europeans had long since stopped honoring extradition requests from North America, so Challoner would be safe if he could make it over there.

But Challoner shook his head. "We don't think so. They shouldn't. We don't know who the hackers are, even. There's nobody in this jurisdiction who knows more than their own cell;

our main communication center is safe over in Asia."

"They send encrypted comm messages, coordinate us all, and they'll never be caught, so it's not dangerous for them to know things." Dar sounded pleased with the system, and Remy had to admit that it made sense.

Challoner was looking thoughtful again; never a good thing. "Maybe that's where you could go, if you don't want to go to Europe. If you want to help. Maybe they could find a job for you at Headquarters."

"With my vast knowledge and skill, I'm sure I'd be really useful," Remy agreed sarcastically. "I could help people relax, I guess, but that'd be about it. But *you* could contribute over there. You could be the chess master, moving all us little pieces around to where you want us."

"Don't get started on the chess talk again," Dar groaned.

"And don't think you're getting rid of me that easily," Challoner added. "I was away from my country for too long, living with my eyes shut. I'm back now, and my eyes are open. I'm staying."

"So we're all here." Dar stood up. "I'm going to stick around, if that's okay. I want to hear the news as it comes in, and you've got higher clearance on your comm. You'll maybe hear some of the government-level stuff. So should we have dinner?"

It seemed odd to go down to the kitchen and serve up the salad, stew, and homemade bread Carralina had left, but there wasn't much else to do. They sat around the wooden table, Dar on one side, Remy and Challoner on the other, and Remy found himself sneaking peeks at Challoner as he ate. There was something strangely fascinating about him; even the way he speared a chunk of carrot seemed genuine and interesting.

"These were all grown here?" Remy asked, using his fork to gesture at the vegetables. He didn't really care, but he liked seeing Challoner's enthusiasm.

And Challoner did seem pleasantly distracted as he peered

around the table. "Not the salad stuff—I already told you, right? No greenhouse yet. But the carrots, the potatoes, the peas, the onions, those are all ours. And the beef too. Yeah, the stew's pretty much ours."

"Except for the salt," Remy prompted.

"Yeah. The damned salt. I should buy a few truckloads of it, dump it somewhere remote, and start mining it."

"That sounds efficient, definitely."

"We lived near the ocean," Dar said suddenly. "Colony Seventeen. Everyone thinks of the colony planet as being one huge continent, but it's half water. And Colony Seventeen was near the ocean. We got salt by evaporating sea water."

"That would be handy," Challoner said easily, but Remy could feel the man's eyes on him, looking for a reaction. "Each family had their own small farm, right? And then contributed to the community with specialized skills? Dar, I know your mother was a metalsmith—the lighter, precision items, she told me. What did your father do?"

"Metalsmith as well, but the heavier stuff. More like a blacksmith, most of the time." Dar grinned. "He'd be grunting away at the forge, hammering with all his strength, practically melting in the heat of the day; and my mom would be sitting there at her work table, using a little soldering gun or something. She definitely had the sweeter job."

"And your parents, Remy?" Challoner prompted.

Remy kept his eyes on his stew.

"Remy? What did your parents do?" Challoner's voice was gentle, but insistent.

Remy looked at him. "My parents?" He didn't understand how they were talking about this. "My parents died. My mother got her arm blown off by a big chunk of shrapnel; she lay there on the floor, bleeding to death, and I tried to stick the damn arm back on. Like she was a doll, and I just had to push the bits of plastic together." He gestured with his hands, showing how the joint should have fit. He knew he should stop, but he seemed compelled to continue. "My father, though, he got set on fire. Did you know they used fire? No reason for it, not that I can think of. Couldn't have been trying to scare people, because they never gave us a chance to surrender. I think they were just trying out new weapons. They shot a little ball in through the window, and it landed there, and he pushed me out of the way and jumped on it, and then he was...." Remy finally stopped. He tore a chunk off the bread slice on his plate and stuffed it in his mouth. It was too big, and he didn't think he'd be able to swallow around the lump in his throat, but he kept working at it, chewing determinedly as he stared down at his hands. They'd returned to the position he'd held them in as he was trying to demonstrate doll repair, and he flattened them quickly on the table, the fingers spread out as if for balance.

Nobody said anything. Remy was finally able to swallow the mouthful of bread. He took a sip from his glass of water, then said, "I'm sorry. I didn't mean to be unpleasant."

Challoner didn't speak, but his chair was loud as it scraped violently across the tile floor. He stood up quickly, and Remy wanted to lower himself to the floor. On his knees, he'd show his contrition, and it was less distance to fall if the punishment was severe. But he stayed still, and Challoner didn't strike him. Instead, he turned and strode out of the room, so fast he was almost running.

Remy looked down at his spread fingers, and he remembered the way his mother's fingers had curled around, as if she were still trying to hold his hand even after that part of her body had been severed from her.

"He's not mad," Dar said. "Not at you. At himself, maybe."

Remy nodded silently. Dar was wrong. Dar didn't understand. Remy knew how these things worked, and he knew what happened when he lost control of his emotions. Challoner might not actually carry out the punishments; Dar was right, Challoner was a kind man. But that didn't mean that Remy didn't deserve the pain. He'd displeased his client, and there was no excuse for it. Challoner had already been tense, and instead of helping him to relax, Remy had made everything much worse. Remy had no contributions to make here. Challoner didn't want to use the one skill Remy had, and Remy had apparently lost control of any sort of social graces or etiquette that he'd ever learned.

He wanted to help. But he couldn't. All he could do was make things worse.

CHAPTER FOURTEEN

REMY didn't want to go looking for Challoner. He wanted to stay in the kitchen, alone, on the floor if possible. But Dar was insistent, and it wouldn't be good if Dar went and told Challoner that Remy was being defiant. Earlier, he'd joked about fighting back when Dar came to get him, and now it was clear just what a joke that had been. Dar was Challoner's friend, and Challoner was Remy's client.

So Remy stood up and followed after Dar. They left the food on the table, and that was wasteful, but the rich didn't worry about wasting food. Remy knew there were families that survived for a week on less than was sitting on Challoner's kitchen table, but those families were far away.

"Adam," Dar said quietly when they reached the office doorway. Challoner was back in his desk chair, staring out the window into the night. "Any news?"

Challoner shook his head. "They're still working on things. I'm not seeing anything on the government channels, but I wouldn't, not until the arrest was made, and maybe not even then." He turned his attention to Remy, who forced himself to stand still instead of shrinking back to hide behind Dar. He was trained, damn it. Just because his discipline had broken once, just because this house and this man made him do things he should never do, that didn't mean he was worthless. He could at least stand still and wait for his punishment.

Challoner was in front of him somehow, reaching slowly for Remy's face. Gentle fingers asked Remy to lift his eyes. "Look at me, Remy. Please."

Remy obeyed, and Challoner said, "I'm sorry. For pushing you to talk about your parents. That was... unforgivably insensitive. I don't know what I was thinking." Remy let his gaze fall a little, and Challoner didn't object. "And I'm even more sorry that you think you have to apologize for being upset about it. For saying things that...." He trailed off, then started again. "For doing what I asked earlier, when I said I wanted to know the truth. I'm sorry for everything that's been done to you to make you think you need to apologize for telling the truth."

"My mother was a teacher and my father was a weaver," Remy said. "That's the truth. That's what you wanted to hear."

"What you said was true too. It wasn't what I wanted to hear, but it's what I *should* hear. It's what every citizen should hear, so they understand what we're fighting against, and understand why it needs to be stopped."

Challoner's comm buzzed, then, calling his attention, but he didn't take his hand away from Remy's face. "I'm sorry, Remy."

"You might want to add 'storming out of the room' to your list of misbehaviors," Dar said firmly. "That's twice today you've done it. It makes him think you're mad at him." His voice was a little softer when he added, "Makes him think he's in trouble."

Challoner's hand was suddenly gone and he turned his whole body away as he said, "Goddamn—" He froze then, and turned back slowly. He brought his hand back to Remy's face. "Goddamn it," he said more quietly. "I'm sorry. I keep messing up. I leave when I'm angry, but I'm not angry at you." He shook his head. "The only thing you've done today that frustrated me was refusing to go to Europe, and you stood your ground on that like my opinion meant nothing." He flattened his hand so his palm was cupping Remy's jaw. "You're a confusing man, Remy."

"I'm—" Remy started.

"Not sorry," Dar interrupted. "You're not sorry. Remember, Remy, you can just tell him to fuck off."

"I'm not sure we need to go quite that far," Challoner said, but there was laughter in his voice.

"You walk out on him one more time, and I'll be the one saying it," Dar replied. Remy felt like he wasn't really part of the conversation when Dar added, "You started something here, and you seem determined to keep going with it. That's great. But don't pretend it's going to be easy, and don't think it's something you can do just some of the time. You'd have been kinder to have not started at all, if you don't do it right. You know what I mean?"

Challoner didn't answer right away, but then he said, "I'm starting to understand, yeah." He slipped his hand away from Remy's jaw, down over his shoulder, gently down his forearm, then wrapped it around his fingers. "I'll do better," he said, and it really sounded like he was talking to Remy now, like he was making some sort of a promise.

The comm buzzed again, and Challoner nodded to its place on the desk. "Grab it, will you, Dar?" Challoner tugged Remy gently toward the couch, and Remy sat obediently. Challoner sank down beside him. Not too close, but near enough that it was easy to keep their hands in contact.

By the time they were settled, Dar had returned from the desk, reading as he walked. He finished whatever he was looking at, then handed the comm wordlessly to Challoner, who took it in his free hand.

Dar pulled one of the wing chairs closer to the couch and sat down. Challoner set the comm down and said, "So. Okay for now." He turned to Remy. "It looks like the security forces tracked down the spot where we introduced the virus last night. We figured they would. It actually took them longer than expected, so that's good news. So they have the device we planted. The scare was because somebody realized that the device itself might be traceable. They should have thought about that before we set it, but... mistakes happen." He looked like he'd like a little time alone with whomever had made that particular mistake, but then moved on. "And there was a security cordon around the zone where our hackers live. No physical movement, but no nonofficial communications, either. So we couldn't be sure they hadn't been picked up. But it turns out the blockade was for someone else. Our guys are safe."

Remy tried not to think about the others who had been arrested, or what they might have done. Or not done. It was better not to think about these things, and he'd never had much trouble keeping his mind away from such topics until lately.

"We're still no further ahead on the larger plan, though," Dar complained. "I mean, it's great that the guys are safe. But what the hell use are they if we can't find a way to deliver their product?"

"We can use my comm. Headquarters seems to think there's a few others out there we could get access to...."

"That's not *ten*, and they said ten was the absolute minimum. Said twenty would be better." Dar looked at Remy and said, "We need to deliver the virus somehow, need to get it into the system. The one we did last night, we physically broke into a server and set it from there. It worked, but the servers are pretty carefully firewalled from each other, so the virus could only spread through that one sector. We want to go national. We *need* to go national, if we're going after the data as well as the cameras, because there are backups in various places. So for this to work, we'd need to hit the whole system."

"You're trying to delete all their data and shut off all their cameras. That's your big plan? How will that help, really?"

"Because it will free key people," Challoner explained. "We've got people placed in the military, in positions of reasonable influence. Their soldiers would follow them if they could, but they can't take the chance because they're afraid of the government. Not necessarily what would happen to the soldiers, but to their families. If the data's gone, the government wouldn't know where their families are, so they wouldn't be able to take action against them."

"That's just one example," Dar said, "but it's a good one. Imagine the same thing spread over every industry. People shouldn't be afraid of their government, and we're trying to make it so they aren't."

"But won't it just be chaos? There's a lot of hungry, angry people out there. If the fear isn't controlling them, what will? Won't they just go crazy?"

"Good question," Dar said. "Best-case scenario, if we have enough worms planted, we'll have most or all of the data transferred to our Asian base. Not to be bastards with it, but to pull out what we need in order to keep things running smoothly. If we do this right, we could have a bloodless coup. A seamless transition from the old government to the new government." He looked over at Challoner, his eyebrows raised mockingly. "The new leader."

"In a purely transitional capacity," Challoner protested. "Just until we can set up elections. *Real* elections."

Remy's brain froze, then stuttered back into movement. "The new leader?" he said quietly. He could tell the other two were waiting for his reaction, and he knew exactly what it had to be. He gave himself a moment until he could be sure it would be convincing, and then he smiled. "That's a great honor. Congratulations."

"It's not an honor. Being chosen by the people would be an honor, but I don't plan to attempt that. This is just a temporary thing. I just... someone needed to step forward, and it ended up being me. But I'm just a placeholder until a real leader can be found."

"I'm sure that's not true," Remy said. "I'm sure you'll do a wonderful job." He thought about Challoner's naiveté and tried not to wince. Hopefully he'd have people advising him. But none of that was Remy's concern, not right then. All he needed to do was keep this man, this man who might someday be more powerful than any of Remy's clients had ever been, happy. He wondered whether it was too late to go back to the Europe option. But then he remembered what a long shot all this was. He'd joined the movement, insofar as he'd been allowed to join, with the clear expectation of failure. He wasn't fighting because he expected to win; he just wanted his life to end with more purpose than it had been lived. And that hadn't changed. Challoner wasn't going to become the North American leader; he was going to die, probably soon, just like Remy. That thought made it easier for Remy to squeeze Challoner's fingers and say, "It'll be a glorious moment, when you take charge." He smiled again, and when he saw that Challoner wasn't returning the expression, he smiled even harder. It was all he had left to do.

CHALLONER and Dar seemed inclined to keep close to the comm, and while the device was highly mobile, Remy could see the advantages of keeping their conference behind closed doors. It was Challoner's house, but that didn't mean much, not to the wealthy. There were probably a dozen people with keys, servants and tradespeople and hangers-on, and they should definitely not have access to the conversations that Remy had heard thus far. The plumber should not know that he was fixing the toilets of a man who aspired, however modestly, to becoming the leader of a newly free continent.

So they sat, the three of them, in Challoner's wood-and-leather office, and they didn't say much at all. Finally, Dar groaned. He'd clearly been thinking, and clearly didn't like what he was coming up with. "They need to find another way. It's that simple. The comm access was a good plan, but it's not going to work, so they need to figure something else out."

It was apparently Challoner's turn to explain things to Remy. "We need to plant the virus in multiple locations. If it just comes from one, they'll be able to shut that sector down before too much damage is done. But if it comes from multiple locations, fast and furious, we'll be in before they know what hit them." Remy nodded; he'd figured that much out from the earlier conversation. Challoner smiled his approval, and continued. "And the way they thought they could get in is through the comms. The upper class, the people close to the government, we have special access. Our comms are wired into the system at a pretty high level, higher than most of the servers, even. So we thought we could use the comms as a way to plant the virus."

"But you can't get access to enough comms," Remy said. "You can't just... I don't know, break into a high-end restaurant on a Saturday night? Or go to a party? That night you saw me with Hesterman, there must have been fifty or sixty of you guys there, and you all carry your comms around like they're a third arm. You couldn't just find another event like that?"

"That was our original plan," Dar admitted. "But it turns out that most people are pretty damned good about turning the security on their comms way up when they go out in public."

"It's an automatic function," Challoner said. "The comms link to our home systems with light security because the home network itself is secure, but once we go out in public, the comms tighten up. It's a pain, because I can't get access to nearly as many sites when I'm not at home. But now that I'm looking at it from this perspective, I understand why."

"So for the attack to work, you need to have access to ten or twenty high-level comms, inside the person's home." Remy shrugged. "That's hard?" He looked at Challoner. "I get that you don't want to implicate your friends, but you could, couldn't you?" Or maybe it was himself Challoner didn't want to implicate. An anonymous attack would be much safer than one that could be traced back to a small group of people. Remy couldn't blame Challoner for wanting to be careful, but he was strangely disappointed, anyway.

But Challoner shook his head. "I don't have all that many friends, Remy. But even if I did... the attack needs to be carefully timed. Synchronized. I can't go to a friend's, infect their comm, go to someone else's and infect theirs... it has to happen all at once."

"You can't put a timer on the virus? Like, have it sit there until activation time?" Remy was in way over his head, and he had the definite feeling that he was making suggestions that the others had already considered and rejected, but they didn't seem impatient, and the conversation was helping him understand the problem.

"We could," Challoner agreed. "But the system sweeps for infections regularly. More or less constantly. Our guys haven't been able to find a way to have the virus be dormant and *undetectable* for long enough to coordinate an attack." He was getting more agitated now, clearly reliving past hopes and disappointments with the plan.

Dar seemed more resigned about it all. "We thought about leaving transmitters in the homes," he said. "We'd store the virus on the transmitter, not the comm, and when the time came, we'd activate the transmitters, they'd infect the comms, and we'd be in business."

"That sounds good," Remy said. "Why wouldn't that work?"

"Well, first, we don't have all that much access to the homes of the very wealthy. It'd be a bitch of a job to get the transmitters placed." Dar took a moment to reflect on the enormity of the task, made a face, then continued. "But we figured maybe we could do it. There'd be a huge risk of discovery, and it'd be slower than we want, because we'd have to watch and wait for opportunities to plant the transmitters. But we figured it might be worth a try. The second problem killed the idea, though. Because in order for us to be certain that the transmitter would find the comm, wherever in the house it was, we'd have to make the transmitter pretty powerful. The houses are big, and the comms are mobile. Like you said, they go wherever the owner goes. And a transmitter that powerful would trigger the house's security as soon as it went off."

"We tested it out here," Challoner confirmed. "I have pretty sophisticated antisurveillance tools, for obvious reasons, but nothing beyond what's widely used by others at my social level. We couldn't get higher than a four-foot range without triggering the security. Which meant an automatic slamming of the firewalls, no data in or out." He shook his head. "Four feet. Where the hell are we going to put the transmitter that four feet would do us any good?"

Remy knew the question was rhetorical, but he was enjoying the conversation. It was nice to talk about something that was just a logistical problem, not a highly charged emotional mess. "You can't put them on the bedside tables, because...?"

Challoner looked at him blankly. "The bedside tables?"

"Yeah. When you go to bed, you put your comm on the bedside table, right? Most of my clients do. It sits there all night. So you could hide a transmitter somewhere on the bedside tables of a bunch of people, and set them to go off at, I don't know, four in the morning, maybe? Sometime that most people would be asleep. But that wouldn't work, because...." Remy stopped and waited for the next piece of the puzzle to be handed to him. But Challoner wasn't even looking in his direction. Instead, he was frowning at Dar.

"Do you?" Dar asked. "Leave it on the bedside table?"

Challoner nodded. "Yeah. Always. It has an alarm to wake me, plus it goes off if there's an emergency. Tells me what time it is. If I can't sleep, I can do work...."

Dar turned to Remy. "All your rich clients do? They all leave them on their bedside tables?" He was starting to sound excited, and Remy searched his mind for any inaccuracies in what he'd said. He didn't want to start something for no reason.

"Not all of them. Some of them pass out drunk in another room, some of them don't even sleep in the same bed two nights in a row. One of them sleeps in one of those hyperbaric chambers. But he leaves his comm right outside it, so... that's like a nightstand." He wanted to be accurate, and he raced through his regular clients. He looked up to see Dar and Challoner looking at him intently. "I don't have a number. But, yeah, almost all of them. Ninety percent, maybe."

"Son of a bitch," Dar said quietly. Then, more loudly, "Son of a *bitch*!" He sounded triumphant, but Challoner was shaking his head.

"Slow down, now," Challoner said. He stood up and took a few steps, stretched, and stared out the window into the night. Thinking, Remy realized. "Maybe...," he mused. "How long could they stay hidden for? How long before I noticed something on my bed stand? If it was inside the drawer? Maybe attached to the back of it? Or the underside. If it was well hidden, if the cleaning staff didn't do a deep clean...." He turned abruptly. "It's worth suggesting," he said firmly.

"We'll still have an access problem," Dar said slowly. "We can try to get in through household staff, I guess, but that's going to be incredibly risky, approaching that many people." He was clearly trying to avoid reaching the logical conclusion. "Well, maybe we can do it. Headquarters can tell us, I guess. Maybe they've already got a team of housemaids lined up and ready to spring into action."

"But if they don't," Remy said, "you'll need to find some other way in." He took a deep breath and made his face relax. "You'll need to find someone who has access to the bedrooms of a lot of rich people."

Dar's resigned "Yeah," came at the exact same moment as Challoner's indignant, "No!"

Challoner seemed to have enough emotion to override Dar's rationality. "We said you were out, Remy. *I* said it. I said you wouldn't have to go back." He gestured at Remy's body. "They beat you black and blue, for no reason. They're insane, and they're cruel, and I will *not* put you back under their control. And that's before we even get to the clients, the disgusting bastards who treat you like—" He broke off and turned away, but this time he didn't leave the room. He just stared out the window again and softly, pleadingly, said, "No," into the darkness.

"We should check on the 'team of housemaids' thing," Remy said quietly to Dar. "That'd be a good solution."

"Yeah," Dar said, but the look he exchanged with Remy made it crystal clear that they both judged the odds to be about the same: there was no chance of a rescue from the housemaids. "Adam, do you want to contact HQ, or should I?"

"You do it," Challoner said. "I'm busy thinking of other ways to get those transmitters in place."

"Think fast," Dar said under his breath, and he reached for Challoner's comm.

Remy watched as Dar sent the message across the ocean, and he watched as Challoner searched the night for answers. And Remy started the process within himself, started rebuilding the walls that he'd allowed to come too far down. If HQ thought the transmitter idea would work, that meant Remy was going back to Baryman, going back to whoring. He needed to be ready.

CHALLONER spent quite a while on the comm. A couple times, he had voice calls, but they were in some language Remy didn't know. French, he was pretty sure, but that basic identification pretty well exhausted his understanding. He was too restless to stay in the office, so he wandered back to the kitchen and put the food away the best he could. Then he remembered that Carralina couldn't see. He tried to remember how many of her tools he'd moved, and from where, but it was no use. He hadn't really been paying much attention to what he'd been doing.

He hadn't known that he was getting comfortable. He hadn't

realized that he was starting to unwind, beginning to get used to the idea of starting a new life, a life where his body wouldn't be used for the enjoyment of anyone with enough money to rent him.

"They won't know." He said it out loud, and then looked around self-consciously. Challoner didn't have any pets, he realized. No living creature in the kitchen to hear him. He raised his voice. "They won't know." That made it better. He'd be doing the same things he used to do, but with a different, deeper purpose. They'd still think they were using him, but *he'd* actually be using *them*. He could do it.

He returned to the office, stood in the doorway, and watched as Dar and Challoner turned to look at him. Dar looked guilty; Challoner, defiant.

"They like the idea," Dar said. "A lot." He waited for Remy to ask, but he didn't have to.

"But there's no team of housemaids," Remy said with a smile. He walked into the room and kept his voice light. "It's fine. I can do it. I've been doing it for most of my life. A little longer is no big deal."

"No," Challoner said. He sounded like he was ready to fight, but also like he already knew he was going to lose. "I promised you."

"I release you from the promise. I appreciate the thought, but things have changed." Remy crossed over to one of the big wing chairs and sat down; he didn't want to be on the couch, didn't want to take the chance that Challoner would sit beside him. "How long am I here for? Just tonight?"

"That was the original plan," Challoner said. "But, no, Remy...."

"Challoner, don't drag it out. This is what needs to be done, and we all know it." Remy knew his voice sounded brittle and tried to modulate it when he said, "So, what do I need to know? How big are these transmitters? Is there going to be a problem hiding them?"

Dar seemed to be waiting for more from Challoner, but finally he crossed to the big desk and picked up something that looked like a fine wire, about the length of Remy's baby finger, with a black orb, smaller than a pea, on one end. "This big. And they won't be active until the preset time, so security scanners won't pick up on them."

"Okay." It was good to focus on the logistics. "Can that wire be bent?"

"It should be straight when it's in place—that's the antennae that will get our activation signal. But you can wrap it around when it's just being transported."

Remy reached out and took the transmitter from Dar. It was strange to think that something so small could be so powerful. "I could wrap it up and put it in a pill casing," he said. "Nobody's going to question a whore with a pocket full of pills."

The mention of drugs seemed to be the last straw for Challoner. He moved abruptly, jerkily, picking up speed as he headed for the door. He stopped short when Dar growled, "Adam." Challoner turned slowly. "Don't walk away, Adam," Dar said. He held his gaze steady until Challoner turned around a little further and looked at Remy.

He came a few steps closer and crouched down in front of the chair before reaching for both of Remy's hands. "Please don't do this," he said softly.

Remy felt like he'd been kicked in the gut, and he had some fairly recent memories to verify that the sensation was accurate. He could have stood up to yelling, he was pretty sure, but this was something else entirely. "I have to," he said. "It might work. And…." He was going to say that it didn't matter. He thought he'd tell Challoner that it wasn't a big deal, that whoring wasn't that bad and he was fine about going back to it. But he couldn't say it. With Challoner looking at him like that, he couldn't lie. So he said, "I can do it. I can get through it."

Challoner raised his hand and brushed the back of his fingers against Remy's cheek. "I want to protect you. I want you to be safe."

"Too late," Remy said with what he hoped was a brave smile. He had the feeling it probably looked pretty gruesome, and he let his face relax. "You woke me up; I can't go back to sleep now. I tried, with the pills, but... it didn't work. And the thing is, Challoner... I don't *want* it to work. I want to be awake. Alive."

Remy had never been kissed by anyone that he cared about, and when Challoner brought their lips together, he could feel the difference. Not in his lips, but in his gut. Challoner pulled away after a too short moment, and Remy wanted to lean after him. They stayed there, frozen, and finally Challoner sighed. "Sometimes I wish I'd kicked you out of that damned hotel room."

"Sometimes I wish the same thing."

Challoner nodded slowly. "Yeah."

"But you didn't. So here we are. And we've got a job to do." He tried to shake the heavy emotions off, turned to Dar and asked, "Are the rest of the transmitters here?" He looked at Challoner to ask, "And do you have any big pills we could steal the casings from?"

"The transmitters are on the way," Dar said. He seemed relieved to be back to talking about business. "I can make an order for pills, as well. Is there a specific kind that would be good? Something that wouldn't catch anyone's attention?"

Remy thought back to Sasha's pill cases. "There's something that's big, and dark purple. Almost opaque. I don't know what those are, but I know that some of the whores use them. I've seen them around. People wouldn't ask questions if they saw me with them, and that transmitter would fit in them, for sure."

"Big, dark purple, used by whores. Okay, I'll see what I can come up with." Dar looked regretfully in Adam's direction before adding, "And can you give us an idea of the timeline? Like... if you were going to plant thirty transmitters...." Another uncomfortable look toward Adam before Dar said, "How long do you think it will take for you to get into that many bedrooms?"

Yeah, this wasn't anything Challoner wanted to hear, but Remy could see why Dar wanted to know. "It's hard to be sure. I don't set my own schedule, or choose my own clients. And not all of them want me in their homes. I'd say... I don't know, no more than one or two a day."

Challoner wouldn't even look in his direction, but Dar nodded. "Okay. We can work with that estimate." He took Challoner's comm over to the desk and started working.

It was a bit awkward, being left there with Challoner, but Remy tried to get past it. He had no confidence in the plan, really, and even if he managed to get the transmitters planted, there was no reason to believe he'd make it out alive once the virus was activated. So this might be one of his last times to see Challoner. He remembered the suicide pill idea, and decided to ask Dar about it when they had a little more privacy. There was no point looking for trouble; Challoner already looked about as miserable as a man could look.

"You woke me up," Remy said quietly. The words from earlier were still bouncing in his brain, and he was pretty sure they made sense. "Being asleep was easier. But it was no way to live, not really. I... yeah, sometimes I wish you'd kicked me out of the hotel room. But mostly, I'm glad you didn't. Really glad."

Challoner managed a smile. "I'm mostly glad too. But I'll be a hell of a lot happier about it all when you're out of this mess and back here where you're safe."

"Yeah, that'll be nice," Remy agreed. "I'll be happier then too." Challoner lived in a fantasy world, but from what Remy had seen of his life on the farm, reality wasn't too far away from a fairy tale, not out there. So if Challoner wanted to imagine a happily ever after, Remy wasn't going to stop him. But this time Remy was going to be more careful. This time, he wasn't going to let himself believe in Challoner's dream.

CHAPTER FIFTEEN

"You should go to bed," Challoner said. "You're tired."

He was right. The pills and transmitters had arrived and been combined, Dar had gone down to sleep in the cottage, and Remy had stayed awake, sitting in the big wing chair and watching Challoner work at his desk. "You should come with me," he said.

Challoner's smile seemed rusty. "That's all I'm getting? Used to be, you'd put a little *effort* into the seduction, Remy."

"I didn't mean you should sleep with me. I just meant you should go to bed. You're tired too."

Challoner nodded slowly. "Yeah. I am." He looked at the desk he was sitting behind, then back at Remy. "I feel like I should be doing something. Doing more. I'm sending you back into that hell, so I should be doing... I don't know. Something."

"Have you actually got anything *to* do?"

"Little stuff. Nothing important. Nothing interesting enough to let me forget that you've got another nine hours here, and then you're gone."

Remy pretended that he hadn't noticed the silent *gone for good* in Challoner's words. It was reassuring, actually, to learn that Challoner wasn't quite as naïve as he seemed. He knew Remy wasn't likely to come back from this, even if he'd decided not to admit it out loud. "So maybe you *should* come with me. Nine hours. That's it. How do you want to spend that time?"

Challoner stood up slowly and walked across the room toward Remy. He stood in front of him and Remy rose to meet him. Challoner took both of Remy's hands in his. "I don't know which is harder," Challoner said. "Letting you go back there, or keeping myself from taking advantage of you before you do."

"'Taking advantage' of me? Are you serious, Challoner?" Remy wasn't sure whether to be amused or disgusted. "Do you know how many men I've had sex with? 'Cause I don't. But it's a big, big number. There's no 'advantage' to be taken. It's long since gone."

"Just because other people have done it doesn't mean that it'd be right for me to do it." The man sounded dead serious.

Remy let himself snort, just a little. "Yeah, okay." There really wasn't anything new to say, or anything more to add, and Remy knew he should leave it. Besides, he'd found a way to contribute now, a way to use his one skill that *didn't* involve getting Challoner out of his tastefully expensive clothes. "That'll keep me nice and fresh for the other clients, I guess. I wonder who'll be the first one, when I'm back? It's been a while... but I'm sure I haven't gotten *too* out of practice. Maybe it'll be Hesterman, if he hasn't come back to his senses yet. We can do the whole 'I love you so much, sweetheart' thing. And maybe he'll take the 'public fucking' kink a little further. That could actually be a bit awkward, if the goal of all this is to get into his bedroom. But I could manage it, probably. First round in public, but he's usually up for at least two...."

"What are you doing, Remy?" Challoner's voice was tight.

It wasn't like Remy had an actual *plan.* "Just talking. Making conversation. Not much else to do, really, since we've done all we can with the transmitters and you don't want to do anything fun."

"For fuck's sake! You still think I don't *want* to? You think I haven't spent the last few weeks imagining you spread out over every surface in this goddamned house, thinking of how good it would feel to just pin you to a mattress and keep you there for days?" He shook his head and his voice lost some of its anger. "I can barely *think* when you're around. And then you go away, and I can't think then, either, because all I want is to get you back." He stood up and walked to where Remy was sitting. "Jesus, Remy. I gave it serious consideration, when I first thought about buying your contract. I mean, the first idea was just trying to get you out of a bad situation. But then I thought about just doing it for real. Everyone else seems to be fine with the idea, and you don't seem to see anything wrong with it. I could buy you, and keep you like a slave, and fuck you 'til you couldn't walk the next day whether you wanted me to or not, and that would be fine with you and fine with everybody else too. Maybe I'm the crazy one, thinking there's something wrong with that."

He crouched and found Remy's hands again, that newly familiar, firm grip that he seemed to think conveyed some deeper meaning. "You know what made me realize what a sick idea that was? It was the date on the contract." He shook his head and tightened his grip. "You signed it when you were nine years old. Your signature... it was little-kid writing. And now I know that it wasn't even your real name. You were just writing a couple words they told you to write. You were a child, and you didn't know what it meant, and if this society thinks that it's okay to enforce contracts like that, then obviously I can't trust the judgment of this society about what's morally okay. And the thing is, Remy...." He paused, and Remy could tell that he was building up to say something Remy wasn't going to like. "The thing is, if *you* think it's okay to enforce that contract, if *you* think that you're not being treated wrongly, then I feel like I can't really trust your judgment about what's morally okay, either. Not in this case. Not... I know it sounds ridiculous, but not about yourself. I know you feel for other people, but when you talk about fighting back, about being part of this thing, it's always about them. It's never about *you*."

"Other people have it worse than me," Remy said quietly.

"Maybe they do. But that doesn't mean you don't have it pretty damn bad."

Challoner had his usual sincere expression on, and Remy really didn't want to look at his face anymore. He stood abruptly, making Challoner rock back on his heels to get out of the way. "So I'm the poor, stupid whore who doesn't even have the brains to know what he wants. I get it. Yeah, I wouldn't want to sleep with someone that stupid, either."

"Oh, give me a break, Remy! Did you hear the first part of what I said? The part where I told you just how much I want you?" Challoner straightened and looked Remy in the eye, and there was a strength in his gaze that Remy wasn't used to seeing. "You say I see you as a stupid whore? I don't, at all. But I think *you* see *me* as a stupid, naïve rich guy who's never seen anything ugly and never had to make a hard decision. You think I'm floating on some innocent cloud of 'let's all be nice to each other,' and I promise you, that's not where I am. This isn't some fuzzy theory I'm playing with, this is the fucking core of my beliefs. People shouldn't be bought and sold—if someone *chooses* to be a prostitute, that's one thing, but you never chose, Remy, and you know that. Children should be cherished, not abused. And people who take advantage of a system that allows those things? Those people are complicit in the abuse, and I will *not* be one of those people, no matter how tempted I might be."

"And no matter what *I* want."

"What you want?" Challoner looked at Remy closely. "Do you actually want me? Because I know what it feels like, what it looks like, when somebody wants to have sex with me. All the little sneaked looks, the way they want to touch me all the time, the way their breathing changes when I get close. And I'm not getting *any* of that from you, Remy. All I'm getting from you is... professionalism. I think you want to do your job, and yeah, maybe you want to make me happy. But can you look me in the eyes and say that I turn you on?"

"You're very handsome. You're fit. You... you seem to have excellent technique, from what I've been allowed to experience. Why wouldn't I want you?"

"Remy, look at me." Challoner waited, and smiled ruefully

when Remy finally complied. "Do you have any reason to believe that if we had sex, you'd actually enjoy it? I mean, beyond simple physical responses."

"'Beyond simple physical responses'? I don't know what that means."

"Like, friction would make you hard, and enough of it would make you come. That sort of thing. Beyond that, would you enjoy it?"

Remy was at a total loss. "Enjoy *what*, beyond that? Like... well, yeah. I'd enjoy making *you* feel good, making *you* come. Is that what you mean?"

"No, not about me. Or... okay, yeah, maybe a bit about me, because that's the idea, right, that you want to do this with one person, not just with any anonymous client. So, what part of me would you really like to touch?"

"What part of you?" Remy was bewildered, and starting to feel as if this was another test he was destined to fail. He knew there wouldn't be a punishment, not of the usual sort, but he still felt his stomach churning with anxiety. "All of you! Your cock. Wherever you want. But, yeah, your cock, or your ass, or... wherever you want. All of you." Surely one of those answers was close to whatever the hell Challoner was looking for.

But Challoner seemed sad. Not disappointed, like he'd been hoping from something better, just sad, like Remy had confirmed his suspicions. "I want to touch your neck," he said softly. "Right there, that little hollow that fills out when you take a deep breath. With just my fingertips, at first, but then my whole hand, and then with my lips, and my tongue. I want to mark you there, suck a deep purple bruise that tells everyone...." He broke off, then looked bitterly at Remy. "Tells everyone that I own you," he finished. "Damn it. That's what I want. Is it really that different from what everyone else wants?"

And now that Challoner needed him to, finally, Remy thought maybe he understood. "You don't want to own me with money.

You want to own me with... I don't know. Something else. And the money gets in the way, because you can never be sure whether it's the money or the something else that's making me yours." He thought about sharing that insight with Baryman; he bet he'd get a gold star for it.

"Love," Challoner said softly. "Or at least lust. I want to own you because you can't help yourself. And, Remy, the thing is, *you'd* own *me* too." He shook his head. "You already do, damn it."

"So I own you, but I can't do anything with you?" Remy tried to lighten the mood with a quick smile. "That doesn't do me much good."

"You can do anything you want with me." Challoner lifted his arms out to the sides as if surrendering, then lowered them. "All you have to do is convince me that you actually *want* it. That *you* want it, not that you're guessing what *I* want."

Challoner looked so open, so vulnerable, and Remy just wanted to protect him. And maybe the thing he needed to be protected from was Remy. "I take pills," he blurted out. "Not just to get high. To get hard. To come." Remy refused to look Challoner in the eyes. It was all matter-of-fact, in Remy's world, but he knew it was taboo to discuss it with a client. It was just one of the many things that the clients didn't want to know. But Challoner wasn't stopping Remy from continuing. "It's all drugs." He shrugged in an attempt to look nonchalant, but he knew there was no real point to the charade. "I don't... the way you want me to want you, I don't feel like that. I don't do that. At all. I'm sorry. I wish I did; for you, I'd like to. But I don't."

Challoner was silent for a moment, and then he stepped a little closer. The arms that he wrapped around Remy weren't demanding anything, just offering comfort. And Remy felt something tighten and then loosen in his chest as he allowed himself to take what was offered.

REMY went to bed alone that night, and for the first time, he wondered what it would be like to share the mattress with someone he cared about. Not for sex. Just for someone he'd be happy to see last thing before closing his eyes and first thing when he opened them again. Maybe someone who'd throw an arm around Remy if the room got too cold, not that the rooms in these houses weren't always climate-controlled within half a degree of perfection. So maybe the arm wouldn't be about warmth, really. Maybe it would just be someone who'd sleep better knowing that Remy was near.

But there he was, again, thinking about the other person instead of himself. Challoner was right. What would *Remy* like? Would Remy sleep better with someone he cared about beside him? And, while he was making himself be honest about that part of the question, maybe he'd better be honest about the whole thing. Would he sleep better with *Challoner* beside him?

Challoner's broad, strong chest, nestled up against Remy's back? That would be nice. Some of his clients were actually okay to sleep next to, except for the part where they'd wake up horny or cranky. If there were no concerns about that sort of thing, just warmth and friendliness. If the person next to him made him feel more safe, instead of less. If the person was Challoner.

Yeah, Remy decided, he'd like to sleep next to Challoner. He thought about getting up and going to find him. Not to invite him to bed. Not necessarily. Just to let him know, as a matter of interest, and if he happened to suggest that maybe he could come up and be Remy's backrest, well, Remy wouldn't object. Remy smiled into his pillow. But it wasn't fair. Challoner was a healthy man, with healthy desires, and he didn't want to snuggle a useless whore to sleep. It wouldn't be fair to ask him to do something like that for Remy. And Remy didn't need him to; he'd sleep just fine on his own.

And eventually he did. He woke up the next morning with the sun, got dressed, and found his way downstairs. Challoner, Dar, and Carralina were already there, gathered around the kitchen table. One look at their faces and he was tempted to ask them who'd died, but he managed to refrain. For all he knew, somebody actually had.

When she heard him in the doorway, Carralina started to stand, but Remy spoke quickly. "I'm fine. I don't need anything. Thanks."

"No breakfast?" Challoner asked.

"I'm good, thanks." He was going to claim that he was still full from dinner, but he remembered how that meal had ended partway through, and decided he needed a better story. "My stomach isn't awake yet." And he'd eaten too much the previous day, too much for someone who was returning to Baryman's exacting standards of body size.

Dar raised an eyebrow as if questioning Remy's story, but the others seemed to accept it. If it had been a big deal, he could have eaten something, but he figured it was a good idea to get back into his regular habits as soon as possible. Which meant he bit his tongue when he wanted to ask about the shuttle's arrival time; that was none of his business, and his client would take care of those sorts of details. Remy was there to serve his client's needs, and that was all.

Right then, it looked like Challoner's need was a serious pep talk. "It's beautiful out there," Remy said with a nod to the large windows. "Looks like spring."

"A few months early," Challoner responded glumly. "There's still plenty of winter to come."

Well, that was true, but not very useful. "Do you have a site in mind for your greenhouse? I've seen some that are attached to the house, so it can be a solarium as well." Surely the man would cheer up if he was talking about his precious farm.

"That sounds lovely," Carralina said. "You're always saying that it doesn't make sense to heat this whole house for just one person to live in… maybe you could take some of that heat and use it for the greenhouse, instead. And it would be nice if I could just walk out and pick a few herbs or leaves of lettuce instead of bundling up for a trip outdoors."

Challoner nodded. "We could look at that," he said. He managed to ask a few questions and share a few ideas, and in general seemed more interested in the conversation, so Remy considered it a victory. Not a huge one, but something.

When an alarm sounded from Challoner's comm and he looked guiltily at Remy, the message was clear. "Time to go?" Remy asked.

"You don't have to," Challoner said. "We can figure something else out. I don't know what... I was up all night, trying to figure something out... but there's another way. There has to be."

"But not a *better* way," Remy said. "Don't worry. It's fine. I can do it. It'll be easier, really, knowing that I have a purpose."

"It'll be death by torture if they catch you with the transmitters." Dar's voice was serious.

Remy could see Challoner tense. He was obviously having to fight to keep himself in the room, and it would have been funny if it wasn't so serious.

Dar gave Challoner a cautious look before continuing. "You asked about that before. About something you could take. You know... if things go wrong." He pulled a small package out of his jacket pocket. "This is your pills—the ones with the transmitters inside. You remember how to install them?" At Remy's nod, Dar added, "And there's two little green capsules in there, as well. They're glass, and they wedge in behind your molar. The guy I got them from...." Dar looked over at his mother, then turned awkwardly back to Remy. "He said you probably already know how to use them, with your line of work. He said you pull it out with your tongue, crush it with your teeth, and inhale. He said the inhalation is the key part."

Remy wanted to make a joke about not getting the capsules confused, not turning "*la petite mort*" into the *big* death, but he didn't think Challoner would appreciate it. "Yeah, okay," he said instead. "Crush, inhale. I guess I don't have to worry about swallowing glass, under the circumstances."

"It's instant," Dar said. "You won't have to worry about anything at all, if it comes to that. Keep a pill on you at all times, and keep it in your mouth anytime you see security guards or think a raid is likely. Hold off as long as you can, though, because there's no antidote. Once you inhale, you're done."

"And take this," Challoner said, reaching into his pocket and then pulling out a rough, deeply carved pendant. It was small, about the size of Remy's thumbnail, but it looked heavy. "It's a transmitter, but it's dormant. It won't set off any security scanners until you activate it." He showed Remy how to squeeze the ends together and twist the top off. "This button, here. If you think things are going wrong, if you need out in a hurry, you activate that transmitter and we'll do whatever it takes to get to you. It might take some time, but we'll get there. I promise."

Remy could feel Dar's disapproval even without looking over, and he understood it. It didn't make sense for Challoner to risk the whole operation for one person, one worthless whore. If Remy pushed the button, and Challoner did what he'd promised to do, the rebels would be launching a full-scale attack with little chance of success. Challoner was a fool. Remy caught Dar's eye and smiled gently, letting his friend know that he understood. He put the pendant in his pocket, and pushed it down deep. He couldn't use it, not for its intended purpose, but he would keep it as a way to remember this time, this place. He could use it to remind himself that there was one man who cared enough to do irrational things in Remy's name, but who also respected Remy enough to let him make his own decisions.

A low tone signaled the arrival of the shuttle, and Remy stood abruptly. "Thank you," he said. "For trying to get me out, and for letting me go back." He picked up the envelope from the table, peered inside at the little purple balls, and smiled. "I can do this. It'll work."

"And you can get out afterwards," Challoner said firmly. Apparently whatever bright flash of realism he'd experienced the night before had faded. "You can make it back here, and you'll be safe. You'll be done with that life, forever."

"Okay," Remy said easily. "That's the goal." He figured he'd be done with that life one way or the other. "I should go, now. They get pissy if I keep them waiting."

He let himself take a long look at the three of them, standing around the table. Carralina, an unexpected connection to a past he thought he'd left behind; Dar, a friend, and someone who saw the world the same way Remy did; and Challoner, standing a little apart from the other two, his face showing all the conflict between his ideals and the demands of the real world.

Remy stepped forward impulsively, bent his head just a little, and found the soft skin at the base of Challoner's neck. The place Challoner had said he wanted to touch Remy. A quick kiss, and then a grin. "Huh. Not bad. Not quite sure what all the fuss was about, but...."

Then Challoner's hand was on Remy's neck, tilting his head, changing the angle, setting up for a kiss that Remy knew would be bruising and intense. But Challoner froze. He took a deep breath as if trying to regain his composure, then leaned forward and gently pressed his lips to Remy's forehead. "Come back," he murmured, "and I'll find a way to make you understand."

Remy stepped backward. Coming back wasn't likely, and he now realized that Challoner, beneath the bravado, was aware of that. "I'll try," Remy said. "I'll really, really try." It was the best he could do, and there was no point in pretending otherwise. He turned and walked briskly out of the room. Down the hall, up the stairs, out to the waiting shuttle, and then he sank into his seat and tried to turn his brain off. He had a job to do, and he would do it. The rest was out of his control.

CHAPTER SIXTEEN

REMY had carefully coached Challoner on how to handle Baryman's people. Challoner wasn't sure about buying Remy anymore, but he didn't want Remy seeing any other clients. He wasn't sure he was going to buy the contract, but while he was waiting, he insisted that Remy be kept off the market. Remy had told him to be as arrogant as possible, to make it clear that if Baryman were a gentleman, he'd understand, but since he wasn't, Challoner would have to explain it to him.

The reverse psychology worked like a charm, and Remy was swamped with clients as soon as he was back in the house. Most of the jobs included at least a brief public appearance, all the better to taunt Challoner, but they all ended up in one bedroom or another, eventually. Well, except for the French diplomat with a passion for outdoor sex. He wouldn't have high-level comm access anyway, since he was a foreigner, so Remy's snow-chapped ass was just one of the costs of doing business.

To his surprise, he was almost enjoying himself. The sex was an annoyance, of course, and he had the usual complement of clients who got off on his pain or humiliation. But his secret gave him strength. With every cruelty inflicted, his resolve deepened; with every transmitter planted, his sense of triumph grew.

He had to be careful about placing the damn things, of course. Some of the bedrooms had cameras, others didn't, and he could never be sure. The cameras that monitored the poor had blinking red lights to call attention to their presence, to remind the people that they were always being watched. The rich, though, were the ones in control of the cameras. They might have their bedrooms monitored for security, or so they could go back and watch the footage themselves, but the cameras weren't there for behavior modification, not in the homes of the wealthy. So these cameras were subtle, hidden, with no lights, no way for Remy to know if they even existed. He just had to assume that they did, and he disguised his activities behind casual stretches or lust-inspired graspings. He'd been sneaking pills for years, and he was more than capable of sneaking transmitters, as well.

In six days, he'd planted nine. It wasn't enough, of course; Dar had given him thirty of the things and suggested that it would be good if they could all find homes. But it was hard to get into more than one bedroom a day. He'd had several calls to hotels, but Dar had said not to bother there; the comms would be on high-level security and the virus wouldn't be able to get through.

When the shuttle dropped him on the roof of Baryman's hotel for his first job of the day, Remy tried not to get discouraged. Nine wires planted. That was good. It was a start. This job wasn't going to do him any good, but maybe the next one would, and he'd just have to focus on that. So he found his way downstairs to the assigned room, on the elite floor, and knocked politely before activating the comm. "David Stone, from the Baryman Agency," he said quietly, and the door buzzed to unlock.

"Come on in," a male voice said. The client sounded young, which wasn't really good news. Old clients wanted whores because they couldn't manage to capture the interest of young conquests on their own; young men often wanted whores because their tastes were too extreme to be accommodated by an unpaid partner. But Remy had no choice, so he smiled as he walked down the short hallway to the main room.

The man was good-looking, which made Remy's concerns all the more real, but he looked friendly enough as he stood up and crossed the floor. "David Stone?" he said, echoing Remy's words.

"That's your name?"

Remy nodded. "Unless you'd prefer that it was something else."

"No, David's fine." He smiled, then said, "David, I've got something a bit unusual I'd like you to do today."

So there it was, Remy's suspicions confirmed. "Unusual?" He used his flirtatious smile. "I'm intrigued. What do you have in mind?"

"Let's go in the other room," the man said. He hadn't offered his name, and Remy knew better than to ask. So they went into the bedroom, and the man said, "Sit over there, on the bed. Your back against the headboard, please."

Remy did as he was told, and tried to arrange himself in a somewhat artful pose, although he wasn't really taking as much pride in his seduction techniques as he had in the past.

"Perfect," the man said. "Now, what I'd like you to do is read to me. But I want you to do a good job. I want you to read it like it's your own words, your own thoughts. Do you understand?"

"Sure. I can do that." He tried to sound more confident than he felt. He'd thought there was nothing new under the sun, but he'd never been asked to do this before, and it was throwing him off.

"I want you to read the words over, carefully, before you start. I want you to really think it through. I'm going to give you my comm, and you can make notes, underline places you want to emphasize, whatever you think will help. You understand?"

"I don't... I'll do my best, but I'm not really sure I'll be able to emphasize the right parts. Do you want to highlight things for me, or something?"

"No. That's part of it. Seeing what you think is important." There was a strange pause before the man said, "That's my *thing*."

It wasn't an unusual phrase, but there was something about the way the man said it, the way he looked at Remy and then nodded down at the comm, that made Remy's pulse quicken. He stretched his hand out to receive the device, braced it so it was tilted toward his chest, and activated the screen.

At first, he just saw the poem. "I Sing the Body Electric" the title said, and Remy wondered whether he was supposed to read that part out loud, or just the verses. He tried to remember any time he'd heard a poem read; was there a special way to do it? Then he saw the different font, partway down the page.

> *R—*
>
> *I couldn't get an appointment with you. You can trust the person who's carrying this. He's a friend. I'm on my comm now, waiting for your reply.*
>
> *Things have gone wrong. We can't wait—we need to act.*
>
> *We've taken measures, and we think we can hold off until late night tonight, but we can't wait any longer than that to activate our plan.*
>
> *How many seeds have you sown?*

It was a bit ridiculous, to bother writing in obscure language. If the security forces got hold of this communication, they'd torture Remy or his mysterious client until they got any information they needed. But it was comforting, somehow, to pretend that there was a safety plan being used. Remy glanced at the client, then keyed in the number 9.

There was a pause, then:

> *Not enough. It won't work. We're*

> *going to get you out of there, and*
> *we'll take a trip together.*

Remy looked at the client again, then back at the comm. He didn't want to give up. All the satisfaction he'd been taking in his work, all the self-respect he'd gained by doing something that was actually useful, and, of course, the hope for a better tomorrow... he couldn't let go of all that. His fingers hovered indecisively over the screen, and then he started to type.

> *No. Not yet. Can you get the cameras*
> *turned off again, like you did last*
> *time?*

Remy could almost hear Challoner's frustrated voice with the words:

> *What? Why? How will that help?*

Remy smiled.

> *I'm not the only whore in the house.*
> *I've been working alone because it's*
> *risky to recruit, but I have friends.*

He did, he realized. The group who met in Sasha's room, the jaded, bitter whores who knew they were on the way out and didn't seem to care: they had nothing to lose. They were almost all serious drug users, and that was a vulnerability, but Remy thought about the lazy disgust in their voices, and he believed they could hold themselves together for at least a day, if they had the right motivation.

Too dangerous, came Challoner's reply.

Too dangerous not to, Remy typed. *I can do it. They can do it. Give us an hour without cameras, and I'll get it set up. Late afternoon would be best.*

There was no immediate reply, and Remy took the opportunity to look up at the client. "It's a beautiful poem," he said. He hoped that it was; he hadn't gotten around to reading it.

"Powerful," the man agreed. "I look forward to seeing your performance."

Remy looked back at the screen and saw Challoner's reply.

> *We can have the cameras off for an hour, starting at five o'clock this afternoon. But I don't like this. I think you should come home.*

Remy couldn't think about that, couldn't let himself savor the word choice.

> *I will, when the job's done. Five o'clock this afternoon. I'll be ready.*

He hit the delete button and quickly closed the conversation window. He didn't want to see any more arguments from Challoner, didn't want to take the chance of having his resolve weakened. He smiled at the client and said, "Okay. I can give it a try."

The client nodded. "Thank you," he said. "I'm looking forward to it."

CHAPTER SEVENTEEN

ON THE way back to the house, Remy wondered whether the man would have taken advantage of Remy's services if he hadn't been Challoner's friend. Maybe Remy wasn't to his taste, of course. This wasn't like the old days, when everyone was expected to choose one sex to be attracted to, and told to live their lives in accordance with that choice. But people still had preferences. Maybe Challoner's friend didn't care for men, or just didn't care for Remy. Or maybe he was another decent human being, another person who wanted his partners to be willing, even enthusiastic.

It was a strange idea, but Remy liked it. He decided that he would believe that about the man until he learned something that would force him to change his mind.

He got back to the house and tried to look bored and cranky as he went to his room and fumbled around with his envelope of pills. Twenty-one still in the envelope, along with the extra suicide capsule, the one that he wasn't carrying with him everywhere he went. He thought about that, and then pulled the lone pill out and stuffed it under his mattress. He felt bad, depriving someone of the escape he planned to take himself, but there was only one extra, and he couldn't think of a way to share it out between the others. He could surrender his own, he supposed, but that wouldn't work. He wasn't planning on taking the pill because he was a coward, he was going to take it to protect Challoner and Dar. He needed to stay silent, so he needed the pill.

He made his way to Sasha's room, knocked on the slightly ajar door, and eased inside. The usual crowd was there, taking a break between their daytime appointments and their evening rush. Remy had chosen five o'clock as the time when the highest number of whores would be around, and he'd chosen well. He sauntered over to his usual spot on the floor, leaned back against the edge of the couch, and counted. Seven other whores, plus Sasha. That was good. If Sasha could arrange the schedule right, making sure that each of the seven, plus Remy, had residential jobs that night, that would be eight more transmitters planted. Maybe more, if Sasha could work some double shifts into the schedule.

Of course, things could go wrong. One of the whores could report the whole scheme, or just get caught. Challoner was right, this *was* dangerous. But maybe not risky, Remy decided, because there really wasn't anything to lose, nothing to risk. The people who'd invented the virus had said that they needed at least ten active transmitters for this to work, and Remy couldn't get that number on his own, not if he assumed that at least some of the ones he'd planted wouldn't be effective. And he wasn't ready to admit defeat, wasn't ready to run away and hide, knowing that he was still just as useless as he'd always been. So, really, he had no choice but to continue and he could just ignore the odds. That made things a lot easier.

So he leaned back against the couch, his eyes half closed, and watched the light on the camera. Michelle was sitting behind him, and she absentmindedly ran her fingers through his hair. He wondered what her real name was, and how she'd come to this life, but he doubted he'd ever find out.

As the time passed, it got harder and harder to stay relaxed. The light was still on, and he took a casual glance at the clock on Sasha's comm. Ten past five. What did that mean? Had Challoner been caught, or was he just hiding, unable to do whatever needed to be done? If he *was* caught, how long would it be before he gave Remy up? He'd fight, Remy knew that. And maybe he'd even be able to get his pill crushed and inhaled.

Remy was surprised by how much that bothered him, thinking about Challoner being dead. An end to the dreams, to the courageous fight against the darkness. An end to the one flicker of hope Remy could remember ever feeling.

He shut his eyes tight and tried to ignore the feelings. He would maintain his composure, and his faith. He'd asked Challoner to engage in a significant act of espionage, with very little preparation time. It was absurd to think that it would happen on a precise schedule. It was probably absurd to think that it would happen at all. He tried to think of a way to still make things work, if he didn't have time to talk to the other whores in private. He couldn't just slip them the transmitters without instructions. He couldn't do it all himself. Could he convey the information, somehow, in a way that the cameras and microphones wouldn't pick up on? There weren't humans monitoring all the surveillance tools; most were being monitored by computers, programmed to be sensitive to certain body language, word choices, and vocal tones. Could Remy make himself explain something this important without betraying himself to the computers?

He'd been keeping his attention, as casually as he could, on the camera, but it still took him a moment to realize that the blinking light had gone off and not come back on. Challoner had done it.

He sat up straight and took a deep breath. "Lance, can you shut the door?" he asked as calmly as he could. Lance gave him a look, then leaned back and pushed the door shut. He followed Remy's gaze to the corner where the far wall met the ceiling, then looked back at Remy with wide eyes.

"The camera's off," Remy said quietly. "I arranged that. I need to talk to you all. But, here's the thing." He scooted around so that his back was to the wall. He wanted to be able to make eye contact with everyone. "I'm about to ask you to do something completely illegal. Something that will get you killed, for sure, if you're caught. And it's something that doesn't really have a huge chance of success, and that *does* have a huge chance of you getting caught." He didn't want to scare them off, but he felt like he owed them the honest truth. "And the only reason I'm asking you to do it is because if it works... it'll change everything. It could be glorious."

No one said anything, so Remy took a deep breath and continued. "The thing is... once I tell you, you're in. I mean, I can't make you do it, but if I tell you about it and you don't report it, they'll kill you anyway. So what I'd like to do... what I'd like to ask you to do... I'd like you to go report me now, if you're not willing to go along. As soon as one person stands up, you should all stand up, and you should go together and report me. That way, I'll be the only one who takes a fall. If this goes any further, and if only one of you reports it... you'll be condemning everyone else in the room."

That was as clear as he could make it, and he looked back up at the camera nervously. He ran his tongue over the capsule lodged behind his molar, and he waited. No one moved. He said, "So, go now. If you won't take the chance, if you don't want to be part of it. If you stay, you're in. You understand?"

He left it for another moment. A few of the whores exchanged looks with each other, but mostly they kept their eyes on him. It was little Elina, who'd helped him with Rheanne at the hotel a lifetime ago, who finally spoke. "We're all still here, Remy. Whatever it is... we're in."

He realized that he hadn't really expected it to get this far. He hadn't really thought that any of them would report him, but he somehow hadn't expected them to go along, either.

"Oh," he said. "Okay."

"Do you have a plan, baby?" Michelle asked. Her voice was gentle but impatient, and Remy realized that he'd underestimated the level of desperation in the room. He'd been so caught up in his own misery that he hadn't recognized it in all of the others.

"Yes," he said. "It's... well, it's dangerous, but you already know that." And they didn't look too concerned. "The idea is to disrupt the network. The entire system." He nodded his chin toward the camera. "Those, for sure, but everything else that they use to control us, as well. Did you know that they insist on soldiers and police giving the home addresses of their families? And if you don't have a family, you don't get a gun. They won't give you any kind of power, if they don't have enough information on you to threaten you into doing whatever they want."

"My brother," Alex agreed, nodding his handsome but graying head. "I wasn't enough, either. He's in the army, but he's just a cook, because we don't have parents or any other siblings to threaten."

"Not bad to be a cook," Michelle said. "Less chance of getting shot."

"Half the pay," Alex said glumly. "He can't save a single cent, so there's no way he'll ever be able to retire. He barely makes enough to pay the room and board they charge him." He grinned. "He can mooch a lot of food, though, while he's working. That's something."

"So maybe not him, but all the guys with guns... if they knew that the government records had been destroyed, if the bastards didn't know where the soldiers' families were... they'd be less likely to obey commands they didn't like, right? More likely to follow an officer who was ordering them to help people instead of hurt them?"

"*Is* there an officer like that?" Sasha asked.

"Apparently so. I don't know names or anything. That wouldn't be safe. But someone I trust says there is. That's all I'm going on."

"That's enough for me," Elina said. She was tiny, but her expression was fiercely determined. She was ready for the fight.

"Okay," Remy said, trying to gather his thoughts. He pulled the envelope out of his back pocket. "Each of these capsules has a tiny transmitter in it. You open the capsule, pull out the little ball and straighten the wire, and it's ready to go. We need the transmitters to be within a few feet of a high-level client's comm, in their home, at about four o'clock tomorrow morning. Like, ten and a half hours from now. We're thinking we should be able to plant them on the bedside tables, where the clients leave their comms while they sleep."

"I have an overnighter tonight, right, Sasha?" Amanda asked. "I can plant the damn transmitter in my ass, and just wiggle it over next to the comm when I feel like it."

"Wouldn't be the only thing you've got stored up there, would it, sweetie?" But Alex's traditional snark seemed almost affectionate. The whores were ready for this, ready to *do* something, and it was pulling them together.

"You can figure out the details on your own," Remy said quickly. "The key thing is to have the transmitters next to the comms, *inside* a client's home. The signal will be sent, the virus will be transmitted, and if we have enough entry points, it'll be all over the country before they catch it and shut it down."

"And then what?" Michelle asked quietly.

Remy frowned. "Uh... well, the people I'm working with, they have plans in place. The army, and an interim president, just until things settle down... they rebuild, I guess, without all the corruption. They redistribute the wealth, make things more fair."

"I meant for us," Michelle said, her voice still soft. "Is this... if Amanda has an overnight, is her client going to know what she did? For the ones who make it back here, is the government going to know? Is Baryman?"

"I don't care," Elina said defiantly. "I'll jump off the roof when the job's done. It's nothing I haven't thought about doing anyway, and this way at least there's a reason for it."

"I don't care either," Michelle said. "But I want to know. Is this it, no matter what? Should we be looking for the ledge, or should we try to get loose and hide, or try to make it back here? I'm in, regardless. But I want to know."

Remy could feel the weight pressing down on him, and felt like his suicide capsule was glowing through the skin of his cheek, a beacon of his cowardice. "I don't know," he said. "If it doesn't work... if the virus doesn't go national, or if the army doesn't go along with the new orders... I'd look for the ledge. If it does work...." He thought about Challoner, and his determination to do the right thing. "If it works, I'd try to make it back here. We'll have friends in the new government, or if there's no real government, we'll have friends who can maybe get us out of here. No guarantees, but...." He smiled as he recognized the simple truth. "But I'm tired of giving up. I plan to keep fighting for as long as I can."

There was a quiet buzz of what Remy hoped was agreement. "Okay, any other questions? You guys know what you need to do?" The whores nodded, and Remy turned to Sasha. "Can you do your part? Can you shuffle the schedule a little, make sure we all have house calls tonight?"

Sasha nodded. "I can. For most of you. But, Remy... you're still one of the top earners. You're still a headliner. And Mr. Baryman is having a party tonight."

A party that Remy would be expected to work. "Can you at least book me to circulate, rather than being in one of the static displays?" Remy wasn't sure what good that would do, why it would be better to walk around and find clients rather than be part of a show, but he knew he'd be able to handle it better. Maybe he was just reluctant to be restrained, now that freedom was finally in sight.

Sasha nodded. "I can do that." He seemed calm about it all, as if it were just one more mundane detail he was being asked to arrange. He picked up his comm and tapped the screen, obviously shuffling things around. Then he said, "Okay. I can set up a couple double shifts, as well, and a triple for you, Bobby, you busy little bitch. So that should help... if everything goes smoothly, we can plant twelve of the little darlings tonight."

"Okay," Remy said, and he nodded. "That would be twenty-one, total. It should be enough, if they're right about... well, if they're right about everything." He reached into his pocket and pulled out the envelope, then doled the capsules out as Sasha directed. Nine were left behind, round and full of promise, and Remy ached to find somewhere to plant them. He'd done his part, he supposed, but he wanted to do more. He looked down at the capsules in his hand and slipped them back in his pocket. The more that were laid, the better the chance of success. That had been clear. So he'd keep his eyes open and look for opportunities. He would do his best to find ways to contribute. He would make Challoner proud.

CHAPTER EIGHTEEN

THE party was elaborate, even by Baryman's standards. A circus theme, complete with animals, clowns, and a trapeze couple that Remy was sure would be having sex up there in the sky before the end of the night. Remy wasn't quite sure what his costume was. There was brilliant green and blue body paint, and feathers. He supposed he was a bird, maybe a parrot, but the choreographer kept ordering him to "Prowl! You're on the hunt! You're exotic and dangerous. Prowl!" Remy didn't know a lot about parrots, but he was pretty sure they weren't dangerous.

The more serious problem was that the costume had no pockets. It had no clothes, really. But the feathers extended down over one of Remy's hands and Sasha helped him tape a transmitter capsule to his fingers. Remy had to spit the suicide pill out in order to make room for his other capsules, but he replaced it quickly and looked up to see Sasha squinting at him.

"That's glass," Sasha said quietly. "Is it what I think it is?"

Remy felt a hot rush of shame. "I'm sorry," he blurted. "I promised. Because I know things. I can't...." He caught himself before he said anything too incriminating. The cameras had been back on for a couple hours.

"It's okay, baby." Sasha smiled sadly and pulled out his own little envelope. "Five or six," he said quietly. "I think I'm going to go with six."

"Not too early. Let it play out."

"I'll try. But I'm tired, baby."

"I know somewhere you can go. Somewhere they'll let you rest, let you get your strength back. Nothing's over, not yet."

"If you say so," Sasha said. "Now, shake your tail feathers on out there." Sasha took a quick look to make sure the choreographer wasn't too near, then said, "Prowl, baby, prowl!"

"Mrowww," Remy purred. "Or maybe squawk? Depending on what the hell I am."

"You're a sexy beast, baby. Go work."

Remy did as he was told. He'd taken his arousal pills, but didn't bother with an orgasm capsule. One way or another, his game was over tonight, and he didn't care if his clients complained that he was insufficiently grateful for their attentions. He didn't know the first man who waved him over, and the client didn't introduce himself. He ran his hands all over Remy as if testing that the paint was dry, then nodded for Remy to follow him to an alcove. The sex was routine, almost mechanical, but as the man was grunting away, Remy's eyes fell on the comm that had been casually left on the table. Right there, inches away from Remy's hand, and it was too good of an opportunity to pass up. He moaned a little, making the man thrust with more enthusiasm, and let himself stumble, then regain his balance with a hand on the table. It was easy to get the capsule loose, a little harder to keep his balance while he used both hands to unwrap the wire, and then just another stumble to let his hand fall on the comm and tuck the transmitter in between the tablet and the leather cover.

He wondered if it could have been this easy all along. Why were they bothering with nightstands when they could be attacking the comms themselves? But, no, clients changed their covers to match their outfits; this was fine for tonight, knowing that the virus would be activated before morning, but it wouldn't have worked long-term.

He managed a few more appreciative sounds while the client finished up, but his mind was absolutely elsewhere. How many more comms could he get his hands on? Was he taking an unacceptable risk? What were the chances of a client finding the transmitter, realizing what it was, and contacting the authorities?

He glanced out at the drugged and drunken crowd and put that last worry to rest; these clowns wouldn't notice if Remy draped the transmitters off their earlobes. His client pulled away from him and slapped his ass, and Remy made himself giggle. "I can find you again later, if you want," he purred.

"Sorry, sweetheart. There's a lot of other little birds out there, and not enough of me to go around."

Remy pouted for just long enough to be polite, then eased out of the alcove and went to find Sasha. "Straighten my feathers and check my paint, will you?" he said in a loud voice. "And check what's missing from that hand, there."

Sasha lifted the feathers away from Remy's fingers. "Lost something?" he asked, and he raised an eyebrow at Remy's grin. "Really? Interesting." He fished another capsule out and put it in place, then fluffed Remy's feathers. "Gorgeous. Get out there."

And Remy went. A blowjob, and that was harder because he was facing the client and was expected to use his hands, but he managed a quick reach and tuck at the moment of climax. A flirtatious lap dance, his feathers ruffling and stroking as his fingers were busy, and another transmitter was in place. Another blowjob, a make-out session that never went any further because the client passed out, and one plant of opportunity, finding an unattended comm and sticking a wire in it before returning it to its completely intoxicated owner.

Remy felt triumphant, and alive. He *was* a parrot-cat, stalking his damned prey. He was a wire-planting animal, and he loved it. "Give me two," he instructed on his next trip to get his plumage repaired. "Dawson and Dupree just came in, and they love the double-team."

"And they love you," Sasha agreed as he attached the pills. "Be careful, baby. Don't get carried away."

"Just doing my job," Remy said with a cocky grin.

He sauntered over to the bar where his targets were ordering drinks and eased his way in between them. "Well, look who's here," he said. "You're back from Australia and you didn't give me a call?" The pouting, flirty look earned him smiles from both men.

"We just got in this morning, David. And we absolutely hoped to see you here tonight."

"I hoped to see you here too. Both of you. Nobody takes care of me like you two." It was mostly true, Remy realized. Neither of the men had ever been cruel to him. They were spoiled children, pushing middle age, with a taste for pretty boys; that was all. They liked their sex rough, but Remy had never complained, never asked them to be more gentle. For all he knew, if he'd asked they would have complied.

For the first time he had a flash of doubt about the whole situation. What would happen to these two and the others like them if Challoner's plan came to fruition? Did Remy want to be responsible for that? Had these men ever done anything truly evil?

Dawson took his glass of scotch from the bartender, sipped it, then held it to Remy's lips. He smiled, let the golden liquid flow over his tongue, and felt Dupree wrap his hands around his chest, exploring. "You're beautiful, David," Dupree said. "Even with all this shit on you. We didn't find anything as beautiful as you in Australia."

"Any*one*," Remy corrected, as if he thought he had a right to be considered a human being instead of an inanimate object. Shit. Who did he think he was talking to? That had been completely out of line, and Dupree's hands stilled. "I've seen pictures of the Great Barrier Reef," Remy said desperately. "It's more beautiful than me. But I believe you that you couldn't find any *person* as fine as I am."

Dupree's hands moved again. "We didn't make it to the coast," he said. "Believe me, where we were... nothing, and no *one* that's even close."

"Well, it's good that you're back now, then," Remy said. "Do you want to find somewhere to show me how much you missed me?" He wriggled his body back into Dupree, then forward into Dawson. "There's bedrooms set up down that hallway. We could have a real party in there."

"Bartender," Dawson said curtly. "The bottle, please."

"And a bucket of ice," Dupree added. "David, you want anything?"

"If I get to have the two of you, I don't need anything else." That was better. Remy was back on his game. He thought about Colony Seventeen, about his parents, and he knew that he'd plant the transmitters and not worry about the consequences.

"You absolutely get to have the two of us," Dupree said, nibbling and then biting Remy's ear.

"Let's go, then," Remy said, and he led the way to an unoccupied room.

The boys were enthusiastic, he'd give them that. He was manhandled all over the room, spread over every piece of furniture, stretched and prodded and bent in all directions, and he didn't get anywhere near their comms until they'd exhausted themselves and passed out on the bed. Once he'd planted the wires, he let the clients sleep for a while, then found their bodyguards and suggested that it was time to escort the men home. The bodyguards, used to this system, agreed, and worked on getting their employers dressed. Remy helped, as he had so many times in the past.

By the time he made it out of the room, the party was winding down, and he was a mess. His paint was streaked, his feathers were mostly missing, spread all over the damned bedroom, and he was exhausted. But happy. He'd planted eight transmitters that night alone, and as long as the clients made it home in the next few hours, they'd be effective. Even if they didn't all go, there had been enough planted to meet the quota, surely. He found Sasha dozing in the costume room and sank onto the couch beside him.

Sasha woke up instantly. "You're back," he said.

"I'm good. Go to sleep. They don't need me out there anymore."

But Sasha stood up and pulled Remy to his feet. "Mr. Baryman wants to see you," he said.

Remy felt his stomach lurch. "Baryman? Now? Why?"

"I don't know. But his orders were pretty clear. He's in his office. He wants you there."

Great. Remy wondered what would happen if he refused to go, but the very thought was preposterous. Remy had grabbed a few little victories, but nothing had really changed, not yet. He ran his hands down over the remains of his feathers, and wished he were just naked. It would be so much more honest. So much less humiliating.

But this would be the last time. Again, one way or another, he'd never be summoned before Baryman again. He smiled tiredly, then raised his feathered hand, exposing his empty fingers. "One more," he said. "The last one."

Sasha's eyes widened. "Remy, no. You've done enough." He looked over his shoulder as if fearing that someone was right behind him, and said, "Not Mr. Baryman."

"*Especially* Mr. Baryman," Remy said firmly. "*Especially* him."

Sasha looked as if he wanted to say more, but finally, he pulled the last transmitter capsule out of his packet and attached it to Remy's finger. "Be careful, baby," he said. "Don't push it."

"Thanks, Sasha. For everything." Remy turned and headed for the main room. He still wanted to get out of this. He still wanted to live. But he wanted to be sure he kept fighting too. Wanted to be sure he gave the plan every chance to work. If he could plant another transmitter, somewhere on Baryman's own comm, that would be perfect.

So there was energy in his step as he jogged up the stairs, enthusiasm for a job well under way but not yet completed. He knocked on Baryman's door, spoke into the comm, and stepped inside.

Baryman was behind his desk, as usual, but there wasn't the usual compliment of goons in the chairs in front of him. Instead, there was one man, and Remy could only see the back of his head. But even that, combined with the smug expression on Baryman's face, was enough to let Remy know what was happening.

He stepped forward in the businesslike manner Baryman preferred, even from grown men covered in paint and feathers, and stopped in front of the desk. "Mr. Baryman," he said with a polite nod. Then he swiveled to face the other man. "And it's good to see you again, Mr. Challoner."

Baryman leaned back in his desk chair and watched Challoner react to Remy's appearance. It wasn't obvious exactly what the game was, here, but it was pretty damned clear that Baryman expected to enjoy it.

"You're looking a little the worse for wear, David," Baryman said, his voice gently scolding. "You didn't fucking think to get cleaned up before coming to see me?"

That trick was all too familiar. If Remy had gotten changed, he would have been in trouble for not responding to the summons immediately. There was no defense, so he hung his head. "I'm sorry, Mr. Baryman." He tried not to think of Challoner seeing his servitude, his lack of self-respect. His lack of clothes.

"What were you thinking, David?" Baryman's voice was still gentle, but Remy knew that this was the turning point. If he found the right answer, he'd be okay. If he guessed wrong, he would be punished.

"I wanted to follow your orders without delay," he said, but he knew that wasn't enough. "And... I'm sorry, sir. I think maybe I was showing off. I wanted you to see how hard I'd been working for you tonight."

Baryman didn't answer right away, but when he did, the

warmth in his voice made Remy's muscles loosen. "You *did* work hard for me tonight, didn't you? How many clients did you serve?"

Remy started to count, but then realized that a much more important message could be sent. He glanced at Challoner as he said "Eight," with a little special emphasis. Eight transmitters set. Eight steps closer to the goal.

"Eight?" Baryman's voice was sharp. "I was told *seven*."

Shit. Eight transmitters, but one of them had been a freebie, planted on the misplaced comm. "I'm sorry. I miscounted."

"Well, maybe you were just seeing into the future," Baryman said. "After all, there's a client here in this room, waiting patiently." He leaned back in his chair. "And there's me. You've been getting a lot of attention lately, David, and it's made me realize that I've never indulged in your services. Maybe it's time I changed that."

"I'd be honored, sir," Remy said.

"*Honored* by which one of us? You can't mean you'll take both of us. I don't think Mr. Challoner is the sort of man to engage in such lewd displays. Are you, Mr. Challoner?"

"I'm not the sort of man for any of this," Challoner said. Remy could hear the rage being tightly controlled, and wondered whether Baryman could sense it as well. "You called me away from important business under false pretenses. You obviously have no intention of selling David's contract to me, or of giving me further access to his services, and you've dragged this charade on long enough." He glanced at his comm. "It's almost four in the morning, and I have a big day tomorrow." Remy tried not to react, tried not to acknowledge the time, or the hidden significance of Challoner's big day. "I'll be taking my leave now."

"So David won't get to choose between us? That's too bad. I was looking forward to seeing him try to squirm his way out of his punishment for making the wrong choice." Baryman shrugged nonchalantly. "But it's fine. If you don't want to be part of the contest, I'll just assume David would have made the wrong decision. Seems pretty fucking likely. So, David, how will I punish you for your mistake? There are so many possibilities...." He broke off and turned back to Challoner. "I'm sorry, didn't you say you were leaving?"

"He's done nothing wrong. You just said he'd worked hard for you tonight. *I'm* the one who's leaving, so why is *he* facing punishment?" Challoner sounded like he was trying to reason with the man, and Remy wished he could explain how useless that was.

But Baryman made it clear himself. "Well, I'd have been happy to punish *you*, Mr. Challoner. But the things I'm going to do to dear David... you'd have me brought up on fucking charges if I did them to you." He reached over and gently stroked David's cheek. "But not David. David knows better."

Challoner was letting himself get sucked in, and Remy couldn't let that happen. Challoner had important things to do, and he couldn't be distracted by some mindless drama over a stupid whore. "I would have asked you to choose for me," he said desperately, and he eased around so he was perched on the edge of the desk facing Baryman, his back to Challoner. "I would have said that I wanted to make you happy, but I didn't think I was your type, really." That was true enough. Remy had never heard of Baryman using one of the male whores. This entire setup was all for Challoner's benefit. But so was the display Remy was putting on behind his back, in Challoner's line of sight but hidden from Baryman. Remy had the capsule off his finger and opened, and he unwound the wire slowly and carefully. "So I would have asked you how I could best serve you, by pleasing you directly or by pleasing one of your valued clients." Remy kept his eyes forward while his fingers fumbled with the cover of the comm resting on the desk. "I would have apologized for being too stupid to figure it out for myself," he said. He tucked the transmitter carefully inside the comm, ran his fingertips along the edge to be sure it was hidden, and then pointed his thumb at Challoner and jerked it toward the door. It was past time for the man to be gone.

"Well, then, that's what you'll be punished for," Baryman said. "Not for your wrong choice, but for your fucking stupidity."

"Of course, sir." Remy knew it was a risk, but he needed to let Challoner know that it was all right. He needed to make it clear that there was nothing Baryman could do to him that should get in the way of Challoner's larger purpose. So he put just a little playfulness in his voice as he added, "How else will I ever learn?"

Baryman frowned. "You're acting pretty fucking chipper for a man who's had the night you've had, and who's looking at the day you're going to have."

"I'm looking forward to the day, sir." Remy jerked his thumb behind his back once more, indicating that Challoner should go. "I'm looking forward to this day very much." There were cameras in this office, almost certainly, and they would eventually show what Remy had been up to behind his back. But none of that mattered, not if the larger plan worked, and not if Challoner played his part.

And, finally, Challoner got the damned message. "Well, I'll leave you to it, then," he said, and his voice sounded pretty good. Not as good as Remy's did, but solid. And it wasn't like Baryman was paying much attention to Challoner anymore anyway. He was too fascinated by Remy.

"Fine," Baryman managed, distractedly waving a hand in Challoner's direction. "Go. If you want to try one of my other whores, let me know. But David... David's going to be out of service for quite a while, I think." His smile was cruel, his gaze roaming over Remy's body as if deciding where to begin, and Remy had to force himself to stay straight and still. He would not crawl. Not anymore.

But Challoner still hadn't left. This was ridiculous. Remy turned his head and smiled. "It was nice to see you again, Mr. Challoner. But you said you were in the middle of something important." He put a subtle emphasis on the last word. "I'm fine here."

Challoner looked almost physically torn, as if two giants were pulling his body, one toward Remy, the other toward the door. And that was when Baryman's comm trilled an alert that Remy had never heard before.

Baryman leaned around Remy and frowned down at the device, then picked it up and tapped the screen. He obviously wasn't pleased with the result. "Fucking piece of crap," he muttered. He looked back at Remy. "Maybe I'll smash it, pull the shards off, and see where I can find a place for them on your body. Sound good?"

Remy's blood was rushing so hard and loud through his ears that he could barely hear Baryman's words. He looked at Challoner and could feel the excitement shooting between them like a bolt of electricity. Had it worked? Was it happening?

"There's nothing in this room as important as what's out there," Remy said as he smiled wide and true and real.

"You're wrong about that," Challoner said. "But maybe what's in this room can take care of itself."

"Yeah," Remy agreed, and he truly believed it.

"What the fuck are you two talking about?" Baryman interrupted. "What's going on?"

Remy heard the fast, heavy steps outside and smiled as someone banged on the door. "I think you're about to find out."

"What the fuck?" Baryman said again, and then Challoner opened the door and a barely controlled security guard rushed inside.

"Sir, I'm sorry to interrupt, but there's something wrong with the cameras. And the comms. There aren't many guests left, but those that are here... their comms aren't working. At all."

Baryman frowned at Challoner. "Is yours?" he demanded.

"I actually left mine at home," Challoner said with a smile. "I should probably go check on it."

Another guard arrived then, poking his head inside, and said,

"There's a call on the emergency channel, sir. The old telephone system. It's for you."

"Son of a bitch," Baryman said. He paused indecisively, then spat out, "Fuck!" and gestured toward Remy while speaking to one of the guards. "Take him and the other whores and get them out of here. Take them back to the house, and keep an eye on them. Especially this one." He stared at Remy. "This little fucker knows something." He strode toward the door, then stopped and turned back to Remy. "This isn't over." Then he was gone, following one of the guards to the old telephone, it seemed.

Remy looked at Challoner. "He's right. It isn't over. You need to go."

"You can come with me, now," Challoner said. He looked at the guard. "Mr. Stone is contractually bound to your employer, but your employer does not *own* him. He cannot legally keep one of his workers from leaving his place of employment, as long as the worker doesn't seek employment elsewhere."

The guard looked like he wanted to call for backup on that one, but it wasn't necessary. Remy shook his head and stepped forward. "No. I won't run away, not when the others can't. I got them into this, and I won't leave them now."

"Damn it, Remy," Challoner started, but he stopped when Remy stepped a little closer.

"You need to go," Remy said. "It's your turn." Then he reached up and touched Challoner on the neck, the spot he'd kissed before, and smiled. "I think this time... this time I want to touch you here," he said, and he laid his fingers gently on Challoner's mouth. He leaned forward, their lips met, gentle and true, and then Remy leaned back. "Maybe more of that later," he said. "For now... your country needs you."

"I don't think I'm the right person...," Challoner started.

"Too bad. Too late. You're it, so get going." Remy smiled again. "You'll be great."

Challoner looked a little surprised by Remy's vehemence, but he moved toward the door. He started to turn around once again, but Remy saw him and spoke loudly to the security guard. "Okay, buddy, you're supposed to be taking us back to the house, right? Let's go, then." And he swept out of the room, ahead of Challoner, ahead of the guard, and led the way downstairs to find the others.

CHAPTER NINETEEN

NONE of the whores on the shuttle knew what was going on and they didn't really seem to care. They were exhausted from their night's work but also from years of being shoved from one place to another without any explanation. This night was just one more seemingly random experience.

For Remy, though, everything had changed. He smiled at the pilot standing outside the shuttle, and almost laughed when the man sneered back. Sure, Remy looked like a bedraggled bird-cat, but he knew he was something different. He'd been part of this. He'd *done* something. The pilot might not know or care, but the pilot didn't matter.

Remy bounded aboard and let the others squabble over the seats; he was happy to stand. Sasha was there, sitting next to the pilot, but he only turned around briefly, gave Remy a tired smile, and then closed his eyes.

The trip to the house was short and uneventful. Remy ripped off his remaining feathers and pulled his clothes, retrieved by Sasha from the wardrobe room, on over the body paint. He reached into the pocket of his pants to find Challoner's amulet. He let his fingers run over it, then pulled it out and hung it around his neck. It felt good there, solid and comforting.

The shuttle landed with a thud, and Remy and Sasha were herded downstairs with the others. Remy looked around and felt like the bubble of joy in his core might actually expand so much that he would explode. There were no red lights, not anywhere. He couldn't keep it to himself any longer. "Cameras are off," he remarked to the whore next to him.

She peered at the nearest device, then scowled. "Or they just turned off the red lights. They could be trying to trick us."

"I don't think so," he said, and he practically skipped down the hall to Sasha's room, Sasha trailing behind him more slowly. Remy could hear the chatter from outside. It quieted when he pushed the door open, then burst into a cacophony of celebration.

"I was there when it happened! His comm just went dead!"

"Did he *cry*? I want to see one of them cry!"

"We were all here, watching the light, trying to look all casual like there was some reason we were still awake, and the fucking thing just blinked out. It was *beautiful*."

Michelle smiled calmly from her spot on the couch and pushed her legs aside to make room for Remy to sit at her feet. Her fingers combed through his hair more energetically than usual, and she bent to whisper in his ear. "Even if this is all it is. Even if it's just an hour without cameras, all over the city, and they come for us and arrest us and it's all over... even if that's all we get, it was worth it, baby. Thank you."

"I hope we get a hell of a lot more," Remy replied. "But, yeah. If this is all there is...." He smiled at her, then turned back to the room and raised his hands in triumph, a wild, primal victory cry rushing past his lips.

The sound was taken up by others in the room. Cheering, baying, whooping in celebration, and it felt like the sound alone might break the walls of the room, might rush out from their prison and knock over every obstruction to freedom.

But Sasha sat quietly. Remy stared at him, and eventually the others noticed and became quiet as well. "Sasha," Remy said. "We did good. It worked." He searched his mind, trying to find a reason for his friend's lethargy. "Maybe it won't last. Maybe it's just a blip. But just a blip is still *something*, Sasha. It's one tiny crack in the dam, one ray of light shining through the walls...." Remy's metaphors started to seem ridiculous, and he finally said, "It's something. And it could be something huge."

"And what if it is?" Sasha whispered. "What if this *is* the beginning of something huge?" He shook his head. "We're whores, Remy. I'm not even that, not anymore, but... that's all we know. It's all we are. If this doesn't work, we're dead. The quicker the better. But let's say it *does* work. Let's say there's a whole new government." His voice was louder, but painfully sad as he asked, "What are they going to do with us, Remy? What *can* they do with us, other than keep us as whores? We're not good for anything else."

"Bullshit." It probably wasn't properly respectful, but Remy didn't care. "A, if this works, we're heroes. We're the ones who made it happen, and they can retire our asses down south as a thank-you. But, B, if we don't want to retire, then...." He smiled again. "Then *we* decide what happens to us. Not the government, *us*. Maybe I really *will* be a corporate event planner, and maybe you'll run a clothes store. Or, fuck it, maybe we'll all still be whores, but we'll be doing it for ourselves, with *us* pocketing the money instead of feeding Baryman's insanity. We *won't* get punished for screwing up, and if someone tries, the government will back us up when we complain about it." He nodded and looked at all the others before turning back to Sasha. "That's the best-case scenario. But the really exciting thing, Sasha? The exciting thing is that I *don't know* what's going to happen. But something is. Something's going to change, and I really don't see how it could change for the worse. I really don't see it."

The door opened then, no knock or warning, and a security guard stepped inside. "Mr. Baryman is in the common room. He wants to see you. All of you."

Sasha turned to Remy. "You don't see it?" he asked. He reached over, slowly, deliberately, and picked up an envelope from the desk. Remy could see the bulging of pills inside it. "Thank you,"

Sasha said calmly to the guard. "We'll be right there." The guard withdrew, and Sasha held the envelope out to the group. "Remy has a suicide pill all ready to go. The rest of us have to look after ourselves. Five or six of these should do it."

"Not yet!" Remy said. "Not *nearly* yet!"

"Ours won't be instant, like yours," Sasha said. "We can't take the chance."

Remy shook his head emphatically. "Take the pills *with* you, fine. But don't swallow them. We don't know what this is; we don't know what's happening." But Sasha was doling out the pills, and the whores were holding their hands out obediently. "You're just taking them with you, right?" he asked.

"It was still worth it, Remy," Michelle said, and the others nodded their agreement.

Remy's tongue knew the routine; he'd pulled capsules from behind his molars thousands of times over the years. This time, he spat the thing out into his hand. "One of you can have this. I have another, but it's in my room, and I doubt they'll let me get it. I don't think I have any secrets anymore, so I don't need it." He looked at the crowd. "So I'll carry Sasha's pills, but I *won't* take them. Not yet. Because I *hope* something good could be coming up." He still felt the bubble of joy, and he made sure it showed on his face. "And because I want to see what happens!"

"You don't know what happens, Remy? Really?" Sasha shook his head. "They win. We lose. That's what *always* happens."

Remy couldn't have done it, not just for himself. But for the rest of them, for the people he'd dragged into it? He had to. He lifted Challoner's amulet up off his chest and made sure everyone was watching as he pulled it apart and pressed the button. "Help's on the way," he said. He hoped it was true. Hoped Challoner hadn't been arrested himself, hoped the signal worked and Challoner got there in time, and hoped he'd be able to do something if he *did* arrive. "We just have to wait it out."

Sasha shook his head. "You're such a dreamer, baby."

"I never used to be," Remy said, "But, yeah. Now, I dream."

The door opened, and the security guard poked his head in again. "I don't want to have to drag you out there."

"We're coming," Sasha said. He put the pills in his pocket, along with Remy's suicide capsule. "God help us, we're coming."

BARYMAN was more agitated than Remy had ever seen him. He was stalking around the room, which was empty of everyone but himself and a couple of his suited goons, and when he saw the whores approaching, he kicked the nearest wooden chair hard enough to send it flying into the opposite wall. The courage that had gotten Remy out of Sasha's room abandoned him in the face of Baryman's rage. The man had tortured Remy, had terrorized and controlled him for most of his life, and he was terrifying. Remy saw Sasha slip something into his mouth, and knew what it was. Sasha was preparing the only escape he could manage. At least it had only been one pill; he had the suicide caplet lined up, but he hadn't actually swallowed the six others.

"Get in here!" Baryman barked. "Line up!"

The whores did as they were told. The bravado from Sasha's room had almost disappeared as soon as they'd been summoned, and now it was gone completely. They were all back to their meek, obedient selves, Remy included. He thought about the amulet around his neck, and he hoped for a rescue. He wanted to live.

Baryman was so angry his whole body was shaking, and he walked down the line of whores until he got to Sasha. "You fucking bitch," he snarled. "You did this. I fucking trusted you, and you set this up, didn't you?"

Sasha didn't even blink. "Yes," he said.

For such a big man, Baryman moved fast, grabbing Sasha's

head and jerking it down just as Baryman's knee drove up. The crunch was sickening, and blood sprayed everywhere, but Sasha didn't make a sound. He'd been prepared for the blow.

Remy was paralyzed. He needed to do something, but what? He looked over at the goons and recognized the one who'd beaten him in the bathroom. The man was standing motionless, expressionless, but ready. And he was certainly armed, just as his friend would be. Hell, Baryman usually carried a weapon or two himself. There was nothing Remy could do.

"We got a list of the people who were hacked," Baryman said, back to his more controlled voice. And the hard kick he aimed at Sasha's kneecap was controlled, as well. He stepped aside as Sasha crumbled to the floor. "They're *all* clients of this agency. Quite a fucking coincidence, isn't it?" Another hard kick, this one to Sasha's back, right around his kidneys. "And you changed the schedules yesterday afternoon, right before the shift. You changed it so all the right fucking whores would go to the right fucking clients." He kept kicking, then, and it was sickeningly clear to Remy that Baryman wasn't going to stop. He was going to beat Sasha to death, beat him *beyond* death if he could, right there in the common room.

And that meant something. Remy's body screamed at him, ordered him to run away, to grovel on the floor and hide. But he was used to forcing his body to do what it didn't want, and it obeyed him when he ordered it to step forward. "Stop," he said with as much authority as desperation could give him. As soon as the word was out of his mouth, he began to relax. He was committed, now, and there was no point trying to escape. So his body gave up on that plan and seemed to be gathering strength for whatever Remy might require of it next.

Baryman turned to him. There was blood splashed up onto his shirt, and more glistened on his dark pant legs. His face was twisted into a feral snarl. "*What*?" he snarled. "What the fuck did you just say?"

"I said stop. You're going to kill him. And the government won't like that. They'll want him alive, so they can question him." Remy forced himself to take another step forward. "And you know that perfectly well. Which means...." God, he hoped he was right. "Which means you don't plan to tell the government about any of this. The government might know who the hacked citizens are, but they won't know they're your clients; you're always so careful with your security, aren't you? You're planning to cover up the agency's involvement. You want Sasha dead so you'll be sure he'll never tell anyone what he did." He looked over at the others. He didn't think there was any point in denying their involvement, but it still felt like a huge risk when he said, "You want us all dead, so none of us can tell." And then the even bigger risk as he looked over at the goons standing by the wall. "But you won't be completely safe unless your boys are dead as well. One of them gets pissed off, or caught for something else, or... anything, really. All it takes is for one of them to open his mouth, and you're in it up to your neck. You're fucked."

Baryman glanced over at his goons and shook his head. "No. My boys are loyal. I'm not worried about them."

Remy tried to sound just as confident as he looked right at the goon who'd beaten him in the bathroom. "He thinks he can trust you. That's kind of funny, isn't it?"

The goon frowned at Remy. "What the fuck are you talking about?"

"Yeah, okay, play it that way. I won't tell him what you did. I won't tell him where it's hidden." Remy had no idea how far he could stretch this lie, but based on the panicked look on the goon's face, he'd taken it far enough.

"He's crazy, Mr. Baryman. I don't know what the fuck he's talking about."

"Shut *up!*" Baryman yelled. The room fell silent except for Sasha's tortured, liquid breathing. Baryman strode over to Remy. "You, you fucking troublemaker, you can shut the fuck up."

"Yeah, I can," Remy agreed. "But that's not going to help you much."

"*Help* me?" Baryman echoed. "What the fuck do you think you can do to *help* me?"

"I can give you a warning. And information. You know how valuable information is."

"What fucking information do *you* have? You're a fucking whore!"

"How much have I reported to you over the years? How much of what I've heard have you recorded?" Remy forced himself to take another step forward, demanded that his body be relaxed and easy. "But that's not the kind of information I have now. *Now*, I've got much more. I'll tell you this: I provided the wires. I know who's behind it all. And if the attack was as effective as it seems to have been, that's information that you need."

Baryman was fast, again, but Remy could have moved. Instead, he stood stock-still, his gaze locked on his employer's, as Baryman pulled a gun from inside his jacket and lifted it to Remy's temple. "So," Baryman purred, "tell me."

"Or you'll kill me? We've already established that you plan to kill all of us. So the gun really isn't a great threat."

Baryman grimaced in frustrated confusion. "What the fuck are you trying to do? What's your plan here?"

That was an excellent question, and Remy wished he had a better answer, although he wasn't sure that he'd share it if he did. Mostly, he was just trying to get Baryman away from Sasha. There had been movement just a moment ago from the crumpled heap on the ground, which suggested that, for some reason, Sasha hadn't yet activated the suicide pill. But he wouldn't need it, not if Baryman kept at him.

Remy was also trying to stall, just in case Challoner actually was on his way. But there was a little something else twisting through Remy's brain, a tiny wave of actual thought burrowing through the fear. "There's a new sheriff in town," he said desperately. "A new source of power. They did this—the comms, the cameras, all of it. And I have no idea whether they've managed to make a permanent change. No idea if they're going to have any real success. But the thing is—you have no idea, either."

He saw the indecision on Baryman's face and took a chance, reaching up slowly to push the barrel of the gun away from his temple. Baryman let his hand drop to his side, the gun with it. Remy forced himself to slow down and take a deep, calming breath before continuing. "Based on what we're seeing so far, I think they did pretty well. Maybe well enough to win long-term, maybe not. But if they do win, if they take power, how do you think they're going to treat the man who killed their friends? The friends who made the whole revolution possible?"

"You're bluffing," Baryman said, but he didn't sound sure.

"There's no bluff. You know all this. You know we were involved. You know there was some success. That's all I'm saying. We want out of here, away from the government and away from you. You want the same thing. Let us go, and we'll disappear. No risk of us talking to the government, if it even still exists, because they'd kill us for what we've done. And if you let us go you'll have done a pretty big favor for a group that might be in a position to pay you back. Killing us does you no good."

"Where the fuck will you go? How can you be sure you'll be able to get away?" Baryman was looking at the technical details. He was sounding almost reasonable. Remy tried not to let his excitement show.

"We just shut down the data systems for one of the most technologically advanced nations on the planet. You really think we can't smuggle a few whores out of the country?"

Baryman frowned and stepped backward, his gun dangling carelessly from his hand. He looked at his goons, then back at Remy. "Fuck," he muttered.

"One shuttle, for one hour," Remy said. "That's all we need." It wouldn't get them to Challoner's, but Remy didn't think it was a good idea to go straight there anyway. If there was still any cover to be blown, he didn't want to be the one to blow it. So they'd get out of the city, and they'd... they'd figure something out from there. Sasha complicated things, of course. He needed medical help, and he'd draw attention to the group wherever they went. But Remy would deal with that once they were the hell away from Baryman.

"Fuck," Baryman said again. "*Fuck!*" He whirled toward the whores as if looking for an escape, or at least an explanation of how his world had gone so suddenly and horribly wrong. He was still quick, but there was none of his earlier smoothness as he raised the gun and pointed it toward Sasha's prone form. "Fuck you all," he growled.

Remy had started moving as soon as Baryman had, and he was just as fast. He managed to get his shoulder into Baryman's side, hard bone meeting fat and buried muscle, and he grabbed Baryman's wrist and pushed the gun up into the air. Remy had the advantage of surprise, but that was all. Baryman grunted, swore, and then his free hand was on Remy's throat, squeezing, choking... and then they were falling, and somebody, somebody lighter than Baryman but still pretty damned heavy, landed on Remy's gut, and there was screaming, and a blur of motion, then more yelling and swearing as bodies tumbled all over Remy, all over Baryman, struggling desperately. Finally, a voice that could only belong to little Elina yelled, "Enough! Baryman, call off your boys or I will pull the fucking trigger, I swear."

Remy managed to peer through the tangle of limbs and see the tiny woman, her face scratched and her short dress torn almost off, pointing Baryman's own gun straight into his eyes. The other whores were piled all over the man, except for a couple who had been pulled off by the bodyguards and hadn't yet made it back to the fray.

Baryman was quiet for longer than Remy liked, but finally he grunted, "Back off," and after only a moment's hesitation, his men obeyed.

They were frozen there, the whores sprawled all over Baryman, the bodyguards poised for action but uncertain about the best course to take, when the door from the roof burst open. Two lines of soldiers streamed in, weapons drawn, their leader yelling, "Everybody, stay where you are! Nobody moves!"

Remy could mostly see feet from where he was lying. Black boots beneath dark green pants, moving in well-rehearsed patterns, fanning out, covering the area, stopping near the bodyguards, and near Elina. Disarming them, Remy assumed.

The voice from the bottom of the pile was only a little strained. "My name is Warwick Baryman. I fucking own this place. I caught these terrorists and they fucking attacked me." His voice was growing in strength, and he pushed himself carefully up to a sitting position. "They were going to kill me. You need to arrest them immediately. They need to be questioned."

"I don't think so," a new voice said from the doorway.

"No pills!" Remy screamed. "Don't take them! We're okay!" He pushed himself up, running his gaze wildly over the other whores. "No pills," he repeated. "It's not the government."

"What the fuck are you talking about?" Baryman demanded, and then he turned and looked toward the doorway. "And what the fuck are *you* doing here?"

Challoner ignored him. He crossed the floor in long, determined strides and crouched down next to Remy, running anxious hands over his body as if checking for injuries.

"I'm fine," Remy said. "But Sasha needs a doctor." He extricated himself from the tangle of bodies and let Challoner help him to his feet. "I'm sorry for calling. I know you must have more important things going on."

"Nothing more important," Challoner said softly. Then, sounding as if he had been commanding soldiers all his life, he said, "These people are heroes. Get a medic up here, and help them with whatever they need." He looked down at Baryman with disgust. "Arrest the suits. Maybe they'll be useful, eventually." Then he looked back at Remy, and his voice was soft again. "I have to go back to HQ, and there's a hospital there for your friend. Will you come with me?"

"Really? I won't be in the way?"

"It'd be easier for me to concentrate if I wasn't worrying about you all the time." Challoner smiled. "I don't want to let you out of my sight. Not for a long, long time."

"That sounds okay," Remy said. And then it felt right to nestle in against Challoner's broad chest, to feel him wrap his strong arm around Remy's shoulder. "Are you guys all right?" he asked the others.

"Absolutely," Elina said. She looked a little dazed still, but her chin was up and she smiled as she said, "We're heroes."

"Yeah. You are," Remy agreed, and then he followed Challoner out into the dawn.

Chapter Twenty

REMY spent the next several days feeling safe, but useless. He visited with Sasha in the hospital, helped him suck his meals around his broken jaw, and didn't talk much. There was too much to say, and both of them seemed afraid to begin. The rebellion was going well but it was still early, and their dreams of freedom were too fragile to stand under the weight of their fears.

Remy tried to apologize for not stepping in earlier at the house, but Sasha waved his words off with his one cast-free arm. "It's okay," he said. "It took you a while, but you did it."

"I was afraid you'd bite the pill," Remy confessed. "I still don't quite understand... why didn't you?"

Sasha's smile was crooked. "You don't know?" He pulled his head up a little and said, "When it came right down to it... I wanted to live. I wanted to see what was going to happen."

Remy nodded slowly. "Exciting things," he said. "Big things."

And that was true, at least on the national scale. The virus had worked almost perfectly. The data had been transferred and then erased, the camera system deactivated, and a provisional government declared, with Challoner at its head. He made speech after speech, broadcast all over the continent, reassuring people that a system was still in place and they were safe. And he was even busier behind the scenes, dealing with the details of the revolution. He had gone from playing chess and running a farming estate to trying to govern a significant chunk of the continent, and it wasn't an effortless transition.

The new government had taken control of all the central systems, but there were still pockets of resistance, areas where the military or the security forces were controlled by men loyal to the old regime. And the areas beyond the cities had fallen into anarchy without the oppressive power of the government to frighten citizens into compliance. Challoner had started working with a governing council, with people who'd been operating in separate cells meeting for the first time, each in charge of their own areas. Don Ackerman was a lawyer elevated to being in charge of the security forces; General Tom Mackie had been key in the revolution and was now running the whole military. But it was Challoner in charge of coordinating them all, speaking for them and making the citizens believe that the new government was committed to serving them. The man had a lot on his plate.

Remy's duties, by contrast, had shrunk quite a bit. About the only role he could find for himself was being Challoner's keeper, bringing meals to the office and insisting that they be eaten, dragging him away for a few hours of sleep whenever there was a brief lull in the chaos.

"There're so many refugees, Remy," Challoner groaned. He'd finally allowed himself to be maneuvered into the makeshift bedroom just down the hall from his office, and he was sitting dejectedly on the bed while Remy tugged at his shoes. "They're trying to get away from fighting between troops who were in the same damned army just a week ago. We knew there'd be a lot of people looking for help. But... *so* many. We're doing our best, but we're going to have a hell of time just feeding them. Why the hell are they all coming?"

"Because they believe. Because they're willing to risk everything for just a taste of what you've created." Remy climbed onto the bed beside Challoner and wrapped himself around the other man's shoulders. "It's *good*, Challoner. It means they see that you can win."

Challoner squeezed Remy's wrist gratefully and his voice was a little lighter when he said, "I've been meaning to ask... what's up with 'Challoner'? Everybody else, it's either 'Mr. Challoner', or it's 'Adam'. I seem to recall asking *you* to call me Adam, as well."

"I seem to recall that I'm not your whore anymore. You can ask what you like, but there's no guarantee that you're going to get it." Remy tugged Challoner's shirt loose from his pants and then pushed his shoulders around and back onto the mattress. Remy snuggled in, his head on Challoner's shoulder, Challoner's arm wrapped around Remy. It had proven to be a good position for getting Challoner to relax, and Remy didn't mind it too much himself.

"But *why*?" Challoner asked. His voice was already blurring into sleep, and Remy knew that it would be easy to ignore the question.

But he didn't. Instead, he found the soft spot on Challoner's neck and kissed it gently. "Because *everyone else* calls you 'Mr. Challoner' or 'Adam'. I don't want to be 'everyone else'."

Challoner didn't say anything; he'd probably already fallen asleep. But then the arm around Remy's shoulders tightened a little, and Challoner raised his head enough to press a kiss to Remy's forehead. "'Challoner' it is," he said.

They slept for a while, and then an aide came to wake them. "Stay here," Challoner said to Remy, his voice soft. "It's the middle of the night."

"It's the middle of the night for you too." Remy swung his legs over the side of the bed. "I don't want to miss anything important." He didn't want to lose a chance to be useful.

Challoner looked like he was thinking about arguing, but instead he took Remy's hand. He didn't say anything, but he didn't let go, either. He stood up, and he and Remy walked slowly out to the office, and as the people there were setting up whatever they had for Challoner to look at, he and Remy walked out onto the balcony that overlooked the city. It was dawn, and all over town, the electric lights were blinking out, made unnecessary by the warm glow of the sun. The air was warm with an early taste of spring, and Remy leaned back into Challoner and breathed in.

"It's all been worth it," he said, and he knew that Challoner would understand. Challoner would know that Remy wasn't just talking about the rebellion; he was talking about *everything*. All the pain, all the struggling and despair. Remy would never forget the dark days, but the memory of them made the current time shine even more brightly. "I can't wait to see what happens next," he said.

Challoner wrapped his arms around Remy's chest and leaned into him, and they stood there together and watched the golden light of dawn spread over their city.

ABOUT THE AUTHOR

Kate Sherwood, Cate Cameron, Catherine Dale... and probably a few new names, eventually. They're all one person.

One person who's lucky enough to get to live a bunch of extra lives through all the characters in her books, and who's trying desperately to keep all the lives organized into some sort of categories... so each name writes a different type of story.

But really, beneath the genre categories? All the stories will have some kind of humour, even in the darkest times. They'll all show characters who are far from perfect, but who are trying to be better.

Basic bio stuff? Kate/Cate/Catherine lives in Cottage Country, the water-filled world north of Toronto, Canada, the land where summers are sunny and crowded with visitors and winters are snowy and isolated. She loves it there. Not that she doesn't sometimes miss the city, especially when her internet is acting up or she wants something delivered!

She works full-time at a non-writing job but would love to shift into a more writing-centred life. There's a five-year plan. It might work....

OTHER BOOKS BY KATE SHERWOOD

For details, see www.booklives.com

Writing as Kate Sherwood (m/m)

All That Glitters – contemporary romance

Long Shadows, Embers, Darkness, Home Fires – four book contemporary action

Feral, Lap Dog, Twice Shy, Pure Bred – four book NA contemporary romance

Sacrati – fantasy/alt history

In Too Deep – NA contemporary romance

Chasing the Dragon – angst and adventure!

Mark of Cain – contemporary romance

The Fall, Riding Tall – two book contemporary romance

The Shift – contemporary fantasy novella – monster hunters!

Room to Grow – contemporary romance novella

The Pawn, The Knight – two book futuristic romance with plenty of angst

Poor Little Rich Boy – contemporary romance

More than Chemistry – light contemporary novella

Dark Horse, Out of the Darkness, Of Dark and Bright – three book contemporary romance with extras

Shying Away – NA romance

Lost Treasure – contemporary romance

Writing as Cate Cameron (m/f, YA)

The Billionaire's Forever Family – contemporary romance

Center Ice, Playing Defense, Winging It, Breakaway – contemporary YA hockey romance

Just a Summer Fling, Hometown Hero – contemporary small town romance

Shining Armor – contemporary romance (originally published under "Kate Sherwood")

Writing as Catherine Dale (YA, contemporary fantasy, general fiction—everything but romance!)

Dark Houses – Speculative YA